her Lovestruck Lord

SCARLETT SCOTT

Her Lovestruck Lord
Wicked Husbands Book Two

For more information, contact author Scarlett Scott.
www.scarsco.com

dedication

This one is once again for my mom.
Thank you for everything.

contents

chapter one

"…love is love for evermore."
-Alfred, Lord Tennyson
England, 1878

MAGGIE, MARCHIONESS OF SANDHURST, knew when to concede defeat, and now was proving just such a moment. She watched the first evening of Lady Needham's infamous country house weekend unfolding in all its raucous glory. How had she ever thought she could find the courage to start a scandal to rival the debauchery before her?

Straight ahead, a masked lady's nipples were nearly visible above the décolletage of her black evening gown as she sipped champagne and flirted shamelessly with a masked gentleman. To her left, a gentleman had a lady pinned to the wall as he feasted on her neck. At her right, another couple's furtive motions suggested they were engaged in something far more depraved.

She'd thought that she was made of stern enough stuff to do what she must to regain her independence. Any man would suffice, she'd told herself, no matter how disagreeable the task. He could be old or young, short or tall, balding, round about the middle. She didn't care. As long as he wasn't cruel or malodorous, she could bear it.

Fool, she chastised herself. *Coward.*

For here she stood, mouth dry, heart thundering in her breast, fingers clenching her skirts. Too afraid to step forward, throw caution to the wind. Too fearful to free herself from the prison of her mistakes.

There was no hope for it. She wasn't cut from the same cloth as her fellow revelers, for watching them only made her want to retire to her chamber, snuggle beneath the covers, and read the volume of poetry she'd brought along with her. If only she hadn't chosen duty instead of love.

With a sigh, she turned away from the swirls of skirts and the dashing sight of masked rakes wooing their eager female counterparts. After two steps, she froze as she heard an unmistakable sound above the laughter and the music and the rumble of inebriated voices. It was the one sound a lady never wanted to hear, the sound that invariably made her shudder in her shoes.

The awful sound of fabric rending.

Her train, to be specific. The lush fall of silk designed by Worth himself. Hopelessly torn. Dismay mingling with true despair within her, she turned to find the culprit. He was dressed to perfection in evening black, taller than she, his identity obscured by an equally midnight half-mask. The lower half of his face revealed a wide jaw, a sculpted mouth. There was no denying that he was handsome, but he didn't appear to notice her, his glittering green eyes instead traveling the sea of iniquity above Maggie's head.

What a lout. Perhaps he was a drunkard as well. Stifling the urge to roll her eyes in frustration, she attempted to gain the man's attention, for he still stood upon the mangled remnants of her beautiful violet silk. "Pardon me, sir?"

He either ignored her or didn't hear her, caught up in the madness of the ball. For a moment, she had the distinct impression his mind was far away from the ballroom crush.

He looked past them all, lost in his own meandering thoughts.

But this man and his thoughts were not her concern. Be he inebriated, enthralled, or distracted, unfortunately he was still on her skirts. "Sir?" She raised her voice, trying not to call too much attention to herself for she was ashamed she'd deigned to attend the notorious party in the first place.

He remained oblivious. Perhaps he suffered from a hearing problem. Oh dear. She had no choice if she wanted to save her train from further damage. Maggie reached out and laid a tentative hand on his arm. "Sir?"

He gave a start and turned the force of that startling mossy gaze on her. "Madam?"

His arm was surprisingly well-muscled, his coat warm with the heat of his large body. She withdrew her touch with haste as if he were a pot too long on the stove that she'd inadvertently touched with her bare hand. He still didn't realize he trampled her gorgeous evening gown. It took her a breath to regain her composure under the force of those piercing eyes.

"Sir," she began hesitantly, "I'm afraid you're standing upon my train. If you'd be so kind?"

"Damn it to hell," he muttered, startling her with his blunt language. His penetrating stare dropped to the floor and he quickly removed the offending shoes. "Ah Christ, it's ripped to bits, isn't it?"

She cast a dreary eye over the effects of his feet. "I expect it will require some correction, yes."

Correction was rather an understatement. Her silk train, complete with box-pleated ribbon trim and a lace-and-jet overlay, was badly torn. She wasn't certain a seamstress's hand could make repairs without them being obvious to the eye. It wasn't as if she couldn't afford a new gown, but this had been her first occasion wearing it, and it had been unbearably lovely.

"I'm truly sorry." His voice sounded cross, drawing her attention back up to his frowning mouth. "If you'll allow it,

I'll be happy to have it repaired for you."

His mouth was especially fine, she noted again, contrary to her better judgment, firm yet sculpted. He had a generous mouth. Kissable. Dear heaven. What was she about, swooning over an unknown man's lips? Hadn't she just decided she was too craven to create the sort of scandal she'd require? She swallowed, forcing herself to recall what he'd just said.

"I appreciate your offer, sir, but I have a wonderful seamstress." She thought of the dressmaker she used in London when in a pinch. Likely, the entire train would require replacing.

"But the fault is mine." He played the gentleman now that she'd finally gained his attention.

"Nonsense." Perhaps her womanly horror at the damage to her gown was foolish. It had not been intentionally done, after all, and she had more than enough coin for Madame Laurier's alterations. "Of all things that need mending, mere fabric is by far the easiest and least costly."

He tilted his head, considering her with a fathomless stare that made her skin tingle to life with a dizzying warmth. "I sincerely doubt truer words were ever spoken."

There was an intensity underlying his words that made her believe he was sincere and not merely another rake plying meaningless flattery. For the first time since stepping into the whirlwind of the ballroom, Maggie was intrigued.

"What have you that needs mending, sir?" A new sense of boldness coursed through her.

His lips quirked into a wry smile beneath his mask. "Would you believe it's my heart?"

So he loved another, then. She tried to ignore the stab of disappointment the revelation sent through her. "I know better than anyone just how difficult it is to mend a heart." She frowned as she thought of the unhappy life in which she had found herself. The realization she had settled on this miserable path was a constant burr beneath her mind's saddle. "Perhaps impossible."

4

"What man would dare to break the heart of a woman as beautiful as you?" he demanded. "An utter imbecile, surely."

She laughed, entertained by his feigned toadying. A man who could laugh at himself and those around him was refreshing. "Forgive me, but I fear you're guilty of dissembling."

"Dissembling?" He pressed a large hand over his heart, feigning shock. "I'm wounded. Why would you say such a thing?"

"Because you can't see my face." She grinned despite herself. Her dainty mask covered her face as well, save her mouth. It was rather the point of a masque, after all. She would have to remove it to accomplish what she wanted. But for now, there was safety in her anonymity.

"Yes, but you have the most extraordinarily lovely eyes I've ever seen," he returned with remarkable aplomb. "I daresay they're almost violet."

Another wave of warmth washed over her. He was somehow different, this man. Dangerous to be sure. "I rather like you," she confided before she could stop herself. Drat. Being too honest had always been one of her downfalls. She'd never been good at hiding her emotions behind a polite veil. Perhaps it was why she'd had such difficulty blending with London society.

He grinned. "You sound alarmed. I'm not all bad, I assure you."

She shook her head, trying to regain her wits. "It is merely that I'd given up on your countrymen."

"My countrymen?" He paused, his eyes crinkling at the corners as he viewed her with dawning comprehension. "You're an American, are you? I thought I detected an accent."

"I am," she acknowledged. "I suppose that renders my eyes less lovely now." Although a number of American heiresses like herself had made their way to England, they were not always well received. She'd had to work quite hard to forge her way, and acceptance from English ladies had not proved an easy or sometimes achievable feat.

"Of course not." An emotion she couldn't define darkened his voice. "Your eyes are still lovely as ever. Would you care to dance?"

Oh dear heaven. Her pulse leapt until she recalled two things. She was an abysmal dancer, and her train was in pieces. She wisely kept the first to herself. "I'd love to, but I'm afraid my train…"

"Bloody hell, I'd already forgotten." He grimaced. "What an ass. Perhaps you'd like another glass of champagne?"

Belatedly, she realized the glass she held was empty. When had she drunk it all? She couldn't recall. Perhaps that was the reason her head felt as if it had been filled with fluffy white clouds. Yes, that had to be it. Surely it wasn't the tall stranger with the gorgeous mouth who kept plying her with sensual looks and disarming smiles. She probably ought not to have another flute of champagne.

"I'd love another," she said. Hadn't she lived her life the way she should? And what had that gotten her but misery and loneliness and a husband she hadn't seen in over a year?

He returned to her side and pressed another glass of champagne into her hand. "There you are, my dear."

"Thank you." She took a fortifying sip, calming the jagged bundle of her nerves. Perhaps there was hope for her madcap plan after all. The stranger before her would certainly do for a scandal. Yes indeed. He certainly looked like the sort of man who would accept an invitation to sin. She forced her mind into safer territory, trying to distract herself from wanton thoughts. "Who has caused your heart to require mending?" she asked him. "A wife?"

He hesitated, drinking his champagne, and for a moment she feared she'd overstepped her bounds. "Not a wife, no," he said with care. "But a very old and dear friend."

"A lover," she concluded aloud, then flushed at her bluntness, which always landed her in trouble. "I'm sorry, sir, if I'm too forthright. I cannot help myself."

"You needn't apologize. Everyone knows that here at Lady Needham's none of the standard society rules apply. You've but to look around you to see that." His tone was wry as his gaze lit on the couple against the wall. The man clenched the woman's skirts in his fist, raising them to reveal her shapely, stocking-clad calves.

Maggie looked away, cheeks stinging. Of course none of the standard rules applied here. Indeed, from all appearances, there were *no* rules here. It was one of the many reasons she'd decided—against her better judgment—to attend. What better place to create a scandal than a party that existed for the express purpose of licentiousness?

"Is that why you're here?" She couldn't squelch her curiosity. "For the...lack of rules?"

Surely it was the champagne that made her so daring. For the real Maggie would never have dreamt of insinuating such a thing to a stranger. She'd all but asked him if he sought a lover, for heaven's sake. But if she wanted to succeed in forcing her husband to divorce her, she couldn't be herself. She had to be someone fearless and bold. Someone without conscience. Someone like the man she'd wed.

"I suppose it is in part." He took another sip of spirits. "What of you? What brings you here? You appear terribly young for this fast set."

"Disappointment, I suppose." She gulped her champagne as he closed the distance between them. He was so near she could see the dark stubble on his defined jaw.

"You're certainly too young for disappointment." He ran a finger from her elbow to her wrist, stopping to tangle his fingers with hers. "Who would dare to disappoint you?"

"My husband." Her mouth went dry. Though truth be told, she was far more disappointed in herself than she was in the marquis. After all, she had known he married her for her dowry in the same way she had married him for his title.

However, she had not anticipated his utter defection and her resulting misery. But there was little need to divulge her inner sins and secrets to the man before her now. This was to be a lighthearted affair. A means to an end.

"He must be an utter bastard to cause you so much distress."

She laughed without mirth. "I would say he is a rather cold and heartless man." Yes indeed, that described Sandhurst perfectly.

He squeezed her fingers. "I'm sorry, my dear."

"You are not the man who owes me an apology." The old sadness bloomed in her heart as she thought of Richard and all she'd left. "But I suppose I'll never have one from him." The best she could expect from him was anger. Perhaps a blinding fury. She meant to cuckold him before all London, to leave no doubt in the minds of the entire *ton*. Only then could she be free. This man could help her. She felt certain of it.

"Do you love him?" he asked, startling her.

His query threw her. People of their class so rarely married for love. She did not love her husband, but she had certainly married him with a hopeful heart. Her mother had assured her that many modern marriages began with respect and led to tender affections after time and diligence. She had hoped to foster a relationship of kindness between herself and her husband, at the least. Instead, their relationship consisted of silence. But it was odd for the man before her to have pondered such a question.

"Of course not," she said at last. "What of you and your dear friend? Do you love her?"

"I did for many years," he said, the admission seemingly torn from him. "Now, I'm not certain what I feel any longer. A need for change, certainly."

She saw them for what they were then, a man and woman who had somehow run across each other's paths at the same ball, both of them lost. Searching. She longed to escape from the gilded prison in which she now found herself. He longed for something. Perhaps distraction. A lover. It didn't matter. What did matter was that the fear in her had at long last subsided. She stood ready, poised to grab the reins of her life and steer herself in a different direction.

"What sort of change do you seek?" she asked, watching him above the rim of her flute.

His sinful mouth curved in a half smile. "I think perhaps it's you."

She nearly choked on her mouthful of champagne. "Me?"

"Oh yes," he told her in that seductive, deep voice of his. His green eyes were fierce and direct on her, trapping her gaze so she couldn't look anywhere else. There was no denying his sensual promise. "You."

She should not have invited the stranger to her chamber. She thought of one of her favorite poems, *The Lady's Yes* and how it cautioned against the flirtations of the ballroom, how inconstant they seemed by bright daylight. Yes indeed, she should never have entertained such iniquity, let alone offered herself up for it.

But she needed a scandal. A scandal of magnitude. A scandal her husband could not ignore. He could provide her with that and more, the stranger from the ballroom. She would make certain that as many eyes as possible saw her for the entirety of the house party. There would be no question as to the sins she'd committed. At the conclusion of the fete, she'd remove her mask, strip herself from the safety of anonymity. Everyone would know the Marquis of Sandhurst was a cuckold.

A small stab of guilt pierced her, for she was not the sort of woman who used a stranger for her own gain. She hadn't been, anyway, but desperation had a way of bringing one quite low indeed. Maggie paced the length of polished floorboards peeking out from amongst thick carpets. Perhaps it was the champagne. Perhaps it was the evening, the man's dancing eyes, his deep voice laden with desire. Perhaps it was the allure of something more, the mysterious relationship between a man and a woman that had never been fully realized for her.

For a wife of nearly a year, she was still, somehow, a virgin.

That made her decision all the more reckless. What would the man think? She didn't know his name, his face. She'd chatted with him in a crowded ballroom and now he would arrive at any moment to take her innocence. *Come to my chamber,* she'd told him, as though it was a sentence she'd uttered to a hundred men before him. Maggie fanned her face with her hand, needing air. What did it all entail? She'd heard murmurings that the deflowering would be painful at best, horridly humiliating at worst. Her friend Victoria said the marriage bed was wondrous, but Victoria was thoroughly besotted with her reformed rake of a husband and her word was understandably compromised by her feelings.

A discreet knock sounded at her door. Two quick raps. He had come.

She flattened her palms over her nightdress, a fairly formal affair of cotton and lace. Upon dismissing her lady's maid, she had retied the mask to conceal her face. After all, she couldn't risk being discovered until her plan was complete. Lady Needham's wicked country house party was the perfect setting for such an undertaking. Guests wore masks for its three-day duration, enabling them to dabble in pursuits that were decidedly more sinful than ordinary society permitted.

Pursuits like fornication in a ballroom. Yes, she was sure the couple to her right had done something most wicked. Before her eyes, she'd seen the gentleman ruck up the lady's skirts to her waist. He'd begun thrusting his body into hers, the lady tipping back her head, mouth falling open. Maggie had watched in rapt fascination, a keen sense of something heretofore unknown crashing over her. And all around them, the revelers had continued, some stopping to watch, others ignoring the spectacle entirely.

She took a deep breath before hastening to the door and pulling it open. There he stood, the man who had trampled her train. He appeared somehow taller now than he had in the ballroom, still wearing his black evening tails and his mask. Heat sluiced through her veins, mingling with uncertainty. For a breath, she thought about snapping the door closed and abandoning her scheme entirely.

"Am I still welcome?" Even his voice was somehow intimate.

Awareness prickled her skin. He was being polite, allowing her to change her mind. She hadn't an inkling of how to conduct an affair. Maybe this was commonplace to him. Maybe he was a rake of the first order. Would that make what she must do easier or more difficult?

But he had asked her a question, hadn't he?

Of course he was still welcome. She hadn't a choice. She stepped back into the chamber, gesturing him inside, using levity to cloak her muddled emotions. "You are most welcome as long as you promise not to do any further damage to my wardrobe."

He chuckled as he strode across the threshold. "I shall do my utmost to keep your gowns in good order, I swear it."

It wasn't her gowns she feared he'd do damage to at this point. She closed the door behind him and spun, unaccountably nervous now that she'd done what she'd set out to do in the first, obtained a lover. If only she knew what to do with him. If only she knew what he'd do to her. Would it be like the couple in the ballroom? Would he pump into her in quick, violent thrusts? An answering pulse throbbed between her legs. Her legs went weak, her breathing shallow. She was ashamed of herself, of her reaction to him, her reaction to this wickedness. For a part of her enjoyed it.

"My lady's maid will be relieved to hear it." She clasped her hands at her waist and watched him. She felt faint, trapped between a desire to flee and a need to launch herself at him and begin this madness. She hoped she appeared poised and confident, a seasoned participant in the game they now played.

He smiled, his teeth visible in a brief white flash before he was once again serious. His eyes dropped. "Your hands are shaking, my dear."

She looked down as well. So they were. Dear heaven. How was she ever going to make it through the night? "I suppose I'm a bit anxious," she conceded.

"You've never been to one of Lady Needham's house parties before, have you?" His voice was knowing. He closed the space between them, catching her worried hands in his large, warm ones.

She was dismayed that he saw through her with such ease. She'd thought she had done an admirable job of portraying the debauched lady. "How did you know?"

"You're a trifle too sincere." He raised her hands to his lips, kissing each with a slow reverence that thoroughly disarmed her. "In truth, I've never met a woman as candid and lovely."

She was breathless. "Never?" Oh, how she hoped he was not merely wooing her with meaningless praise. A foolish thought, a foolish hope, for she had no claims upon the man before her, nor would she ever. He was a means to an end. Through him she'd gain her independence. That was all.

"Never." He turned her hands over and dropped a kiss to her palms, then her wrists. "It's bad of me, but I'm deuced glad I trounced your gown."

A shiver of pure desire skittered down her spine. Her body felt heavy and warm, weighed down with the delicious possibility of what was to come. "It seems fortuitous." All her earlier bravado failed her. She was desperate to know what was about to unfold and yet simultaneously terrified.

"Am I overstepping my bounds, my dear?" He yet held

her hands in his. "You haven't stopped trembling. I wouldn't dream of frightening you."

"No," she hastened to assure him. "This is all new to me, I fear, and rather daunting."

He stilled. "Am I to be your first lover, then?"

He'd guessed. Likely, she hadn't made the assumption a difficult one to make.

"You are." Embarrassment made her long to crawl beneath the lovely carved oak bed taking up the opposite wall. Somehow, she hadn't imagined as much conversation. How had she ever supposed seducing a man would be easy? How had she ever believed it wouldn't affect her?

"I'm honored," he said, his voice deep and velvety. He reached up to touch the corner of her mask. "Do you wish to keep it on?"

"Yes." The barrier made their intimacies somehow more manageable. "If you don't mind, sir. At least until the lamps are out."

"If it pleases you." His fingers lingered on her chin, tipping it upward. "I'm going to kiss you now."

She placed her hands upon his broad shoulders. "Please do." She closed her eyes, waiting. The other kisses she'd experienced had been chaste and flat, a mere perfunctory brushing of lips over hers. Richard had been the perfect gentleman. The Marquis had never even bothered.

But if she'd expected the same sort of brief peck now, she'd been entirely wrong. Delightfully so. His mouth pressed against hers, hot and firm, his upper lip fitting naturally into the seam of hers. He drew his arms around her waist, anchoring her body to his. The hardness of his long, lean form was a pleasant surprise. She leaned into him, hungry for more, gasping when his tongue teased her lower lip. The moment she opened to him, he swept inside her mouth. Tentatively, she ran her tongue against his, tasting him. Champagne and sin.

The warmth pervading her senses all evening escalated into a fire that began in her belly and echoed in her sex. Her skin tingled. A steady ache thrummed between her legs. She'd never experienced a more heady mix of pleasure and longing. *At last*, she thought as she mimicked his kiss.

He dragged his mouth from hers, his breathing ragged, before dropping tantalizing kisses over her bare neck. He made a path to the hollow at the base of her throat where her pulse galloped at a frantic pace. His silk mask scraped against her, equally exciting. She tilted her head back to grant him greater access. His fingers went to the shell buttons on her cotton nightgown's bodice, unhooking them from their moorings one at a time.

Dear heavens. For all the times she'd lain awake in her bed, imagining this moment of capitulation, she'd never had any idea how thrilling and horridly frightening it would be all at once. He was disrobing her. She didn't know his name. Somehow, impossibly, that heightened the allure.

He worked his way to the button between her breasts and paused, glancing up at her. The intensity of his stare nearly made her knees give out. "Are you utterly certain, my dear?"

He was giving her the opportunity to change her mind, she realized through the dizzying desire clouding her rational brain. Of course she wasn't certain. She'd never been more hopelessly uncertain of anything in her life. But that was part of what made sharing heated kisses with a masked stranger so enticing. She felt free for the first time, empowered by her anonymity. She could be anyone she wanted to be in the magic of the night. She could do anything she wanted.

"Yes. I'm certain."

"We shall go slowly." He cupped her breasts through the fine fabric of her nightdress. "I want to make you mad with wanting before I take you."

His words sent a fresh surge of heat and wetness to the apex of her thighs. His thumbs rubbed in lazy circles over her nipples, hardening them into aching nubs. She wanted desperately for him to touch her without the barrier of cotton. She reached between them, attempting to help undo the endless line of closures with fumbling fingers.

"All those damn buttons." He gave her nipples a soft pinch that made her moan. "What do you women think when you purchase these blasted fripperies?"

She'd certainly never thought of a sinful stranger peeling it from her body. Maggie freed a few more buttons until her nightgown was open to her waist. She pulled her arms from the long sleeves, baring her bosom to his heated gaze.

"Do you find this preferable, sir?" Her voice was throaty, almost as if it belonged to another woman entirely.

"Hell yes, I do." He palmed her breasts. "This is a vast improvement."

Her heart raced, every part of her body focused with maddening intensity on the place where their skin met. Her need for a scandal no longer drove her. Instead, it was him. His touch, his scent, the forbidden. She arched into him. Their gazes clashed and he kissed her again, his mouth open and voracious. Claiming. She kissed him back rubbing her tongue against his as he plundered. She wanted more.

He squeezed her nipples between his thumb and forefinger and dipped his head to kiss her throat. She placed her hands on his chest, longing to feel his masculine form without his formal evening clothes. He dragged his mouth lower, sucking her nipple. He flicked the bud gently with his tongue in quick, sweet strokes. It was wicked. It was wanton. Of all the times she'd envisioned carrying out her plan, she'd never once imagined she would actually enjoy the act of sin that would grant her the freedom she so desired.

He paused and looked up at her, a mischievous smile curving his lips. The contrast between her pale skin and his black silk mask was as seductive as his glittering gaze. "Do you like my tongue on you?"

The boldness of his speech shocked her. No one had even referred to limbs in her presence before. Bodies were things to be covered and hidden, not meant for unveiled adoration. But she rather liked this naughtiness, the venturing into the forbidden. "Can't you tell for yourself?" she returned, joining in on his game of teasing.

He suckled her other nipple, dragging deeply until he wrung another moan from her. "I want to hear it from your proper, lovely lips." He laved her with his tongue, bent on reducing her to a complete wanton. "Say it."

"I like it." She sighed, her fingers sinking into his too-long, midnight hair.

He stopped, blowing air over the taut nub he'd just pleasured. "What do you like? Tell me."

Maggie's mouth went dry. She didn't know what she liked. All she knew was that she liked every wicked thing he did to her. But she couldn't say such words aloud. "I don't know."

He caught her nipple between his teeth and nipped playfully. "Tell me. If you want more, you must tell me, darling."

Fine. She wanted more. "I like your tongue." She pressed her breast into his cheek. "I like your mouth on me."

He kissed the plump mound she'd offered him. "You're learning."

"I did warn you against my forthright nature." She was breathless as his mouth seared a trail back up to her neck and at last her lips.

Their hungry mouths met. He drew her against him, pushing the crumpled remnants of her nightgown from her waist, down over her hips. It landed on the floor about her ankles, sending a brief draft of air up her naked legs. One of his hands cupped her bottom while the other skimmed over the curve of her belly and settled into the mound at the apex of her thighs. His long fingers dipped into the folds of her sex. All thought fled from her mind.

"I'm grateful for your nature." He nipped at her lips and rubbed the hidden pearl between her legs, the one she'd only dared touch once or twice in the bath. Pure bliss surged through her body, along with a yearning for more.

"Please," she begged, uncertain what she was asking him for. Completion. A joining. Anything that would satisfy the crescendo of longing that was driving her as mad as he'd said he wanted to make her. She'd never known anything so potent and incredible was possible between a man and woman. Revenge, freedom, right, wrong…everything fell away. All that existed for her was this moment, this man and the way he made her feel.

"Tell me what you want." His ministrations continued, his pace increasing along with the pressure he exerted upon her.

She was going to fracture, to collapse. Her breathing was hitched. Her heart was poised to leap from her chest. Sensation built to a wild pitch as his fingers worked between her legs. It was as if he knew she was about to come undone.

"I…" she began, only to falter. She didn't think she could speak. He lowered his mouth to suck a hard nipple once more, and the dam within her burst. She writhed against him, desire rippling through her body in waves of unadulterated pleasure. Her hips ground against him as she cried out, head thrown back.

"Do you want me to fuck you, darling?" He licked a path around the pink tip of her breast.

As the ripples of passion began to subside, she felt a new spurt of wetness between her legs. He continued teasing her there, and her flesh was sensitized by his touch so much that she feared she would reach her peak again in another breath.

She'd never heard the word *fuck* before, and she had a feeling it was terribly bad, but she loved the way it sounded on his lips. Whatever it meant, she was quite certain she wanted it very much.

"Do you?" he asked again as his fingers moved over her with a practiced expertise.

She gasped at the heightened sensation. If the pleasure he gave her had been strong before, it overwhelmed her now. "I do," she said. She wanted more of that, wanted to be filled. By him, with him.

Just when she was on the brink, he withdrew, startling her. In the next instant, he took her in his arms. She threw her arms about his neck for purchase. No man had ever scooped her up thusly before, as if she weighed no more than a feather pillow. And she weighed far more than a feather pillow.

"I'm too heavy." It wasn't as if she was overly large, but she possessed the requisite feminine curves. She was no willowy miss, that much was certain.

"You're a perfect armful." He looked impossibly rakish with his black mask and seductive smile.

She couldn't shake the feeling that beneath the silk shielding his face from her view there hid a dangerously handsome man. He was the opposite of the only other man whose attentions she'd ever wanted aside from Richard.

Her husband.

Sandhurst had been far too busy to say more than a handful of sentences to her after he'd secured her fortune. Having won her, he'd promptly abandoned her in favor of his beautiful mistress. A year had passed since she'd last seen him. And how dare he intrude upon her thoughts now, when freedom was within her grasp? To the devil with him.

She forced all unhappy thoughts from her mind and instead focused on the man who carried her across the room to deposit her on the bed with a gentleness that suggested he thought she was fashioned of the finest porcelain. He was everything a gentleman ought to be, and she was thankful she'd been given this one night to spend in his arms. With hearts in need of repair, they had somehow found each other. And with his unwitting help, she'd gain her escape.

Maggie watched him as he shucked his coat and silk tie and made short work of his white shirt. In a breath, his chest was bare to her seeking gaze. He was broadly built, well-muscled, his stomach taut, chest dotted by a tantalizing amount of dark hair. She'd never seen a bare male torso aside from the marble slabs and oils applied to canvas in the name of art. No artist's rendering had ever been so perfect, at least not in her eyes. She longed to touch him.

And then, he unfastened his trousers, allowing them too to fall. His manhood jutted from between his firm, horseman's thighs. Thick and hard, it rose in proud relief against a small whorl of hair and his sac. Her mouth went dry as she stared at his shaft. She knew a bit about men and women, both from her married heiress friends who had dared to share treasured secrets and from the saucy novels she read in private. She was aware that he was about to put himself inside her. It was daunting to be sure. How painful would it be? She stiffened as a new wave of nervousness assailed her. She'd tried to prepare herself in advance, but preparation and reality were starkly different.

He sensed her sudden discomfort. Still wearing his mask though not a stitch else, he lowered his strong body to the bed. He cupped her face and gave her a lingering, tender kiss.

"You needn't fear me, my dear." He broke away from her. "We shall do only what you want. Tonight, I am yours. Do you understand?"

She stared at him, at a loss. He was giving himself to her. Completely. "Mine?" she asked, doubting him.

"Yours," he repeated. "Your servant for tonight. I seek only to bring you pleasure."

"You already have," she said foolishly. She didn't know what he wanted of her. He imagined her a woman who knew the ways between a man and woman. Perhaps when he had guessed he was her first lover, he had meant her first lover outside her marriage. Most married women had lost their maidenhood, so his was not an unreasonable assumption. "I haven't done this before," she added for good measure.

"I know you haven't." He smiled and kissed her again.

"No," honesty compelled her to say. "It is not as you think. While I'm a married woman, my husband has not…that is to say, I remain…chaste."

"Oh Christ." He stilled, his gaze searching hers, his mouth going taut. "You've never lain with a man before?"

She shook her head, flushing from head to toe. The words refused to form on her tongue.

"Ah." He leaned into her, pressing his hard body to hers, and kissed her lingeringly. "That simply means that our rules have altered."

She rolled toward him so that her breasts crushed into his hard chest and his manhood prodded her belly. "I haven't an inkling as to what rules you speak of." She was well aware that she was out of her depth.

"The rules between you and me as lovers," he said, cupping her bottom and pulling her into him more fully. "You must promise to tell me exactly what you want. Do you promise?"

She swallowed. This was so much more than what she had imagined. She wasn't certain she could find it within her to give voice to the wicked things he did to her. But with those vivid eyes swallowing her whole, she knew she would do anything to please him.

"I promise," she agreed at last.

A sinful smile flirted with the corners of his lips. "Good." He kissed her again, nipping at her lower lip before working his way back down her body. "I want to taste you everywhere."

His tongue flicked out against the fullness of her breast, then lightly over her aching nipple. But he did not take her into his mouth again as she wanted. Instead, he moved lower still, to her navel. He paused, glancing up at her, looking every inch the part of a highwayman of old come to plunder. He was perilously near to the wet heat of her center. She longed to feel him there.

"Open your legs for me, darling," he coaxed, his hands on her hips, caressing.

She obeyed, shivering with anticipation, watching him.

He groaned, his eyes going to that most private part of

her. Cool air hit her humid skin, heightening her awareness even more. "I want to taste you. Do you want my tongue on you, darling?"

Dear heaven. He had a filthy, frank way of speaking. He meant to... Her mind couldn't form a coherent thought. She was shocked and titillated at the same time. She hadn't known men did such sinful things. She should tell him no. But his stare and his naughty words had combined to send another delicious pulse of want to her core. She wanted him to lick her. Maggie swallowed, stricken by the realization. She was a wanton.

"Yes," she whispered at last. "Please."

His eyes swung up to hers, pinning her with the naked desire she saw reflected in their mossy depths. He lowered his head and sucked the responsive bud of her sex into his mouth, holding her gaze all the while. The sight of him pleasuring her, his masked face buried between her thighs, only served to heighten her passion. She tipped her head back and moaned as he continued sucking, occasionally using his teeth to ever-so-gently rake against the plump nub so eager for his every attention. It was pure poetry, singing through her body and setting her aflame. This was the answer to the troubles plaguing her, she thought, this sweet distraction. At least it could warm her body if not her soul.

"Mmm, darling." He lifted his head, stopping the sensual torture. His lips were shiny with her juices. "Do you like when I lick your cunny?"

She flushed, still embarrassed by his words even now that he had actually done the deed. She didn't know what to say. A helpless slave to her own need, she watched as he pressed a kiss to each of her thighs, then flicked his tongue out to toy with her. She bucked against him, dangerously near to falling apart. So many new, wicked names to match the sensations he unlocked.

He stopped again, blowing on her swollen, slick flesh. A truly seductive smile curved his lips. "Tell me, my dear. Tell me what you like. Say the words."

He wanted to hear her affirmation, wanted that power over her. And he had it. He could make her say whatever he wanted, could make her do whatever he wanted. She'd strayed too far from her intended path. She struggled to force her mind to function. "I like your mouth on me." While this was indeed a night of firsts, she still couldn't bring herself to repeat his wayward words.

He groaned once more, lowering his head to her sex. His tongue worked over her in a maddening dance, flicking her tender button back and forth. She couldn't hold herself together. The wild feeling between her thighs rippled through her entire body, making her tense beneath him. Suddenly, the pleasure whirled out of control, slamming into her. She shook, arching into his knowing mouth, crying out with helpless release.

"You came for me twice, darling." He dropped a kiss on her sex, then rose.

His manhood jutted from him, hard and long. He had enjoyed giving her pleasure as much as she had receiving it. She reached for him, clutching at his strong, broad shoulders. His skin was hot and smooth, his muscles flexing beneath her touch as he angled himself over her. His dark head bent to suckle her nipple. Wetness trickled down over the folds of her sex. Want of him made her mindless.

Maggie pulled him to her, moaning. She didn't understand what was happening between them. Nothing in her life could have prepared her. Good heavens. Perhaps she was dying of pleasure. It seemed possible as he took her other nipple into his mouth. His hands ran up over her hips to settle on the nip of her waist. He dragged his lips to her neck, kissing just below her ear. She shivered, loving his every touch, his every action.

"I want to go slowly for your sake, but I'm going mad with wanting you." He caught her earlobe between his teeth and gave a soft, playful tug. "Christ, what you do to me, woman."

She was already beyond rational thought, but not so

much that she didn't know what she wanted. What she needed. She captured his face between her hands, pulling him to her until their noses nearly brushed. He was devastatingly handsome, that much she could discern even with the obstruction of his silken mask. "Do not go slowly on my account," she urged him, breathless.

A beautiful smile curved his sensuous mouth. "I love debauching you, my dear."

Debauching her? She did her best to ignore the phrase, for perhaps lingering upon it overlong would induce an attack of conscience. Of course, she shouldn't have any conscience at all in terms of her husband, that insufferable lout who likely didn't recall what she looked like. But she had not been raised to be a fast lady with an impenetrable heart. Her parents, for all that they were alarmingly wealthy, had always enjoyed a love match. She'd foolishly expected the same respect and love in her own marriage. She had been terribly wrong.

He lowered his mouth to hers for a devouring kiss. She opened to him, her tongue flitting against his. He tasted sweet and musky, a blend of himself and her both. His hands went between them, skimming down over her rounded belly to her cunny, to use his ribald word for that part of her body. She found she liked the wickedness of it. He worked her nub, and she tipped her hips up and into him, loving his every touch on her starved flesh. She wanted more.

"I've never wanted to take anyone the way I want you." His breath was a warm puff of air fanning over her lips.

"Take me," she said against his mouth. "Tonight, I'm yours."

"Fuck." He lowered his forehead to hers. "I'm going to lose my head if I'm not inside you soon."

She wanted him inside her. Mindless, she moved against into his finger, hungry for more of him. Deeper. Harder. Oh good heavens, yes. "Please," she begged. "I want you."

"It's going to hurt." He kissed her lingeringly. "When I

enter you, I'm given to understand there will be pain."

She didn't fail to notice his phrasing. "Am I your first virgin?"

"Yes." His tone was velvety. "We are each other's firsts, it would seem, in different ways."

She rather liked the notion, she found. It was fitting somehow. "I have never been faint-hearted," she said, referring to the pain. "When I was a girl, I broke my arm falling from an apple tree and I never even cried." Surely his entrance couldn't cause as much pain as a broken bone had, she reasoned.

"Brave girl," he said, kissing her. "I don't want to hurt you."

"You won't," she said with more bravado than she truly felt. "Make me yours."

He ceased his delicious torture. His cock, large and full, pressed into her instead. "Wrap your legs round my waist, darling."

She did as he asked, allowing him to settle comfortably between her thighs. He moved against her, not yet entering her. Warm pleasure hit her like a wave from the ocean.

"How does that feel?" he asked, sounding strained.

She was touched by his concern but frustrated too. She didn't want him to be restrained and careful. She wanted him to lose himself inside her. "Wonderful."

He thrust into her, slowly at first, and then with increasing pace and vigor. The pain began, an unpleasant burning. This was what she'd been warned about, but once her maidenhead was gone, she would never again experience the discomfort she knew now. Biting her lip, she jerked into him, taking him deep inside. A sharp ache cut through her.

And then he began moving. The pain ebbed with each long, slow thrust of his cock. As she adapted to the new sensation of him filling her, she moved along with him, adjusting the angle of her hips for comfort. Soon, pleasure overtook all else. Nothing could have prepared Maggie for a man pleasuring her in that elemental way. It was incredible.

He reached between their bodies to stroke her and increased the pace and the pressure of his thrusts, his breathing coming faster. His heart was a rapid thump against her breast. She sank her fingers into his silky hair, inhaling deeply of his potent, male scent. Just when she thought nothing in the world could possibly compare to the sensations sparking through her, she was proven wrong. He anchored her hips and slammed into her, bringing her intense waves of pleasure. She was going to come yet again, she realized, twisting up, wanting more of him, wanting to consume him.

Her sheath tightened on his cock as she found her release, and he abruptly withdrew from her. He pressed himself against her belly and a warm, wet spurt landed on her bare skin. His seed, she realized.

He collapsed at her side, wrapping one possessive arm around her, his breathing heavy and fast. Maggie had never felt more alive. She was awash in fantastic sensation, her entire body throbbing, her sex wet and swollen. She turned to him and pressed one last kiss to his lips, knowing that from this moment forward, she would never again be the same.

A woman, she thought with what little coherence remained in her fogged mind. She was at last a woman. A woman about to gain her revenge.

chapter two

*H*E WOKE TO A WOMAN, warm and sweet-smelling, pressed to his side. For a moment, he thought it was Eleanor, until he recalled that Eleanor had told him to go to hell and was likely off riding her balding, red-nosed husband somewhere in London. Damn it.

Simon blinked open his eyes. Perched on her side, his bedmate slept opposite him, her back a bare slice of tempting skin, long red curls curved over her creamy shoulder. The bedclothes had pooled around her narrow waist, leaving the small dent at the top of her buttocks visible to him in the early-morning light.

Ah yes, his mystery woman. His cock stirred as recollection filtered through his sleep-fogged mind. He'd taken a virgin he'd met at Lady Needham's house party. Hell. She sighed in her sleep and settled on her back, revealing her full, pink-tipped breasts once more. Her nipples were hard, begging to be sucked. He groaned, his hand going to his already rigid cock and stroking. Hopefully she wasn't too sore, for he longed to take her again. He'd done his best to ease her into lovemaking, but he'd never had a virgin before, and there was no telling how her body would react.

He moved his hand beneath the covers, brushing his fingers over her rounded thigh before settling in the damp, hot folds of her cunny. Ah yes. She certainly felt ready. He glanced up to her face as a gauge. Her mask still covered the upper half of her face, but in her slumber it had been knocked askew. Curiosity pricked him then.

Who was she? He had to know her face, this untutored virgin who'd made him come undone with the ease of a practiced courtesan. He wasn't about to let her out of his sight any time soon. She was just the sort of distraction he needed. He slid the mask away. She was beautiful. Familiar. She was...

Good, sweet Christ.

She was his *wife*.

He stilled, willing his eyes to see something different. It had been some time since he'd last been in her presence— perhaps even a year—but there was no denying who she was. The small, pert nose, the lush lips, the riotous red curls. She appeared somehow wilder, more vibrant and womanly now as she lay nude with him. But the face of his mystery woman, the woman who had altered his world with her innocent passion, was undeniably the woman he had wed.

Margaret. Lady Sandhurst. Christ, all this time he'd thought she was a quiet, bookish bluestocking sitting at home building her library and sending him petulant letters, and instead she'd been about the business of making him a cuckold. He took back his hands as if he were a street urchin caught stealing. What a cunning little wench she'd turned out to be. He never would have guessed.

He rolled away and rose from the bed, his ardor effectively dampened by the revelation that he'd been about to make love to his wife. Again. Bloody hell, he'd never wanted to consummate their union. He'd been forced to marry her as a matter of circumstance, but he'd vowed never to make her his wife in truth. And now he unwittingly had done precisely that. His gut clenched at the realization.

"Fuck." He searched for his discarded clothes. "Bloody stupid prick."

He had to leave before she woke and discovered who he was. Good God, it would be better to allow her to think she'd tupped some stranger. He should have known it was her. How had he missed the signs? He bent and stuffed his legs into his trousers. She was an American. Her hair was the same color, all rebellious curls. Of course there'd been the matter of her mask, and that he'd never once dreamt his mild-mannered wife would deign to appear at a house party renowned for its sexual decadence and freedom. How the devil had she garnered an invitation?

He found his shirt and didn't bother with the buttons. No questions would be asked if anyone passed him in the corridor, as they would more than likely be equally guilty parties. More so, actually. He'd only bedded his wife, after all.

Raking a hand through his hair, he tiptoed from the chamber. He closed the door at his back with a sigh of relief. There was no reason she ever need discover the truth. It was best for the both of them, really. He had no intention of playing the part of husband. Ever. He had come to the house party for distraction, a respite from the torment eating at him ever since Eleanor's defection. He may have been forced to sell himself to an American fortune, but he still possessed his pride, by God.

He stalked back to his chamber. It would be best if he left Lady Needham's before seeing her again. He didn't think he could stomach it.

Maggie woke to the sound of a door being snapped tightly closed. It must be her maid, she thought in her sleep-clouded mind. She rolled over, aware of cool air over her naked breasts. And a distinct yet new soreness between her thighs.

Good heavens.

She sat up in bed as if a gong had just been rung beside her ear. Maggie looked around, relieved to find her chamber empty in the early-morning light. She was alone. It wouldn't do for her lady's maid to find her in such a state of...she looked down at herself to find she was utterly nude and promptly yanked the bedclothes all the way up to her chin.

Her heart tripped over itself. She'd actually done it. Her plan to force Sandhurst into divorcing her had sprung into motion. Now all she needed to do was wage a war of public humiliation. All she needed to do was use a man she scarcely knew to further her cause. The unwanted thought sent a pang of guilt through her.

She didn't know his name or his face. He had pleasured her in ways she'd never imagined possible. And then, apparently, he had disappeared. She glanced about the chamber, searching for a sign of her impassioned lover and finding only a rumpled scrap of fabric.

His necktie.

Had she not pleased him? Was her untried state too much for him? Or was this standard practice for the wicked? Perhaps the fast set all shared life-changing evenings of desire and then never saw each other again without compunction.

Who was he?

Unable to sleep, she rose from the bed in search of her nightgown. She didn't want her lady's maid to find her in such a state. With a sigh, she threw a linen shift over her head, straightening it before wrapping herself up in a dressing gown. Her bare feet crossed the carpet to the mirror at the vanity on the far end of the chamber.

Her hair was a wild tangle of curls about her head. She appeared pale. Different. She was a woman on her way to regaining her life. The biggest step had been taken, and now all she needed to do was continue what she'd begun. Two days of sin in return for her lifetime. If only her moment of triumph didn't feel so dratted empty.

Maggie found herself seated beside Lady Needham herself at breakfast. Her ladyship was without a mask, in defiance of her own rule that all guests were to remain incognito for the entire weekend. Her reputation preceded her as a woman with a complete disregard for the strictures of polite society, a woman who sought pleasures regardless of the cost and encouraged others to join her in her iniquities. But in truth, Lady Needham was a small woman with a smart sense of dress and a habit of speaking more plainly than was fashionable.

Maggie thought her hostess to be rather American at heart, and she admired her bravado. She didn't have much appetite this morning, but Lady Needham buoyed her flagging spirits with her clever quips over the other guests' fashion choices.

"Blessed angels. Would you have a gander at that atrocious nest of hair?" Lady Needham whispered to Maggie, inclining her head toward the unfortunate woman in question. "I daresay an entire flock of birds could get lost in that monstrosity."

Maggie giggled into her napkin, keenly enjoying the distraction her hostess's unbridled tongue provided. Of course, she agreed with her, but Maggie would never venture such observations aloud.

"What do you think, my dear?" Lady Needham asked *sotto voce*, giving her a friendly nudge.

"Her dress is a ghastly shade of yellow," Maggie offered.

"Ah, I love your accent, dear girl. Say 'ghastly' again, do."

"Ghastly," Maggie complied.

"A New York lady, obviously." Lady Needham took a sip of juice and studied her with a lively blue gaze. "Did you enjoy the ball last night?"

Maggie swallowed. "I did, yes, my lady."

"You needn't stand on ceremony here, dear." Lady Needham smiled. "You're not in New York, and you're not in London. You're free to do whatever you want and to be whomever you want. My rules. And I daresay those are my only rules."

"I like your rules." They were freeing. A prelude to her future without the manacles of marriage.

A gentleman stalked into the breakfast room just then, stealing Maggie's eye. After what they'd shared the night before, she'd know his figure anywhere, that masked, handsome face and dark hair. It was him. The man who had made love to her all night and then vanished by morning.

Her breath escaped from her lungs in a slow flight.

His cold gaze did a tour of the breakfast room, traveling over the occupants until it landed upon her. Maggie froze. Unbidden, the sinful magic he'd worked on her body rose in her mind. She imagined him licking her, sucking her nipples, recalled the feeling of his cock hard and demanding inside her. Flushing, she looked away.

"Handsome devil, isn't he?" Lady Needham asked softly. "I must say I had my eye on him, but he's been in love with another for ever so long."

"You know who he is?" The question had left her lips before she could think better of her eagerness.

"Of course I do, my dear. But I can't tell. It would spoil the fun." Her hostess raised a brow. "And what good is the world without a spot of fun?"

Her mystery man inclined his head, acknowledging her ever so slightly. A spot of fun indeed. She couldn't look away from him. It was as if no one else in the breakfast room, none of the other glittering, tittering masked revelers, existed.

"Ah, it would seem that our gallant has eyes for one lady only this morning." Lady Needham's voice was still quiet, but an edge of curiosity had crept into her smooth drawl. "Lucky, lucky Lady New York."

"Sandhurst," Maggie corrected her without thought. She forced herself to look away from the man who had so easily set her world on end. "I'm Lady Sandhurst," she admitted to her hostess. She would begin small. Share her name with a few of her fellow guests, test the waters.

Lady Needham gaped at her. Maggie supposed she was something of a recluse in society, certainly not known for much of anything save having a husband who was desperately in love with Lady Billingsley. She'd grown accustomed to that unfortunate bit of fame. And of course there was the matter of her having convinced her friend the Duchess of Trent to provide her with the invitation. Lady Sandhurst had not been invited.

"Sandhurst," her hostess repeated at last, sounding utterly perplexed.

Unfortunately, she hadn't anticipated such a reaction to her *faux pas*. "I do apologize, my lady, for accepting on behalf of the Duchess of Trent. I'm aware the invitation wasn't meant for me, but I was in greater need of it than she."

Lady Needham waved a dismissive hand. "Nonsense. Everyone knows they may pass along an invitation to any interested party they like. It keeps the company from growing stagnant. It's merely that I'm familiar with your...situation, my lady."

She shifted uncomfortably, her corset pinching her waist. "I'm aware my husband's reputation precedes me."

Lady Needham stared. "You don't know, do you?"

Maggie frowned. "Of course I know, my lady. It is exceedingly difficult to avoid gossip in London, try as one might."

"Just so." A small, indecipherable smile played at Lady Needham's red lips. "I'm pleased you've joined us for our naughty revelries, my dear. Welcome to the wicked." She held up her diminutive glass of juice in a petite toast.

"Thank you." Maggie supposed she ought to express gratitude, even if it would seem she'd been given her initiation to the wicked the evening before. A most thorough welcoming that had been. Trying to stifle the heat that particular thought produced, she raised her glass of freshly squeezed juice from the orangery as well. Guilt pricked her conscience then, but she swept it aside as well. She needed to become wicked to escape the most wicked of them all.

"I've just had a depraved thought, my dear Lady S."

"Call me Maggie," she invited her newfound friend. She'd never grown accustomed to her married name, especially since it was a mantle she'd never worn in truth. In her heart, she was still plain old Margaret Desmond, who'd been something of a wallflower in New York society and had remained one in London.

"Maggie, then." A full smile blossomed on Lady Needham's face. "And you shall call me Nell. I've a delightful game of naughty charades planned for this afternoon, and I'd love dearly for you to join us. Will you?"

Good heavens. She'd never dabbled much in parlor games, and especially not the iniquitous sort. "I'm afraid I don't know how to play. I'm something of a newcomer to the wicked, if you'll recall."

"Ah, that can be easily remedied. I'll teach you." Nell winked. "Besides, the stakes aren't necessarily high. They're only what you wish them to be."

Maggie pondered her hostess's mysterious reply as she turned her attention back to her plate. Somehow, she suspected there was something more to Nell's invitation, something she was too untried to comprehend. There was no hope for it. She supposed she would have to rediscover her old sense of adventure if her plan was to succeed. Perhaps she had allowed it to lapse for far too long.

Bloody, bloody hell. Simon studied his wife in her stunning afternoon frock of violet silk. She wore twin diamond stars in her artfully piled hair. Her waist was cinched to a perfect silhouette, emphasizing her generous bosom, which was revealed by the deep cut of her bodice. She laughed at something a no-account blackleg said to her. He wished it didn't sound so deuced inviting. He wished she wasn't so damn beautiful. He wished he'd never known the exquisite pleasure of making her come the night before. More than anything, he wished she wasn't his wife. Wanting her would have been so much easier if she were anyone else's wife but his.

But she was, and for some stupid, mutton-headed reason, he'd decided to stay on at Lady Needham's den of vice. And for some equally stupid, mutton-headed reason, he'd allowed himself to be cozened into a game of naughty charades. Of course, when his hostess had first presented the invitation, he hadn't realized his wife would be a part of the games. If he had, he'd likely have run in the opposite direction, arse-on-fire style.

Or would he have?

He couldn't seem to stop staring at her. Why the hell couldn't he have made love to another woman in her stead? Any other woman would have done. Every other wanton society woman was present, and he'd had to choose her. What a duffer he'd been, rendered too oblivious by his lust to see what was plainly before his nose.

She glanced at him then, and damn if her blue stare didn't send a surge of lust straight to his traitorous cock. He thought of how lovely her breasts were, pert handfuls with luscious nipples that tightened when he sucked them. He thought of how she tasted, sweet and musky, how she had cried out and writhed beneath him in her introduction to pleasure.

He'd taken his wife's maidenhead.

The thought was still enough to make him ill. Almost. It would have if it hadn't also made him so painfully hard. Desperate for distraction, he turned to his lovely hostess, Lady Needham. She was an old acquaintance, blonde and petite, ineffably lovely, old enough to know the rules of jaded love and just the sort of woman a man could dally with free of consequence. She and Lord Needham had been living separate lives for some years. She never spoke his name. He hadn't ever thought it odd, but for some reason he did now.

"I must say I haven't indulged in charades since your last party, Nell." He allowed his fingers to trail for a moment at her elbow. "I haven't forgotten."

She smiled, fine lines forming at the corners of her eyes. For all that she was an acclaimed beauty, even she was not goddess enough to avoid time's unforgiving hand. "Ah yes, I believe you had Lady Billingsley as your companion then."

He stiffened at the mentioning of Eleanor, still painful. "And you wound up dancing on the table."

Her expression turned sly. "Did I? I daresay I don't recall."

"I saw your drawers," he drawled, recalling every moment of her impromptu performance. No one could hold a candle to Nell when it came to daring.

"Odd, that." She pursed her lips. "I don't ordinarily wear them."

He grinned back at her, glad for the levity. He'd had such few opportunities for it of late. If only her revelation had some effect on his cursed lust. But though Nell remained alluring as ever, she wasn't the woman causing his blood to race to the wrong end of his body. "Are you wearing them today, my dear?" he asked mildly, trying to divert his attention from his inconvenient attraction to his wife. "Lord knows I'm in need of a pleasant distraction."

Most women would have swooned at such a question. Nell threw back her head and laughed. "I suppose that is for you and the rest of the company to discover." She tapped him on his coat sleeve. "Now do come along. It's time to start the festivities, and if it's a diversion you need, I have just the thing for you, Simon darling."

Dear sweet heavens.

Maggie twined her hands together nervously and paced the length of the chamber she'd been assigned by Lady Needham. It was a man's chamber. Of that much she was certain. But whose? She feared that naughty charades was a great deal too naughty for her sensibilities.

Nell, as she was wont to be called, had blithely explained that each lady was to retire to an appointed chamber and await the partners she chose to send them. Upon the arrival of their partners, charades would ensue. They were to keep score and announce the winners at dinner. Of course, Nell had added with a wink, the naughty portion of the charades was left to the imagination of the players themselves.

Naughty indeed. She fanned her heated cheeks with her hand. Perhaps it wasn't too late to escape. She was decidedly in the rabbit hole and most definitely over her head. One scandal ought to suffice. She had no wish to create a second. Her decision made, she rushed for the door, her silk mules clipping on the carpet.

The door opened, stopping her completely. Her heart fluttered, her stomach feeling as if it were tipping like a runaway carriage. And then the nervousness quickly melted into a far more heady sensation.

Anticipation.

It was *him*.

He too stilled, his gaze burning into hers. His sensual mouth flattened in apparent displeasure. Had he been hoping for someone else? Perhaps the night before was all he had sought from her. Perhaps she had disappointed him in her clumsy innocence. There was also the troubling matter of the woman he'd loved. Even Lady Needham knew of his past, and he had told Maggie himself that he had loved the woman for many years. Such strong emotion wouldn't dissipate easily. Mayhap he harbored regrets.

"You," he said, the lone word filled with emotion.

Anger? Irritation? She couldn't tell. "Sir," she said lamely, dipping into a curtsy. It was likely a silly show of formality in their circumstances, but she was unbearably nervous. What was the proper protocol for greeting the man who had made passionate love to her the night before, the man whose name and face she didn't know?

"Damn Nell for this," he gritted. "She thinks she's being clever."

He wasn't pleased. In fact, he seemed wound as tightly as a watch spring. She faltered, at a loss. "Clever?" Did Lady Needham know what had transpired between them? The prospect was mortifying, even if it was what she required for her scandal to take root.

"Never mind." He snapped the door closed at his back before stalking into the chamber. "It would seem we're at the mercy of our hostess's whims."

She watched him. "I'm sorry you find my company so offensive."

He frowned, his eyes darkening to a deep, glittering emerald. He stopped a mere foot away from her, clenching his fists. "Not precisely offensive. There are things at work here that you don't understand."

It was her turn to frown. "You are correct in that I don't understand the reason for your sudden discontent. But perhaps you could enlighten me."

"I could." He spun on his heel and gave her his back, striding in the opposite direction. "But I don't wish to, and I find I'm too bloody old for a game of naughty charades."

He reached for the door, preparing to leave her, and in that moment the realization that he could easily dash her plans to bits struck her. That everything she'd already done, every risk she'd taken, could all be for naught if he chose not to play his role in the scandal. That after all this, she'd still wind up miserable and alone, unable to divorce Sandhurst and move on with her life.

She hurried after him, desperation coursing through her. "Wait."

He stopped but didn't turn to face her, didn't say a word. His head was bowed as though he waged some sort of inner battle.

Uncertain now that she'd given him pause, she laid a tentative palm on his shoulder. Freedom was within her reach. She couldn't allow it—couldn't allow him—to slip away. Before she could rethink her actions, she stepped closer, her skirts brushing his trousers, and wrapped her arms about his lean waist. She laid her head against his back, breathing in his spicy scent, relishing his nearness, his seductive heat radiating into her.

"What are you doing?" His voice sounded thick.

How lowering. "Embracing you."

"Why?"

"Because I couldn't let you go without touching you one more time." She flushed although he couldn't see her face. In more than one sense, it was the truth. She couldn't let him go, couldn't give up on her dream of escaping her intolerable marriage. But she also enjoyed touching him. He made her feel things, sensations that not even Richard had inspired.

He tensed. "You don't know what you're playing at, my lady."

"You're utterly right. I don't." But he hadn't extricated himself, and that had to count for something.

He trapped her hand and dragged it to the placket of his trousers. He was already hard, but as her fingers tentatively traveled over him, he became positively rigid. He sucked in a breath. An answering heat bloomed through her. "Is this what you want? Is this what you came here for? To cuckold your husband?"

"Yes." Another truth, torn from her. "Will you help me?"

"No, goddamn it." His voice was low. "Enough damage has been done."

But he didn't move away, and nor did she. There was something potent and heavy about the moment. Her heart thudded against her breast. "Please? I need to take a lover."

A strangled sound emerged from his throat. "You *need* to take a lover?"

"It's a necessity." He didn't understand, but neither did she require him to. "My future depends on it."

He released her hand, his entire body stiffening. "Perhaps I know your husband, madam. Perhaps he's even a friend of mine. Did you ever think of that?"

Of course she hadn't. But Sandhurst hardly seemed the sort of man to have friends. He was a heartless rake. A cold, unfeeling scoundrel. "I doubt you would be friends with such a blackguard."

"You don't know me, my lady." He gave a dark, bitter laugh. "Or mayhap you do. Which would be worse, do you think?"

With their masks firmly in place, it was easy to imagine they were strangers who had never crossed paths. Suspicion pricked her. What was behind his sea change? Why would he pose such questions? "Have we met?" she asked, curious.

"I believe we have," he answered cryptically.

It seemed as if he knew her identity despite her mask. Had Lady Needham told him? "Do you know who I am?"

"No." He turned around at last, slipping his arms around her waist. "I begin to think I do not."

He took her mouth in a ravaging kiss then, hot and hungry, open and possessive. She kissed him back, locking her wrists around his neck and pressing her body to his. Their tongues tangled as she welcomed him once more, tasting him. Her nipples hardened beneath her chemise and the stiff abrasion of her corset. Her fingers sank into his thick, soft hair. Oh good heavens, she was on fire for him. What did this man do to her? She had lived twenty-two years without ever feeling as if she were about to burst into flame. And yet now, here she was, helplessly in this stranger's thrall.

He dragged his lips down her neck, sucking at her sensitive skin while he undid the delicate shell buttons lining the front of her bodice. She was instantly grateful that she'd chosen to wear her purple silk Worth gown. The bodice was separate from the skirts, allowing for easier disrobing. She hadn't had a thought for it that morning when her maid had dressed her. But now she was incredibly glad. Being disrobed by him was wholly delicious, a world away from being circumspectly stripped by her servant.

This man relished each opened button, every exposed inch of her skin. She helped him by untying the elaborate bows at her elbows and shrugging her bodice from her shoulders. He whipped it away as if it were no more important than a fly, dropping it to the floor in a whisper of sound.

She was before him in her linen corset cover and her elaborate skirts. Never mind how she would redress herself. All she could think about was succumbing once more to their mutual passion. She hadn't expected to enjoy her fall from grace or to revel in it. She'd thought to be stoic, to close her eyes and separate her mind from her body. She'd never imagined *this*.

He kissed her, long and hard. She met him with all the longing clamoring inside her. When at last he dragged his mouth away from hers, she stared at him, unflinching. She'd always counted herself a woman of courage. "Will you be my lover, my lord? Or do I need to find another?"

He became rigid, his expression hard with anger. "There will be no other. Leave here. Nothing awaits you in this den of debauchery other than disappointment. Go home, my lady."

A chill settled over her that had less to do with the drafty chamber than with his cutting admonishment. "I suppose I'll need to find another, then. There are any number of other gentlemen who would suit."

That was a lie, of course. She didn't want another gentleman. For reasons she didn't care to examine, she wanted the cold stranger before her with the sensual mouth and strong jaw. But he didn't want her, it seemed, and she had precious little time to waste. She couldn't shake the feeling that Lady Needham's was the chance she needed.

He gripped her waist, pinning her to him when she would have retreated. "Was I not clear? There will not be another gentleman. You've had your pound of flesh."

Defeat settled heavily over her shoulders. He was a conundrum, this man, ready to plunder her one moment and crying conscience the next. For her part, she chose to remain unashamed. Her husband had no conscience, so why should she? Her heart had been toughened long ago.

She squared her shoulders and stared up at him in defiance. "One could argue that it was you who had his pound of flesh. Perhaps this was a mistake after all."

"Of course it's a mistake." His fingers tightened on her. "But we've gone too damn far now, and we can't undo what's already been done."

She had a sense once more that he spoke beyond her ken. He knew something she didn't and that rather nettled. Perhaps she'd uncovered the reason for his odd question about her husband the night before. "Is it her?" she asked before she could think better of it. "The woman you love. Is she your wife?"

His lips tightened. "No."

"You must love her very much."

He stared. "I don't bloody well understand you, woman. Only moments ago, you were rubbing my cock like a seasoned courtesan, and now you want to talk about my past as if we're having tea and muffins."

She blanched and wrenched away from him. Perhaps she had mistaken him entirely. "Nor do I understand you, my lord. But I can see now that you are not the man I thought you were." Tears threatening to humiliate her by pooling in her eyes, she sank to recover her shucked bodice. She stuffed her arms into the sleeves and pulled the gaping silk together in a poor attempt at modesty. Her pride wouldn't allow her the time required to fasten the buttons. "I think you ought to find another partner for naughty charades."

He sneered. "You want me to fuck someone else? Would you care to watch? Is that it? Has Lady Needham's little party corrupted you so thoroughly already?"

Maggie gasped at his crude words. "No. How dare you?"

"How dare I?" He laughed, but it was a bitter, jaded laugh. "How dare *you*?" He caught her around the waist once more, anchoring her body to his. "How dare you make me want you so much that you're all I can think of? How dare you kiss me and touch me until I want to take you so badly I ache with it? You aren't an innocent in this wicked game we play, my dear, and you know it."

His mouth swooped down over hers, possessive and firm. She didn't want to enjoy his kiss for it was laced with anger, but she couldn't deny the way he made her feel. It was elemental, primitive. Potent. She too was angry with him for his sudden coldness toward her, willing her lips to remain still. She would not return his kiss. She didn't want ugliness between them.

He drew back, staring down at her. His eyes had darkened with such stormy passion that they were more hazel than their ordinary true green. "Kiss me, damn you."

"Who are you?" she asked, her fingers traveling to the edges of his black mask. She wanted to know with a desperation that tugged at her heart.

"No one to you." He tugged her hands away. "Have you changed your mind so quickly, my lady?"

"You changed it for me." Her gaze never wavered from his. "You insulted me, my lord."

He traced her lower lip with his thumb, staring at her intently. "I'm sorry for insulting you."

"Are you?" She wasn't certain she believed him. Desire was one thing. Self-respect was another entirely. Her husband treated her as if she were nothing more important than a speck of lint on his coat and she'd be damned if she'd allow another man to do the same.

He inclined his head. "I am. You affect me, and I don't like it."

She heard a rough thread of honesty in his voice. For some reason, she believed him. He seemed as lost in their maze of seduction as she. His thumb still absently rubbed her lip. She wanted to kiss it but somehow stifled the urge. "That is not an excuse for abominable behavior," she pointed out.

His jaw clenched. "I'm aware, but there are other factors you cannot know."

But she wanted to know them. He didn't wish to share. Was it that he didn't trust her? Something was afoot, and she was determined to weed it out by its insidious root. Now, however, was not the time. She took a breath. "I accept your apology."

He appeared to relax, his mouth tipping up into a smile. "Thank you."

"But I don't wish to play charades any longer at the moment," she forced herself to say. "Naughty or otherwise. I think it best if I return to my own chamber just now."

His smile disappeared. "As you wish."

She stepped away from him again, clutching her mangled bodice to her as if it were a shield. "I shall see you at dinner, my lord."

With that, she all but fled from his chamber before she did something horridly foolish. Before she turned around and threw herself back into his arms.

chapter three

$\mathcal{D}$INNER THAT EVENING WAS A SUMPTUOUS AFFAIR served *à la russe* and laden with oysters, trout, pheasant, aspics, hothouse fruits, fresh cream, and endless stores of wine. In short, Nell had concocted yet another indulgent delight featuring anything a man could possibly want. As the night wore on, the company grew steadily louder, the women laughing with increasing gaiety, the men chortling and winking as they sized up their next conquests. Simon wished he could enjoy the hedonistic display, but his mind was too damn preoccupied by thoughts of *her*.

He still didn't want to think of her by her given name, and certainly not by the diminutive she preferred, for that would render his folly far more real. He took a gulp of his wine, then another. She was seated opposite him. Yet another instance of Nell's immoral machinations.

He glanced up from his plate, his gaze unerringly going to his wife who was dressed to perfection in a completely black evening gown that complemented the fieriness of her hair. She was doing her best to flirt with the man seated to her right, who he was convinced was the lecherous Duke of Dunsmere. He'd recognize the bastard anywhere. Damn the man, whose reputation as a rakehell of the first stare preceded him. Simon found himself scowling at the pair as they laughed over some nonsense or other.

Dunsmere was not fit company for any lady at all, and certainly not for the Marchioness of Sandhurst. Why, she had a reputation to uphold, blast her. She'd better not take the man on as a lover. She was on a mission to cuckold him, after all. What was it she'd said? *There are any number of other gentlemen who would suit.* An uncomfortable sensation pierced his gut, and it felt remarkably like jealousy.

Jealousy?

Absurd. He had bedded his wife and enjoyed it. Nothing more. What did he care if she took up with Dunsmere next, as long as she did so quietly? He didn't, he told himself firmly. He had no need for heirs from her. If she cuckolded him, it hardly mattered. His pride had overruled him earlier, but now his head was much cooler. He was relieved that she was showering the louse with such attention, truly he was, for that released him from his burden. He was free to find another woman and lose himself in her.

His wife laughed, the sound throaty and alluring, and his cock was instantly hard. Damn, damn, and damn again. He was lying to himself. His patience fled him. "Do share the reason for your levity," he bit out rather loudly. The pair turned matching shocked gazes to him. He fought down a flush, aware he was behaving boorishly.

"Pardon me?" His wife's violet eyes were upon him, pinning him to his seat as if he were a preserved insect on display.

He resisted the urge to fidget, feeling a bit like a lad being reprimanded by a dragon governess. "I merely inquired as to the source of your merriment."

The duke raised his glass in a mock salute, seemingly laughing at him. "You, old boy."

The hell he had. Simon clenched the stem of his wine

goblet with so much force he wouldn't be at all surprised if it snapped. "I'm sure I've mistaken you."

"No." The blackleg took a jovial sip of his wine, grinning. "I don't think you have. I very clearly said just now that we were laughing at you."

Simon didn't think twice. He stood. Yes, pistols at dawn was long since outlawed, but fists certainly hadn't been. He was going to bloody well beat the blighter to a pulp. Break his hawkish nose. Split open his sneering lip.

"Meet me outside," he demanded. "Now."

His nemesis grinned even more, appearing to contemplate his demand. "No," he drawled at last, sounding as if he hadn't a care. "Don't think I shall, old boy. Do sit back down and smooth your ruffled feathers."

He shook his head slowly. By damn, the last two days had put him through the paces. All he had wanted was a bit of peace and companionship, a way to distract himself from Eleanor. Instead, he had discovered the most beguiling passion of his life with a woman he had spent the last year resenting. And now this scoundrel dared to laugh in his face before everyone, suggesting he had feathers as if he were some sort of old rooster strutting in the barnyard. It was the outside of enough.

"I won't," he snarled. "Be a gentleman and meet me outside."

"That's the odd thing." The bastard had the gall to wink beneath his mask. "I'm not a gentleman. Anyone who knows me can tell you that. Indeed, I pride myself on my lack of gentlemanly conduct."

"Oh blessed angels' sake." Nell popped up from her seat at the head of the table, twin patches of pink on her cheeks. She appeared to be in fine dudgeon. "I'll not have all this ridiculous masculine posturing ruining my dinner. Sit down at once, Simon."

He gave her a warning stare. There could be an infinite number of Simons in the world, but she'd better not reveal his full name. Good God, they'd all be better off if his wife never knew the identity of the man who had taken her innocence.

But he still wasn't about to allow Dunsmere to insult him before the entire company without reparation. "I've been gravely insulted," he said at last.

"What tripe. You've been on the arse-end of a joke." The duke tossed back the remnants of his wine and gestured for a footman to refill it. "Nothing more. This is meant to be a lighthearted party, is it not, Lady Needham? In truth, we were speaking of my lovely companion's misplaced attempt at ice skating back when she lived in the barren wasteland of New Jersey. Were we not, my dear?"

Her eyes were still fixed to him. He couldn't tell if he read horror or dismay or disgust or a combination of all three in her gaze. "New York," she corrected quietly. "And yes, we were. I'm sorry, sir, for the misunderstanding."

He'd been the arse-end of Dunsmere's little sally all right, and now he *felt* like an arse. He sat because there was nothing else to do short of marching around the table and punching the duke in his obnoxious, laughing countenance. Surely the latter had its fair share of appeal, but there was no need to further make a fool of himself.

"Lovely, my lord, Your Grace. I'm relieved it was all in good fun." Nell's voice was wry. "Now do calm yourself, Sandhurst. I daresay nothing untoward was meant."

Sandhurst.

Bloody, bloody hell. She'd slipped and spoken his name. He tensed, his gaze swinging back to his wife. Her ivory skin had taken on a sudden waxy pallor. She stared at him with such intensity he feared she penetrated the contents of his black soul. And he had no doubt she didn't like what she saw.

She knew. Those violet orbs darkened to a violent, stormy blue. The lady was not pleased. Indeed, he'd never seen a woman look more irate than she did in that moment. As quickly as her face had paled, her cheeks went crimson, her mouth compressing into a stern frown. If she'd been equipped with a weapon, she likely would have hurled it at his head with every intention of maiming him.

"Christ." The die was cast. There was only one Sandhurst. He couldn't prevaricate his way out of this one. He told himself it shouldn't matter, that he didn't plan to see her again after this country house party anyway. He loathed having been saddled with a wife he neither wanted nor loved. Certainly, he detested the reminder that he'd been forced to sell his title to her papa or face financial ruin.

But as she stood, pressing a hand to her midriff as if she were about to be ill, he a knifelike stab of compassion hit him. They had made love and that simple act had forever altered the way he saw her, whether or not he liked it. He'd never intended to consummate their marriage. He'd thought that if he couldn't bear a child with Eleanor, he had no need for one, hadn't cared if his title passed to a distant relative from the gutters. But now, he had done the very thing he'd sworn to never do, and in so doing, he had hurt her. Unintentionally, but he had hurt her all the same.

She offered a mumbled apology to Nell and, her other hand pressed to her mouth, she fled from the dining hall before the shocked and tittering onlookers. He watched the swirl of her black silk train disappear around a corner, wondering if he ought to follow her. Did he owe her an explanation? He told himself that he did not, that she was just as guilty as he. After all, she had flirted wickedly and invited him to her chamber, had declared her intention of taking a lover and making him a cuckold. If she had not, he would have found someone else, someone very much not his wife, and enjoyed her charms instead.

Only it wouldn't have been the same. She had found her way past the walls he'd built between them, sneaking over the barrier as if she were a thief. For some reason, her name worked its way into his mind at that moment, the name she had asked him to call her on their wedding night just before he'd left her. The name he'd refused to even think.

Maggie.

He looked to Nell, who appeared as stricken as he felt. "You must go after her, Simon," she said quietly. "I'm sorry. I never meant to——"

"But you did, damn you." His voice was more cutting than he'd intended but he didn't care. "You did, and now I shall have to bear the consequences."

He stood, knowing Nell was right. He had to at least follow Maggie. Perhaps he did owe her that much. He wasn't completely made of stone. He had a heart, but it had been taken by another. Christ, he was confused. His life was falling apart as if it were a poorly constructed shirt, gaping at the seams. Damn it, he had to try to put an end to the madness.

Maggie hurried through the halls for the sanctity of her chamber, running as fast as the heels of her evening slippers would allow. Her surroundings were a blur as her mind raced to comprehend the devastating truth that Lady Needham had unwittingly divulged. The man who had shown her the pleasures hidden within her body, who had kissed her and made love to her with a passion she hadn't dreamt existed, was the man she was trying to escape. He was the husband who had not spoken to her in over a year, the aloof but handsome stranger who had boldly proclaimed his love for another woman and refused to consummate their marriage. The man who had been living in sin with another man's wife.

Sandhurst.

Her husband. Why hadn't she known? In the wake of her discovery, everything began to make sense. Nell had known, she realized, recalling her hostess's reaction when she'd introduced herself as Lady Sandhurst. *You don't know*, she'd said.

Of course she had not, foolish woman that she was. She had been too blinded by a handsome smile and a knowing touch and the promise of her plan coming to fruition to see what everyone else had already known. Including Sandhurst. His words replayed in her mind as she continued her determined retreat.

You.

There are things at work here that you don't understand.

Perhaps I know your husband, madam.

She felt ill as the full ramifications hit her. Blessedly, she reached her chamber door and threw herself inside, slamming it at her back. He had duped her, lied to her, seduced her. But why? What could he have possibly had to gain? If he had wanted to consummate their marriage at last, he could have done so at any time. He needn't have disguised himself and trifled with her. It made no sense.

With a cry of pure rage, she whipped her silly mask away from her face. Some good it had done her. This was to have been her one chance for escape from the loneliness of her marriage. And he had ruined this as well as he had ruined the last year. For one miraculous day, she'd been given hope again, and now he had taken it all away. Betrayal sliced through her.

She pulled off her earrings and slammed them down on the dressing table, then undid her necklace before going to her hair. While she knew she ought to wait for her lady's maid's assistance, she was overcome by the need to escape from the shams of elegance. She wanted to shout and beat her fists. Instead, she systematically plucked pins from her dramatic coiffure. A fat curl fell, brushing her shoulders.

Suddenly, her door swept open.

She spun, heart pounding with disbelief, to find Sandhurst striding inside as if he belonged there. He slammed the door behind him, eliciting a wince from her. She tried not to notice what a handsome figure he cut in his evening tails, tall and debonair and lean. Drat him, she was drawn to him as ever, the longing she felt for him elemental and undeniable even as she wanted to rush at him and pummel his broad chest.

"Maggie," he began in that familiar velvety drawl of his, "this can all be explained."

She crossed her arms in a show of defiance and pinned him with a glare. "Do not call me that. Only my family and friends are permitted to refer to me thusly."

He stopped halfway across the room, his eyes searching hers. "I'm sorry."

She let loose a bitter laugh. "Sorry for what? Sorry that you were caught out? Sorry that you lied to me? Sorry that you pretended to be someone other than the husband who has abandoned me for the past year?"

He flinched. "I suppose I deserve your scorn."

"You suppose?" The man's temerity knew no bounds. "What you actually deserve is a punch directly to your supercilious face, not scorn. You should consider yourself fortunate that I am not a violent woman."

"I'm sure I deserve all that and far worse. But would you care to listen to me, or are you going to continue your aimless railing against me?"

"I hate you." She couldn't contain herself though she knew she was acting more as if she were a young girl in short skirts rather than a woman grown. "You may as well remove your mask. I know exactly who you are, much to my shame."

He tore it away, tossing it to the floor. For a moment, her breath stopped, for she had forgotten how gorgeous he was. He was truly a fine-looking man, with his dark hair, rigid jaw, aristocratic nose, and sculpted lips. But his looks hid a cold and devious soul.

"I didn't know it was you." He effectively ruined the moment. "You were wearing a bloody mask."

She wasn't moved by his protestations of innocence. "I don't believe you."

"We haven't seen each other in some time, Maggie." He stalked toward her, cutting the distance between them in half. "You didn't recognize me, either. You were only too keen to reveal your intentions of cuckolding me."

51

"I told you not to call me that." She was determined to hold her ground. "If by 'some time', you mean an entire year, then you're correct. Of course I didn't recognize you. I scarcely even recalled what you look like. And don't dare to be outraged by my actions, sir, as it would make you the worst sort of hypocrite. You obviously knew who I was. I could tell by your reaction at dinner. I'm not a complete fool."

"I did know, but I only discovered who you were this morning." He ran a hand through his hair, leaving it askew, and sighed. "I removed your mask while you were sleeping."

She contemplated what he'd said, and she had to admit it did make sense. His reaction to her during charades had been vastly different from the passionate lover of the evening before. He'd discovered who she was and he had not wanted her any longer, at least not in the same way as before. Yes, it made devastating, awful sense.

She stared, trying not to notice how near he stood to her or that she could smell his masculine scent of soap and musk. "Why have you come here, Sandhurst?"

"To Lady Needham's?" He appeared uncomfortable. "I should think for the same reasons as you."

"No." She shook her head, her anger deflating inside her like a hot air balloon going limp. "Why have you come to my chamber?"

"I don't know." An underlying tone of honesty edged his voice.

She turned away from him, the sight of him hurting her too much. "You may go. I shall return to the townhouse in London at first light." She preferred London to the country estate, always would, and did not care for the fashionable custom of leaving the city at summer's end. "But make no mistake that I want a divorce, Sandhurst. I'll create the worst scandal you've ever known if you don't willingly grant it to me."

He followed her, catching her bare upper arm. His touch was a hot brand on her skin. He spun her back to face him.

"I never intended to hurt you."

"Your intentions are a moot point, for you already have hurt me. But this will be the very last time." And she had never meant words she'd spoken more than those. She would avoid him at every opportunity. Good heavens, if she needed to, she would return to New York. The life she'd been living in England held nothing for her save disappointment and solitude.

"I'm sorry," he said again, still holding her to him. "There will be no divorce, Maggie. The scandal would be greater than any misdeed you could commit by bedding some worthless rakehell like Dunsmere."

"I'll bed him and a dozen others," she swore. "I'll bed footmen. I'll bed your prince. I'll do anything to be set free."

"You'll do nothing of the sort, damn you." His expression was harsh and bleak, somehow condemning and compelling all at once. "*There will be no divorce.*"

She thought of what he'd told her the night before when he hadn't known who he was plying his charms upon. His heart had been broken by a very old and dear friend, he'd said. Lady Billingsley. The reminder cooled her blood. He'd never cared for Maggie. It had only ever been his mistress he'd wanted in his life, and he'd made that fact abundantly clear. She had given up the man she loved to wed him, and she'd been left with nothing.

"Go back to your Lady Billingsley." She dug the heels of her palms into his shoulders, trying to free herself. "I'm sure that whatever heartbreak you've suffered at her hands can be mended."

"Lady Billingsley has returned to her husband," he told her, his voice rough.

"It was her decision," she guessed, understanding him just a little. Perhaps he wasn't an unfeeling cad, for it appeared as if he had been hurt by the woman's defection. But he was still a horrid, amoral husband, and she must not soften toward him.

He inclined his head, his expression impassive. "The

decision was not mine."

Precisely as she'd thought. He would never have ended his affair. Lady Billingsley had left him, and instead of returning home to his wife, he had gone in search of another woman to bed. How dare he?

"I'm afraid you'll have to find another woman to serve as your whore," she said coldly. "I'll not be her replacement."

"I'm not seeking a replacement, damn you." His eyes glittered into hers. He pulled her into his solid frame.

She kept her hands between them, a bracing wedge. "Then why are you here?" she asked him again, sensing that the undercurrent between them had once again snaked into dangerous territory. She was pushing him and she knew it, but she wanted to shake him in the way he had her. She wanted to know why, after all he had done to her, he still made her feel quivery inside.

"Because I can't seem to stay away."

The acknowledgment sounded torn from him. She stilled, studying his expression for any hint of subterfuge and finding none. He didn't want to feel anything for her, that much was apparent. But their night together had meant something to him. She could see it reflected in his gaze and knew he saw the same in hers. She couldn't help herself. Such an odd dichotomy, to have developed feelings for a lover only to discover that lover was a loathed spouse. Little wonder she felt as if she were an amnesiac slowly relearning the pieces of her life that she'd forgotten.

Everything was new, different. Nothing was as it seemed, not Sandhurst, not Maggie, not what she'd once believed. For this man had set fire to her blood. He wasn't cold. He wasn't hateful. At least, not when he'd thought her someone else.

But none of that was enough. He had still been an abysmal husband, and he had still lied to her, humiliated her. "I don't understand you."

"Christ, I don't understand myself." He lowered his

head until their noses nearly brushed. "You're the last woman in the world I wanted to make love to, and now all I can bloody well think about is how it felt to be inside you." His breath fell hot and wispy over her lips. "And how I want to be inside you again."

The air felt as if it had been sucked from the chamber. His blunt admission shouldn't have affected her. But her pulse pounded. Heat slid between her thighs. A pang low in her belly left her tingling.

How had her anger fled her so easily? When Richard had courted her, she'd never felt the incredible tumult her husband produced in her. She desired Sandhurst and yet she knew she shouldn't. Loving Richard had been easy, sweetness and light. Sandhurst affected her in an entirely different manner, dark and consuming.

She wanted him to kiss her but she knew she must not allow it. Her chin tipped up of its own will, sealing their mouths together. He took her invitation, molding his lips to hers in a passionate, claiming kiss. She opened to him, sliding her tongue against his. He tasted of the wine he'd been drinking at dinner, sweet and vibrant.

She wound her arms around his neck, her fingers happily sinking into his soft hair. She ached for him. As impossible and illogical as it was, the desire she felt for him was as strong as ever, perhaps the only truth between them. She dragged her mouth from his, desperate for a breath, and kissed a path down the side of his neck. His hands went to the buttons lining her bodice, pulling them open.

Then sanity returned to her. Surely giving in to him now would be worse than reckless. It would be stupid. She had to stop. They had to stop. Even if stopping was truly the last thing she wanted to do.

She pushed at his shoulders. "We cannot."

He halted his efforts at whisking away her bodice, but his fingers didn't stray from the buttons. "Why?" His harsh, ragged breathing filled her senses. Frustration and desire mingled in his voice.

"Because you don't like me," she forced herself to point out, "and I do not like you."

He raised a brow, looking down at her as if he were a god who had just been told he was mortal after all. "What has liking to do with it? We're husband and wife. I want you and I know you want me, Maggie. I can taste it in your kiss."

She steeled herself against his potent persuasion. "Of course I'm attracted to you, or rather, to the man I thought you were. The problem is that now you are once again you, not him."

He stared at her. "Damn it, I haven't a bloody inkling what you're prattling about."

"What I feel for you is not real," she explained. "It's meant for the mystery man I met last night."

"Goddamn it, I'm that man." He frowned, appearing perplexed by her logic.

"No." She willed herself not to pull him to her for another kiss. *Just one more*, her evil body cajoled. *One more kiss, caress. One more night.* "You're the man who is in love with another. You're the man who has treated me as if I were no more important than a dusty book in your library. You're the man who abandoned me."

"I didn't abandon you. I gave you a home and *carte blanche* to buy whatever fripperies you desired. Ours was never a love match."

What an arrogant brand of reasoning he possessed. Did he not know her father was a real estate tycoon who owned nearly half of New York? It wasn't dresses and baubles that she wanted. "I've had fripperies and homes all my life. I wanted a husband."

"Christ." He exhaled, his voice sharp, irritated. "I *am* your husband."

"In name," she insisted, though it was no longer true.

"No." He caught her chin in a firm grip, forcing her to look at him when she would have turned away. "I am very much your husband in deed as well as law after last night."

She was trapped in his gaze, heat simmering through her

traitorous body at the reminder of what they'd shared. "It was for one night only."

"I don't think so, my dear. You may hold on to your self-righteousness this evening, but we both know that I will be back in your bed. There will be no other lovers." He slid his free hand inside her gaping bodice, unerringly finding her breast beneath her corset. Only the fine fabric of her chemise separated her skin from his. Her nipple pebbled. "You want me. You can rationalize it however you like in your mind, but I'm the man who made love to you last night. There is no mystery man."

He was right, drat him. Her mystery man had been a fiction. The man who had set her aflame stood before her, rolling her nipple between his thumb and forefinger. How could she reconcile her heated lover with her icy husband? She was in a hopeless muddle, and the worst part was that he made sense.

"But what transpired between us last night has nothing to do with us as husband and wife." She needed to resist him for the sake of her self-preservation.

"Perhaps." He still toyed with her breast. "Or perhaps not. I have a proposition for you. Forget about your madcap scheme to make a cuckold of me. For the next month, let me bring you pleasure. We've barely touched the surface. There's much, much more I could show you if you'll but say the word."

He was a devil. And she was a fool, for his offer cut through her determination to free herself of him, undermining it. "I don't think it would be wise," she forced herself to say.

"Few pleasurable endeavors are ever wise," he pointed out. "Drinking too much wine? Great fun but great misery the next morning. Overindulging at table? Delicious but the older you get, the more it lands round your middle. I'm afraid wisdom has little to do with anything worthwhile, my dear."

He once again spoke undeniable truth. Still, where the

notion of taking him as a lover had held appeal for her when he'd been a stranger, it now seemed treacherous. She couldn't afford to become more involved with a man who had proven himself to be a cad of the first order. She'd suffered too much loneliness and misery at his hands already, and surely he could only bring her more.

"And after the month is over, what is to happen then?" she demanded. "Are we to simply go our separate ways as if none of this has ever occurred? Am I free to return to my life in New York?"

His gaze became shuttered. "You will still be my wife."

Not particularly reassuring. She frowned, disentangling herself from his arms with a heavy heart. "I'm afraid that isn't good enough for me."

"But you suggested just such an arrangement earlier today." He sounded vexed. "You said you required a lover."

"To make you a cuckold." Defiance made her bold. "I wanted to create such a scandal that you'd be left with no choice but to rid yourself of me. Living in purgatory ill suits me, Sandhurst. I want to go home if I'm not to be a wife. I'm weary of the pitying looks of strangers." Everyone knew she'd married a title and Sandhurst had married a fortune. Just as everyone knew he'd spent their entire year of marriage living apart from her, cuckolding Viscount Billingsley.

His jaw tightened. "To hell with strangers. You're my bloody marchioness. Last night, I took your maidenhead. There's no going back from that, damn it. We are irrevocably joined. There will be no scandal."

She refused to allow him to intimidate her. "Everything in life can be undone, my lord. My father taught me that."

"Your father is wrong."

"I don't think he is on that score."

They stared at each other, reaching an impasse.

He circled her nipple with his thumb, and she couldn't deny the sharp wave of longing the simple, single touch sent through her. "You want me."

58

"I want the man I thought you to be." The distinction was important to her.

"How fortuitous." He tugged her nipple between his thumb and forefinger. "For I want the woman I thought *you* to be. Let's lose ourselves. Let's forget who we are and why we're here and everything that's come before. A month, Maggie."

Tempting indeed, but she refused to wave the flag of surrender. "It must be on my terms."

"Your terms." His voice was flat.

He didn't want to grant her a divorce. That much was apparent. Perhaps there was another way of getting what she wanted. "Yes. My terms. I'll agree to a month. During that time, you may not pursue any woman but me." She took a breath before continuing. "And after the month is over, we may both pursue anyone we choose. If I like, I may return to New York. I'll not ask for a divorce as long as I'm free to live as I see fit."

He didn't appear pleased with that idea. "Both of us?"

She would not budge on this. She had no intention of ever being miserable and lonely again, trapped in a life and a place she didn't want. "Both of us."

"Promise me you won't pursue Dunsmere," he muttered. "I couldn't bear it."

"I'm afraid I don't know him," she said sincerely.

"He was..." Sandhurst shook his head. "Never mind. It doesn't matter any longer. Fine. I agree to your terms. But I have one of my own."

She should have anticipated as much. "Go on."

He pulled another of her buttons from its mooring. "During this month, your body belongs to me. I'm free to take you as often as I wish, in whatever manner I wish."

Your body belongs to me.

"I agree," she said quietly, lest she change her mind.

After all, she had come to Lady Needham's country house weekend in search of wild and wicked scandal. She'd been seeking a lover, a means to secure her freedom. And she had found that, albeit with the last person in the world she'd ever expected.

Her own husband.

chapter four

H E HAD JUST SECURED HIMSELF A NEW MISTRESS, albeit the last woman in the world he'd ever expected. His bloody wife. He stared at her, wondering if he'd gone utterly mad.

Yes, by God, he had. Why else would he be about to embark on the most preposterous *affaire* in the history of bed sport? His wife, who he had neither wanted nor cared for since the their wedding day, was somehow making his skin go hot as a tea kettle set to boil and his cock hard enough to hang a bucket of coal. He wanted to be inside her again, pounding her sweet, wet cunny until he filled her with his seed. The mere thought was enough to make him groan.

She looked unbearably luscious in her black silk gown. Her breasts were a creamy temptation popping out of her bodice. He wanted to suck one of her perfect pink nipples into his mouth. Madness had never seemed more compelling. Damn. She'd bewitched him.

He kissed her then before he said something mutton-headed like she was the most gorgeous woman he'd ever seen. Because somehow, she was. He'd been so busy keeping his distance that he'd failed to notice. Maybe he hadn't allowed himself to notice.

Her soft lips were as eager as his, every bit as hungry. He had to have her. And he could have her as many times as he wished for the next month. It should have appalled him, the bargain he'd just struck with her. He'd resented her ever since he'd found it necessary to marry her to restore the coffers his wastrel father had drained. On their wedding day, he'd wished it had been Eleanor at his side instead of a copper-haired American heiress. He'd spent the last year ignoring her existence, acting as if he hadn't a wife at all. Indeed, he'd sworn to himself that he'd never consummate their marriage.

Yes, the thought of bedding her for a month should have left him cold and disinterested with a withered cock. Instead, it sent a fresh wave of urgency straight to his groin.

Simon dragged his lips from hers. He cupped her lovely face in his hands, mesmerized for a moment by the pure beauty she was. He had missed her, looked through her, had seen her as a means to an end. He supposed he'd been too caught up in his bitterness to pay attention to the gem that had fallen into his lap. He would not make the mistake again.

"I want you naked." He was free to do whatever he wished, to want her. And what he wanted now more than ever was to fill her with his cock, to lose control, spend himself inside her. Nothing else mattered now. He'd already fallen off the bloody ledge the night he'd taken his wife to bed. There was something animalistic about the way she made him feel, as if he wanted to brand her as his, fuck her so hard and so deep that she could never think of another man again. Yes, his conscience could bloody well go to hell.

Her luscious mouth was swollen with his kiss. Maggie was his in a way Eleanor had never been, would never be. He'd been the first man to take her. He slid a hand down to her tiny waist, anchoring her to him. The hectares of fabric between them had to be done away with, of that much he was certain.

"Do you want me?" He had to know.

"Of course I want you." Her eyes seared his. "Even though I should not."

No, she shouldn't want him. Just as he shouldn't want her. But everything had changed. Or maybe nothing had, and in the morning he'd wake with a clear head and never want to bed her again. Either way, nothing was going to stop him now.

He longed to remove her garments, to pull away her trappings and get to the lush woman hiding beneath. Eleanor had often been prepared in some sort of naughty creation, or completely nude and waiting for him. She'd been well aware of what she was doing. With other women, it had been the same. But he found there was something incredibly arousing about Maggie, who little knew how to employ the expected. Her innocence prolonged the anticipation and heightened the pleasure.

His fingers unerringly found the buttons on her bodice. He tore open several more before he grew tired of the lengthy process and began tearing.

"Sandhurst." Maggie's hands stayed his, "this is a very expensive gown."

For a spoiled American heiress, she was certainly cautious. He frowned, his cock raging to be inside her. "Call me by my given name."

She worried her lower lip, looking utterly adorable. He wanted to tear her gown from her in shreds and carry her nude to her bed. "I've forgotten what it is."

Christ. She didn't know his name. He supposed he couldn't fault her. They'd been strangers for the entirety of their union, but somehow he had never forgotten hers. "Simon." His hands seized the separation in her bodice and yanked, successfully rending the remaining buttons from their moorings. Several of them popped to the floor. He pushed the fabric down over her shoulders and she shucked it even as her expression became pinched.

"You are a dress murderer," she murmured. "First my train and now my bodice."

Yes, when she put it that way, it quite seemed he was bent upon destroying her wardrobe. But the truth of it was that her wardrobe was merely an innocent barrier keeping him from what he wanted. Her.

"Apologies," he said with patent insincerity. "Your dresses have too damn many buttons."

"Fashion decrees it," she returned, her hands busy at work on his coat.

He allowed her to divest him of it. "Fashion never had to stand about with a randy cock while having to suffer through a thousand buttons keeping him from the woman he desires."

She stilled, her eyes meeting his again. "Surely the other women you've known have worn just as many buttons as I, if not more."

Her words gave him pause, because damn her, irksome as her insights often proved to be, she was once again right. He hadn't ever been so irritated by trappings and buttons. True, those women had often been at the ready. But during the times when they had not been, what then? He had attended countless soirees and balls with Eleanor when she had been buttoned and corseted to perfection. Still, he'd never once been so frustrated, so eager to undo her every show of propriety.

What was it about Maggie that turned him into a ravening madman consumed by lust? Christ, if only she were still the cowering, naïve girl of their wedding day. It all would have been so much easier. But so much less delicious.

"I don't give a damn about them," he told her at last, as his mind worked its way through the havoc she wreaked upon him. "The only woman I want in this moment is you."

He meant it. Maggie was his present. A present he had never imagined himself wanting, but his present nonetheless. And looking back over all he'd done, he could honestly tell himself he would not wish for a different outcome.

Her gaze remained on his, demanding and haunting at the same time. He wanted to blink, hide. He didn't know what she wanted from him. Worse, he was afraid he couldn't give her whatever it was she desired, beyond a mere mating of their bodies.

"And you're the only man I want in this moment, Simon," she said, an echo of him.

She was incredible. His. For the month. What the bloody hell had he been thinking? How would it ever be enough? He didn't want to feel this mad pull he felt for her, but it was as if she had cast a spell on him.

"To hell with your fripperies." His hands went to her corset cover. He had no more patience for fastenings. He tore the whole damn thing apart, delighting in the sound of destruction. The unveiling of her corset gave him pause. It was canary yellow, trimmed in seductive black lace. "Yellow?"

She flushed, lowering her gaze. "I couldn't resist."

"I'm glad." His voice went thick. The color somehow complemented her bold features to perfection. He wouldn't have thought it, but the vibrancy of the yellow coupled with her pale skin and bright hair was astoundingly beautiful. He reached behind her, fingers unerringly finding the laces of her corset and loosening them. "You continually surprise me, Maggie."

"Just as you have surprised me." Her fingers went to the hook-and-eye fastenings of her corset, undoing the bottom pair first. A small patch of her white chemise was visible beneath the restrictive garment.

His mouth went dry as he thought of how few layers there remained between them. "Allow me." He placed his hands atop hers.

"You needn't play lady's maid." She moved to the next set of closures.

"I'm not playing." His voice was hoarse. "Allow me, Maggie." He couldn't voice the myriad of emotions playing through him. Perhaps he sought to do penance for the year he had acted as if she hadn't existed in his world. For the first time, the word 'wife' held meaning for him. Wife. His. Maggie. They were all the same, each taking his breath.

"Very well." She held her arms to the side. "I'm yours."

Damn it, her words made his cock so rigid that he nearly lost his ability to function. He coughed to disguise his distraction and set his hands to work on her elaborate trimmings. "You're so very beautiful."

"I am?" She sounded surprised.

He searched her face for a sign of prevarication but found none. She truly didn't seem to know the full extent of her womanly power. "Of course you are." His hands found the fastening of her skirts. They were at her back and naturally brought his arms about her, their mouths once more close together. He nipped her lower lip between his teeth, savoring the dilation of her pupils, the flush on her cheeks. "You must know that."

She appeared dazed, running her pink tongue over her full lips. "I know nothing of the sort. If I were so lovely, surely you would never have thrown me over at the first possible opportunity."

He winced. It was only fair, he supposed, that his past treatment of her would not be altogether forgotten. He had been a bastard. He hadn't thought of her as a person but rather as a means to an end, a way for him to repay the debts that his father had left him, debts that had continued to mount over the passing years. That she could even allow him to touch her at all was an amazing feat of her understanding. He wished there was something he could say to absolve his sins, but this was new to him, possessing compassion for his unwanted wife. *She* was new to him.

"You are unbearably lovely." And she was. He realized he needed to open the closure on her skirt before he could proceed. His fingers traveled around her waist, but he couldn't find the hidden prize he sought. "I can't open your damn skirts."

She laughed, brushing him aside to find the opening herself. As she released them, her skirts pooled on the floor with a swish of silk. She stood before him in her chemise and corset and petticoats, her bustle pad an odd skeleton clinging to what he knew to be a lush bottom.

"You're not being fair." Her violet eyes traveled the length of his body and lingered—unless he was mistaken— on his cock.

He swallowed. "What do you mean?" Christ, he hoped she didn't want to engage in a lengthy debate of some sort. All he could think about was tearing the remaining coverings from her full breasts and losing himself in the inviting wet folds of her cunny.

"You're still wearing all your evening finery, and I've been reduced to the rubble of my ladylike trappings." She smiled hesitantly, reaching beneath his black jacket and helping him to shuck it from his shoulders.

Ah, so the lady wanted to be bold. Perhaps she was intent upon making him embarrass himself by coming before he removed his clothes. Her tentative caresses, even through a layer of fabric, were nearly enough to undo him. "How kind of you to remedy the situation," he said gruffly, trying to hide the tumultuous feelings at war within him. He felt much like a boat at sea taking on water.

His coat joined her skirt on the floor. She worked on his tie next, fumbling with a lack of familiarity. He couldn't blame her, for without his manservant, he was deuced hard put to disrobe himself. He attempted to help her and the result was only more confusion. Their eyes met and they shared a laugh. He leaned in and kissed her. The moment was so awkward and yet so tender, so familiar. It was as comforting as it was arousing. He had to admit that he'd never indulged in a mutual session of disrobing with another woman. He found he rather enjoyed the intimacy, the shared commitment to lovemaking that it signified.

She kissed him back, her mouth opening to his questing tongue. Her hands sank into his hair in that way she had.

His mouth worked over hers, perhaps harder than it ought to, but he couldn't seem to rein himself in. She did things to him, powerful things that were as impossible as they were undeniable. Had it only been two days ago that he hadn't been bothered to think of her without the bitter sting of resentment? It seemed a lifetime ago instead.

He tore at his necktie, finally undoing it, and returned his attentions to her corset. At last, he undid the final fastener on the offending garment and tossed it to the floor. Her chemise was not much of a barrier. He cupped her breasts through its delicate fabric, gratified by her pebble-hard nipples hungry and eager for his touch. Damn but he was going to enjoy each second of making her his again and again.

Maggie was about to make love with her husband.

The knowledge set her adrift, made her feel as if the room spun about her. Oh, her body wanted him. But her mind balked at the deal she'd just made with the devil himself. One month for her freedom. Of course she'd accepted. She'd had no choice.

He tugged her chemise over her head and she helped him, tossing it away without a hint of shyness. Cool air made her nipples tighten to harder peaks. The way he looked at her made her belly tingle. He lowered his head and sucked an engorged nipple. She moaned. His mouth on her was her undoing. She clawed at his shirt, wanting to feel his well-muscled chest without the hindrance of garments.

No choice. That was why he melted her. That was why he made her ache. She would've laughed at herself if she could. But she was beyond laughter. Beyond anything but following her animalistic need.

He grinned and looked up at her. "Patience, my dear, is a virtue." His tongue flicked against her, prolonging the sweet tug of arousal his ministrations produced. But even as he chastised her, he tore his shirt from his body.

At last. She ran her eager hands down his chest to the whorl of hair on his taut belly that led to his trousers. When she cupped the rigid outline of his cock, the breath escaped from his lungs. He nipped her other nipple with his teeth, exerting just enough pressure to send a new, poignant sensation directly to her core.

Her nimble fingers found the fastening on his trousers and opened them. He was wonderfully naked beneath, his member hot, hard, and smooth all at once. She gripped him, gratified when he grew larger in her hand. Touching him brought a sweet blossoming ache to her sex, a need for him to be inside her.

"Ah hell," he swore against the generous swell of her breast. He licked a naughty path around first one nipple, then another. "If you insist upon playing with my cock like that, I'm going to come in your hand like a lad with his first woman."

She faltered, releasing him. "Do you not like my touch?"

"Quite the opposite." His tone was gruff as he pressed her hand back to him, urging her to move up and down his shaft. With his other hand, he cupped the nape of her neck. His eyes melted into hers. "I like it too much."

His mouth crushed down on hers for a hungry kiss. She leaned into him, still stroking his ever-growing cock. He felt so beautiful and long in her palm. She thought of how much pleasure he would bring her and dampness spread between her thighs. Their tongues mated, their breaths becoming almost as one. His scent consumed her, that blend of musk and spice that was innately his. She pushed his trousers from his hips and barely heard him kick away his shoes and the remnants of his evening finery. Now he was naked and beautiful.

He broke off their kiss, his breathing as erratic as hers. His gaze was dark and verdant, rivaling new grass in the spring. "The bed," he said. "Now."

They moved as one across the chamber. When they

reached the high tester, he gently lifted her bottom on the mattress. "Lie down."

She scooted back into the center of the bed, conscious of her nudity yet still aroused by his smoldering air. Watching him silently, she sank into the soft, sweet-smelling coverlet, her mostly intact coiffure a bit of an uncomfortable lump behind her head. He eyed her as if he were a starving man and she the feast laid out before him. She shivered with anticipation as her eyes traveled over his fine form, lingering on the cock that rose proud and full between his thighs. She was anxious to once again feel him within her.

He joined her on the bed then, parting her legs with his muscular thighs. His head dipped near to her sex as he pressed a kiss to the top of her mound. And then, his mouth was on her. He sucked, dragging on the bud at her center in the same way he had the night before. She writhed beneath him, glorying in the raw sensations he evoked in her. His tongue swept over her wet folds, down to her entrance, before sinking into her.

She snagged handfuls of the bedclothes, mesmerized by the sight of him between her legs. He met Maggie's gaze and flicked his tongue against her, alternating between sucking and entering her with his tongue. Just when she feared she could no longer bear the pleasure, he switched from his mouth to his fingers, working her into a frenzy as he kissed a path from her belly to her neck. He dropped open-mouthed, ravenous kisses upon her while his long fingers slipped inside her slick passage. She arched into him, clutching his broad shoulders. He kissed her earlobe, his breath sending more pleasure flitting through her. Then he caught her hand and lowered it between them, settling her once more on his cock.

"Put my cock inside you," he murmured against her skin.

She rubbed her cheek against the stubble of his whiskers. "I don't know how."

"I'll show you." He pressed her fingers around him and

guided them to her aching sex. "Can you feel me, darling?"

As he asked the question, he thrust forward until his tip grazed her. "Yes," she said, barely able to manage coherent speech any longer.

"Take me inside." The pressure of his large cock increased.

She tipped her hips up to accommodate him while simultaneously pulling him into her. He filled her, stretched her. There was a moment of pain as her body adjusted to the still-new invasion, but it faded as he pushed himself all the way inside. Pleasure shot through her like a huntsman's arrow finding its expert mark. He buried his face in her neck, kissing her still as he found his rhythm, sliding gradually into her, then out again. She sensed he went slowly for her benefit, allowing her to accustom herself to him.

But she wanted it faster. Deeper. She arched against his every thrust, matching his pace. Her thighs fell apart to welcome him more fully. His fingers went into her hair as he dragged his mouth back down to her breasts. He sucked her nipples while he drove into her again and again. The pull on her highly sensitized breasts was enough to send her careening into climax. She shuddered as pure bliss overtook her, making her tighten around his cock.

He groaned and plunged deeper, harder, quicker. Soon, he pumped into her, finding his own release. He cried out, throwing his head back, and the warm spurt of his seed filled her. She clamped her legs around him, milking his cock for each drop. Her heart beat a thunderous rap against her chest. Her body tingled with a potent glow of sated desire. They had claimed each other.

They remained entwined for a few breaths, and then at last he rolled to his side, removing his weight from her altogether. She was fairly certain that none of her limbs were in working order, but her neck obliged her by moving to the left so that she faced Simon. He lay on his back, beautifully naked and spent, staring at the ceiling. His profile was exceptionally handsome, she noted, more handsome than a man's profile ought to be, really. Almost beautiful.

It was difficult to believe that after a year of icy abandonment he was at her side of his own volition. Her feelings for him were such a confusing jumble. The old resentments and hurt remained. How was she to ever make sense of this new, passionate husband who had taken her life by storm? She couldn't forget their past, but neither could she deny their incredible passion.

He turned to her, his expression guarded now that their needs had been met. "I expect I should return to my chamber before we start tongues truly wagging."

That was not what she wanted to hear. She frowned at him. "You know as well as I that everyone has been about the same business. There's no gossip here."

He absentmindedly stroked his stomach. "I'm fairly certain everyone guessed who we are after the spectacle I created at dinner. I'm afraid there will be a great deal of gossip now."

"Ah." Coldness replaced the wonderful warmth she'd been enjoying. "You wouldn't want news to reach Lady Billingsley, would you?"

"I simply don't wish to be fodder for the gossip mill," he said, but he looked away from her.

Would the dreadful woman never cease plaguing her? Maggie wished he had fallen asleep instead of choosing to speak. His words were like tiny daggers being sunk into her heart.

"Do what you must," she said coolly. If he wanted to leave, she would not beg him to stay, particularly if his heart still remained elsewhere. In a month's time, she could return to New York and forget she'd ever known his name. She was strong, strong enough to bear anything. He couldn't break her. No one could.

He didn't speak as he rose from the bed. She turned her back on him, not wanting to see him sneaking out of the chamber as if he were no better than a thief. Or a rogue sampling a kept woman's charms for the night. She

72

supposed he had rather a great deal of experience at just such a thing. The rustling sound of fabric reached her ears.

They were strangers once more, it seemed.

His abrupt defection hurt her. She wanted to cut him with words. Say something ugly, something that would dig beneath his arrogant façade and go straight to the bone. "If you were this cold with your whore, I'm surprised she didn't grow bored of you much sooner," she said before she could stop herself. It would seem she possessed precious little control where he was concerned.

All sounds of rustling fabric disappeared as though they had never been. Her words had hit their mark. Though it was cruel of her, she relished the brief moment of power it gave her over him.

"She was never my whore," he said at last, his tone tight with restraint.

"Nor was she your wife." She still refused to give in to her inner fool and glance back at him.

"I'm more than aware, Margaret." She had displeased him enough to earn the use of her full name, it appeared. The sound of him dressing resumed. "I'm going to join in the after-dinner festivities, and I suggest you do the same. But stay the hell away from the Duke of Dunsmere."

She didn't respond, keeping her back to him as he stalked from her chamber and slammed the door. It occurred to her that she really ought to discover precisely who the Duke of Dunsmere was. And then, like an unwanted gift, it also occurred to her that she was going to have to suffer the embarrassing fate of ringing her maid to assist her in dressing once more. Damn him.

Damn her. The drawing room was ripe with possibility, laden with inebriated women wearing scandalously low-cut bodices who wanted nothing more in the world than to be fucked later that evening. But he had eyes for her alone. He couldn't decide which was worse, his having agreed to her mad concept of no other lovers for a month or the sad fact that it didn't matter. Regardless of his promise to her, he didn't want another woman. He only wanted the red-haired siren flirting her head off with the Duke of Dunsmere.

Clever minx. He had no doubt she had sought him out intentionally. Earlier, he had been itching to get away from her, frustrated with himself for allowing her to compromise him so completely that everything he'd stood for since their marriage had been obliterated. His reaction to her scared him. He wanted her in a way he had not wanted any other woman in a long time, perhaps ever. Including Eleanor.

Men and women were pairing off by the moment, disappearing from the drawing room in search of pleasure. As he looked on, a pair of buxom blondes escorted a masked man he was certain was the Duke of Eversleigh from the room. Lucky blighter.

"I must apologize," purred a familiar voice at his side.

He turned to find Nell watching him. "I'm afraid your apology doesn't matter."

She winced. "I didn't mean to muck it up for you, Simon, truly."

"There's nothing to muck up," he lied. "I didn't know who she was but now I do."

"You must have had a lovely time smoothing her ruffled feathers." Her eyes narrowed as she considered him with thinly veiled skepticism. "You disappeared for two hours."

"I was napping." He kept his tone bland.

"Rubbish. You were bedding her."

A guilty flush crept over his cheekbones. "Go to hell, Nell."

"Such poetry." She laughed. "You're not the only man who's smitten by her, you know. Dunsmere appears to be prepared to kiss her very hem."

His gaze went back to his wife. She stood deuced close to the duke. Her breasts were nearly brushing against his arm, for Christ's sake. "I'm going to kill him," he vowed.

"I'll not have bloodletting at my soiree," she admonished firmly. "Tell me, Simon. How is Eleanor?"

He stiffened at the mention of her. "I wouldn't know."

But Nell was ever a dog with a bone. "I've heard she's living at Billingsley's country estate and that she's breeding."

Breeding. Eleanor was with child. The revelation hit him with the force of a fist. But there would have been a time when he'd have been hit with the force of a raging stallion. She had done her duty by Billingsley, then.

"Then she ought to be happy," he forced himself to say, though he didn't think it was true. Billingsley was a notorious brute and given to drink. The thought of Eleanor at his mercy had once been enough to make him ill. He'd been prepared to do anything to keep her from going to her husband. But she had not wished it, and in the end, he'd let her go. He had no rights where she was concerned, and he never had.

"Are you happy, Simon?"

Nell's unexpected question shocked him. No one had ever, in his recollection, asked him such a thing. He wasn't certain how to answer her. "I suppose that depends upon whether or not my little wife is planning on leaving your drawing room with Dunsmere."

A smile played with the corners of Nell's lips. "You're jealous," she observed. "That settles it. You're definitely smitten with your little wife, as you call her."

Smitten. Devil take it. Was he? Obsessed, perhaps. Consumed by lust and the need to be inside her, absolutely. But the word smitten suggested something deeper, something based on emotions that didn't exist. His eyes sought out Maggie once more. She was resplendent in her evening gown. There was no sign to suggest that she had been naked and in his arms a mere hour before. That he'd been inside her. But he knew. He knew what she tasted like. Where she liked his teeth to nip. Where she preferred his tongue to lick.

"I don't like this," he grumbled, more to himself than to

Nell.

"I daresay you don't." There was humor in Nell's voice.

He was going mad. There was no doubt about it. He tore his gaze from his wife and looked down at the woman at his side. He tried to summon a crumb of the desire he felt for Maggie and could not. Damn it, he could not allow another woman to ensnare him as Eleanor had done. He took Nell's hand in his and raised it to his lips for a leisurely kiss at the sensitive turn of her wrist.

"Go to bed with me," he suggested on a whim. A dark voice in his head told him he'd be better off if he forgot his wife and his promise to her. After all, he owed her nothing. The past two days had been an aberration.

Nell's smile didn't reach her eyes. "I'm not the woman you want."

Of course she was right. But he was foundering. "I don't know what the hell to do."

"I shall tell you." Her tone was frank, pure Nell. "You'll go to her side and make your claim upon her. Why bother playing silly games? Let yourself free, Simon. You aren't encumbered by Eleanor any longer."

Eleanor and Nell had been friends once, but something had happened to change all that. Though she had continued to extend invitations to himself and Eleanor over the years, Nell had not bothered to hide her dislike for her sometime friend.

He considered Nell's edict now, eager for the distraction. "Why do you harbor such ill will toward Eleanor?" He had often wondered, but Eleanor had never wanted to discuss their falling out.

Her expression became shuttered. "Some secrets are best kept."

"Nonsense," he dismissed. "Can you not tell me now?"

"You don't wish to know." Her ordinarily lush mouth drew into a pensive frown.

He was more determined than ever to have the truth. "Tell me, Nell. Our friendship demands it."

"Very well." She tipped up her chin in a show of defiance. "She bedded my husband."

"Needham?" But that was impossible. Eleanor had only been intimate with two men, himself and of course Lord Billingsley, out of necessity only. She had told him so herself. "Surely you must be mistaken."

Nell's gaze never wavered from his. "I saw them together."

He felt as if the breath had suddenly been sucked from his lungs. He had never known Nell to be a liar, and she would certainly have no cause to dissemble now when he and Eleanor were no longer speaking. He thought back to the time when Nell and Lord Needham had first become estranged. Two, perhaps three years. "When?" he asked, needing to know.

"It doesn't matter." Nell shook her head as if to dispel the memory from it. "This is very difficult for me to discuss, and we cannot change the past however much we might wish to."

Her refusal to answer told him his suspicions were true. Eleanor had bedded Lord Needham while professing her love for him, while she had been Nell's trusted friend. The realization of her betrayal still hit him like a fist to the gut, even if his ties to her had already been cut. "Jesus," he said at last. "Why didn't you ever tell me? Why did you allow us to attend your house parties as though nothing had occurred?"

"You would never have believed me." She patted his arm in a consoling fashion. "I know too well how love makes us oblivious to the faults of our lovers. And as for allowing her to attend my parties, I was too proud. I would die before I'd allow her to see how deeply she'd wounded me."

His heart hurt for her as much as for himself. He put his hand over hers and gave it a reassuring squeeze. "I'm sorry."

"You needn't be. It was a long time ago, and my life is different now." She drew herself together, replacing her vulnerability with her cheerful hostess's façade once more. "Now unless you act with haste, I'm afraid the duke is about to make off with your wife."

Christ, the barbarian appeared ready to throw her over his shoulder and cart her from the room as if she were spoils of war. An unholy rage came over him, a potent mixture of suppressed anger toward Eleanor and confusion over the way one saucy redhead had overtaken his mind. "I will kill him. I swear it."

Nell directed her best impression of a displeased governess his way. "I've already told you. Absolutely no bloodletting. You'd do best to whisk her away from all this, Simon. She's too innocent for our jaded lot."

She was right. Maggie didn't belong here in this den of lotharios eager to take advantage of her naiveté. Damn it, he wasn't certain he belonged here either. And if anyone was going to avail himself of his wife's naiveté, it would be him. Damn Dunsmere and Eleanor, and for that matter Needham, straight to hell.

A quick inquiry with Nell had led Maggie to the Duke of Dunsmere, and she'd sought him out, all the better to irritate Sandhurst. Maggie found the duke deceptively witty and charming. Perhaps too charming. She was aware of his clever attempt to steer her from the drawing room without her being the wiser. His hand was firm on her elbow, lingering too high, his thumb a deliberate pressure on her bare skin. He smiled down at her, his eyes twinkling with mirth, and she couldn't deny his amusement was infectious. Even if she was only using him as a pawn in her war against Sandhurst.

"I'm afraid your husband is bearing down upon us just now," he told her abruptly, *sotto voce*. She wasn't surprised that after the disastrous altercation at dinner, everyone appeared to know who she and Sandhurst were, despite their masks. Gossip loved to travel. "If you but say the word, I shall have you out of here in a trice. Beyond his insufferable reach."

She was tempted by the offer, but not foolish enough to accept it. "While I thank you for your concern, I daresay that would be like slipping into a cage with a tiger rather than a lion."

He pressed a hand to his broad chest in mock indignation. "I'm wounded you only consider me a tiger."

Maggie laughed, taking the opportunity to glance casually to her side and confirm that Sandhurst was indeed headed their way. Nor did he appear to be pleased. Good for him, she thought. After all, he had been unkindly cozy with Nell for quite some time. Indeed, she'd surreptitiously watched their interlude and could only presume there had been an intimate conversation between them. Had he grown weary of their bargain already?

"Are you certain you prefer him?" Dunsmere released a sigh. "I dearly love women with fiery hair and luscious bosoms. It's a particular weakness of mine."

Mere days ago, his words would have shocked her. But she found she enjoyed the freedom of expression at the house party, whether in the bedchamber or in the drawing room. It took her back to her younger days, when she had been a carefree scribbler of poems the world would never see. How long had it been since she'd last written a verse? Far, far too long.

"I hadn't realized my bosom could be described as luscious." A wild streak in her made certain that she drawled the words just as her husband came abreast of them.

His eyes were dark slits of emerald ice beneath the silken mask that he had once more donned. "My lady." The bow he offered her was scornful at best. "Dunsmere."

"Sandhurst," the duke acknowledged. "I do hope your ruffled feathers are now smoothed, old boy."

"Remove your paws from my wife," he bit out by way of response.

Maggie swallowed, watching him with new eyes. She'd never seen this particular side of him. Oh, she was no stranger to his anger. But this time he was different, much like the lion she had described him as. "Sandhurst," she cautioned. Dear heavens, she didn't want them to come to blows. "His Grace was merely being courteous."

His lips thinned. "Whilst discussing the merits of your bosom?"

"Dear me." Dunsmere's voice was deceptively mild. "You seem irritated. I daresay we were merely finishing the delightful discourse we shared at dinner."

"I'll thrash you," her husband roared. "Come outside with me now. I've promised Nell that I won't trounce you in her home."

"How kind of you, but I'm afraid my pugilism days are over. One too many broken noses." He tapped the knot on his otherwise perfect feature. "The ladies don't prefer it, or so I'm told."

She nearly groaned aloud. He was digging her a hole with his words, and soon she would be buried in it up to her neck. The rigid set of her husband's jaw told her she would not escape her antics unscathed. She had to remove herself from the situation unfolding before her and could only hope that Simon would follow. After all, she hardly wanted him to engage in a bout of fisticuffs with the duke. Even if she secretly enjoyed the jealousy evident in her husband's rigid stance and dark tone.

"As much as I've enjoyed the evening, I'm afraid I'm weary and must retire," she said, hurrying to fill the conversational gap lest the two men decided to continue trading potentially lethal barbs.

"I shall escort you," both men offered simultaneously.

Good heavens. She winced and accepted her husband's proffered arm. "Good evening, Your Grace. Thank you for the conversation."

Emitting only a raw sound of possessiveness, Sandhurst all but propelled her from the room. If the duke responded, Maggie would never know. Her husband was too busy hauling her to her reckoning.

chapter five

H E TOOK HER TO HIS CHAMBER RATHER THAN HERS, perhaps for fear the duke would seek her out in the quiet of the night. Maggie would never know the reason behind his decision for certain. The door was barely closed at his back before he turned on her, his hands gripping her arms as he hauled her up against the wall, pinning her with his large body so that there was no escape.

Maggie blinked, startled by the virulence of his reaction. She reached for his shoulders. "What in heaven's name are you doing?"

"Punishing my wayward wife," he told her in a tone that was at once velvet and whisky to her senses, seductive and shocking. He pulled up her skirts and wedged a hard thigh between her legs.

She felt the unfamiliar abrasion of fabric against the open slit of her drawers and couldn't keep herself from straining into him. She was hungry for him already, warm and wet and willing. But she wasn't about to give in to him easily.

"What have I done?" she asked on a half-gasp, prolonging the inevitable. She had expected to spark jealousy but not anger. Then again, perhaps the two were not that far apart in the realms of emotion.

His hands were at work beneath her skirts, finding the closure on her drawers and sliding it open. "You know very well. Don't play the innocent with me."

She stiffened as he swept a hand over the bare skin of her upper thigh. Her drawers slid down over her limbs. She forced herself to protest. "Simon."

"You intentionally sought out Dunsmere." His gaze skewered her, holding her to the wall as surely as his body did. Fingers skimmed her inner thigh, tantalizing her.

"You were doing a fine job of monopolizing Lady Needham," she pointed out, having difficulty forcing her brain to function properly with him so near to her aching center.

"I told you to stay away from him." He ignored her completely. His expression was drawn with a combination of desire and irritation. "Were you intending to make me jealous with your little tête-à-tête?"

Of course she was. "Not in the slightest." She squirmed when he continued to dance around the hungry flesh where she most longed for his touch. "What were you and Nell discussing so intently?"

If he wanted to question her as if he were her jailer, surely she could do the same. It had seemed to her that he and Lady Needham had been discussing something serious. Indeed, she hadn't liked their proximity or the gravity of their expressions. She had seen the moment Simon took Nell's hand in his, and she hadn't been particularly warmed by it.

He stilled. "What Nell and I discussed is none of your affair. We are merely old friends."

Yet another of his old friends. An awful part of Maggie wondered if he had ever bedded their hostess in his past. Or if he wished to in his future. The heat building inside her collided with ice. "What manner of old friend is she?" She had to ask, though she didn't truly want to know the answer.

"She's not the sort you'd like the bloody duke to be." His hands curled around her thigh in an almost punishing grip.

"Stop," she cried out, trying to shrug from his grasp. For the first time, she realized she had been playing a game she hadn't the experience to play.

"Stop what?" He lowered his head, his lips grazing hers. "This?" At last, he took her mouth with his, claiming her in a kiss that punished as much as it incited her need. He cupped her bare bottom, grinding her sensitive cunny against his rigid thigh. "Or this?"

She moaned, unable to keep herself from feeling the delicious sensations he stirred. But she wasn't willing to be thrown from her course so summarily. "Stop being unkind to me. I did nothing wrong."

"Aside from consorting with the biggest lothario in England?" he scoffed, lowering his mouth to explore her neck. "I'll be damned if I'll share another woman."

She had tipped back her head to allow him better access to her throat, but his words gave her pause. Who else had he shared? She had been given to understand that Lady Billingsley had been his exclusive paramour for the last few years. "I don't understand." She wondered if perhaps his rage had not been solely provoked by her after all.

"It's nothing." His lips grazed her skin again. "We made a promise to each other. A month, yes?"

"Yes." One moment, he was about to devour her, the next he was angry, telling her half a story she'd never read before. "But what has that to do with this moment?"

"I want you." His mouth opened on her neck, sucking. "Do you want me?"

But she was determined not to be swayed. Her mind swirled with questions. Had Lady Billingsley been the topic of his conversation with Nell? Perhaps she had revealed an ugly side of his former paramour's past?

She sighed, trying not to enjoy the delicious heat of his mouth over her, nearly impossible though it was. "I want you to tell me the truth."

"I've told you already." He pressed a series of kisses down to her bosom. "We were merely conversing."

Did he think he could elude her so easily? She frowned, sinking her fingers into his thick, soft hair and forcing him to meet her gaze. "What other woman have you shared?"

He exhaled, his breath hitting her chest like a warmed blanket. "Why must you be so bloody persistent?"

She didn't know. "It's in my nature, I suppose."

"A man must be allowed his secrets."

Maggie didn't particularly care for the sound of that. "I detest secrecy."

"I'm sorry," he startled her by saying. He didn't strike her as the apologetic sort. "I merely don't wish to discuss it. It has no bearing upon you and me."

She had the sense that his concession had cost him a great deal more than was readily apparent. He was a proud man, that much she had learned quickly in the short time they'd spent together. Maggie took pity on him. "Very well. You needn't tell me just now."

"Good." His fingers traced a path of heat over her thigh before sinking into her wet folds to tease the aching bud that most yearned for his attention. "Because now, the only thing I'm going to do is fuck you, my dear. Hard and fast until you come."

She lost her breath. The iniquitous words made her all the more hungry for him. No man had ever dared to speak such sin to her. It rendered her quite weak in the knees. "Don't we require a bed?" she dared to ask.

He applied just the right amount of pressure with the perfect amount of speed. And then he sank a finger inside her. "Not when you're so wet and ready for me."

Her hips pumped against his rhythm. Her instinct took control of her. She wanted him so much, despite the unknown between them. Nothing mattered but the way he made her feel, as if she were about to shatter into a thousand singing shards of herself.

He stopped to open his trousers, and she caught sight of him, rigid and tantalizing. "Hook your leg round my waist." He guided her then, opening her to him more fully. His mouth came down on hers, crushing and possessive.

His cock pressed against her, hot and stiff. She arched her back to help ease his entrance. While his tongue plunged into her mouth, he slid inside her in one long, delicious thrust. She moaned, sucking on his tongue, her hands going to his firm buttocks to drive him even deeper. This time, their passion ran at full gallop. There was no steady canter, no time for soft kisses and gentle caresses. Nor did she want that. She wanted him to take her, hard and fast as he'd said, make them both explode with their mutual desire.

He withdrew from her only to slide in again, increasing his pace, going faster, wilder. With his thumb, he continued to exert pressure on her nub, and the wave of her first release washed over her. Her cunny clenched on his cock and they both moaned, lost in the sensations, the need to become one.

He dragged his mouth back to her neck, nipping at her with his teeth just enough to make her shiver. Tonight, she reveled in his ferocity, in the way his hands were almost rough upon her, in the way he took her as if he couldn't wait another moment to fill her with his seed.

While she still shook with the effects of her passion, he rocked against her, flattening her to the wall. A warm burst of sensation rushed inside her, and she knew that he too had found his release. She clasped him to her as they plummeted from their cloud of pleasure as one. His breathing was as ragged as hers, his heart a rapid thrum against her chest. He kissed her neck, then dropped a lingering kiss on her mouth before gently returning her foot to the floor and slipping from her body. They stared at each other.

"We leave tomorrow morning," he said at last, his voice almost hoarse. "Together."

She nodded. While days before, leaving with her husband would have seemed inconceivable if not altogether impossible, now it seemed perfectly normal. She wasn't certain she could yet manage rational conversation, so she busied herself with rearranging her skirts. Only her drawers, discarded on the floor, remained as a sign of their frantic lovemaking. He refastened his trousers while she attempted to collect herself.

"I suppose I ought to return to my chamber," she said when at last she rediscovered the ability to speak.

"You'll stay here with me this evening," he said, more decree than request.

His pronouncement startled her. Hadn't he just been concerned with observing a false sense of propriety? What had changed? She blinked, wondering if she'd heard him properly above the mad thudding of her heart. "I beg your pardon?"

His expression was impossible to decipher. "I want you to remain in my chamber," he elaborated. "Please."

Maggie supposed he wasn't accustomed to asking for what he wanted. After all, he was a man and a lord both. Even so, his request was hardly tender, and though she was not impervious to his lovemaking, she was still quite stubborn in her own right. "You might ask me rather than issuing a demand."

He frowned. "I didn't demand. I said please."

"Silly me." She almost laughed, but he was serious. "Thank you for issuing a polite demand."

He raked a hand through his hair, looking vexed. "Damn it, woman, you're as prickly as a rosebush sometimes. I merely want you to stay here in my chamber."

"Why?" she persisted.

"Because I don't trust that blackguard who calls himself a duke," he thundered, his eyes darkening.

Ah. So he *had* been jealous of Dunsmere. She was secretly pleased. Still, there were logistics to be considered. "What of my lady's maid? She won't know to find me here."

"I'll damn well be your lady's maid for the night," he growled. "In the morning, I'll have her sent up for you."

Another thought occurred to her just then, and she had to know. "Do you trust me?"

His gaze searched hers. "I'm not certain. I've misplaced my trust far too many times, it would seem."

How paradoxical that he should make such a confession to her, of all people. She stared at him. "So too have I, my lord."

He inclined his head, accepting the insult wordlessly.

She was more convinced than ever that he and Nell had been speaking of Lady Billingsley. A tiny sliver of triumph sliced through her at the thought. Perhaps his old and dear friend had not been the angel he'd believed her to be after all. And while Maggie couldn't compete with a paragon, she could certainly compete with a mere woman. If she wanted to compete at all, that was, and she wasn't entirely certain she did. Indeed, her brain was doing a fair job of convincing her that she ought not to, though her passionate heart felt otherwise.

But in the end, she was tired, and giving in to a small battle didn't seem too foolish a decision. "Very well," she capitulated. "I shall stay."

Early the following afternoon, they arrived at Denver House, Simon's country seat. The visit was Maggie's first, since they had wed in London and he had not bothered to provide her with a honeymoon. Instead, he had run off to the arms of his mistress. It had been a cold revelation to Maggie, who had been naïve enough to believe her husband would treat her with the respect she deserved. She had imagined settling into a comfortable life, getting to know her husband, exchanging pleasantries over dinner, raising children. She had not imagined abandonment, though she had been warned by her mother in advance that not all men proved faithful husbands.

Her mother, she'd discovered, had been woefully inept at warning a young bride about the realities of a society marriage. An odd mix of feelings assailed Maggie as Sandhurst handed her down from the carriage and she took in the imposing façade of the home she'd never seen. Her heart went to her throat. Lady Needham's country house had been impressive indeed, but Denver House was magnificent.

She stared at the immense structure with its rows of windows flanked by an east and a west wing at either end. Doric columns stretched across the front as if they were a row of soldiers at the ready. Twin curved stairs descended to the gravel thoroughfare. Bas relief carvings decorated the stone walls.

The entire scene took her breath.

"Welcome to Denver House." Simon's voice was grave.

She had seen many a great building in London and New York, but this place was somehow different from all the rest. She forced her gaze back to her husband, who watched her with an impenetrable expression etched on his handsome face. "It's unbearably lovely."

"It's a crumbling pile of familial rubble." His voice was cool.

She supposed that if she had been raised in such a structure she too could have been unaffected by its majesty. Her father's townhouse in New York was grand, but not nearly as regal. "You don't like it here?"

"I will present you to the staff," he surprised her by saying, skirting her query with neat precision.

Although she knew she ought to be stern with him for not having brought her to Denver House before, she couldn't help but be pleased by his announcement. It was far too late in coming, and under all the wrong circumstances, but she was once again choosing her battles. "Thank you. That would be wonderful indeed."

He offered her his arm, looking uncomfortable. "I'm

aware it should have been done well before now."

"Yes." She would not allow him to escape her censure, for although they had created a tentative truce, it hadn't swept away a year of his bad behavior. "It most certainly should have."

A self-derisive smile curved his lips as they walked to the entrance. "You're not the forgiving sort, are you?"

"Only where forgiveness is well-deserved." She kept her voice prim. She did not wish him to think that lovemaking was a panacea. Of course she enjoyed the wicked things he could do to her body, but that hardly meant she'd forgotten the stark realities of their union. Now that they were away from the dream world of Lady Needham's party, it was easier for their difficulties to reemerge.

"Is there a way it can be earned?"

Their shoes crunched on the gravel in time. Despite her caution, she was enjoying this slice of life as it could have been for the two of them, as it perhaps would have been had he not already found love elsewhere. She had to admit that she longed for the simplicity of companionship, the ease of friendship, that she knew some women found with their husbands. This was not the life she'd ever envisioned for herself, even when she'd accepted her duty and agreed to their marriage of convenience.

Maggie considered his question then, forcing her mind to the conversation at hand rather than the emotions surging through her at their odd homecoming. "Do you wish to earn my forgiveness? Truly?"

"You doubt me?"

She couldn't stifle a mocking laugh. "Of course I doubt you. A year of absence doesn't procure a great deal of faith in a man, you know."

"I daresay it wouldn't." He patted her gloved hand where it rested upon his arm. "I admire your tenacity, my dear. It's so very American."

"Thank you," she returned. "I suppose."

"Allow me to introduce you to the staff, and then we can

discuss just how a sinful man might go about winning the forgiveness of a beautiful woman." The glance he gave her was scorching, igniting an answering fire deep within her.

She had an impression that his idea of a discussion involved sin and a bedchamber rather than a dialogue. But though she'd agreed to his bargain, she still possessed a memory and a mind. Both recalled what it had felt like to bear his icy civility followed by abandonment. Both recalled the pitying stares and whispers that followed her wherever she went. And both recalled that he had left her for another.

"Forgiveness must be earned, my lord." She met his gaze with a frank, unflinching stare. Let him not think himself an exception to that particular rule. For he most certainly was not.

Simon had disappeared. Maggie frowned as she wandered through the immense confines of Denver House on her own. While they had spent the evening in heated lovemaking, he had left her bed before dawn. He had not appeared to break his fast, nor had he deigned to share an afternoon repast with her. Tea too had been ignored. She had done her best to dismiss his abrupt and confusing desertion. She had made tentative friends with Mrs. Keynes, the housekeeper. She had come across several footmen and maids. But her husband was another matter. And by the time six o'clock had arrived, she was feeling rather perturbed with the man.

Truly, she was left with no recourse but to find him. She had already intruded upon a study, a library, several bedchambers, and the drawing room, to no avail. Her dudgeon growing ever higher, Maggie clipped down the hall and selected the door nearest to her, throwing it open.

Furniture shrouded in coverings greeted her, a sliver of sunlight emerging from a distant pair of windows. She was about to move on to the next room awaiting her inspection when it occurred to her that the curtains ought to have been drawn together. Instead, they appeared to have been deliberately opened to allow a small bit of light to enter the otherwise somber chamber.

Awareness struck her, a sense of being watched. She hesitated at the threshold, suspecting she had at last found Simon, but uncertain if she dared to enter. There was a solemnity to the chamber, as if it were cloaked in secrecy, that made her wonder if she trespassed. After all, if he had hidden himself away, there was undoubtedly a reason.

But what?

She was startled to realize that she cared enough for him to seek an answer. Drat him. When had she begun to develop a *tendre* for the man who had happily run off with his mistress? He certainly didn't deserve her affections. He didn't deserve her body or her time. She owed him nothing but a month.

Her frown grew more severe as she stepped into the chamber at last, prodded by her self-disgust. She had thought she was made of sterner stuff. Maggie forced herself to recall that while his kisses melted her bones, he had treated her abominably. He was a cad.

She was in control. Yes, she was. She had to be, or else she was hopelessly in his thrall, and that wouldn't do. Not for one moment. Her husband could not be trusted. His latest misadventure had reminded her, in somewhat mocking fashion, of precisely that.

Double drat him. She cleared her throat, summoning up an impression of her fierce mother. "Simon?" Her gaze darted about, but she could see precious little other than the hulking silhouettes of chaises and settees that were likely long since out of mode. No answer. She strode deeper into the room, swearing that she could smell him. "If you are in this chamber, it would be in your best interest to show yourself at once."

She attempted to peer into a dark corner, waiting for his response. None was forthcoming until, after what seemed forever, his familiar voice stroked over her senses like a lover's caress.

"What shall become of me if I don't?"

A shiver of anticipation danced over her skin. At last. He had certainly led her on a merry chase for much of the day. She spun in a slow circle, still unable to locate him. "Where are you?"

"Perhaps you ought to find me." An undercurrent of humor laced his voice.

He was amused, was he? Her gaze narrowed as she skirted what appeared to be an escritoire and ventured into the quadrant of the chamber where his voice seemed to emanate from. "You are a beast. Have you no conscience?"

At her question, she shook her head, answering herself. "Foolish, wrong-headed me. Of course you haven't a conscience."

"I have a conscience," he spoke up, sounding a touch indignant. "I simply ignore it."

"I'm well aware of that, my lord." Where in heaven's name was he? She swept aside a particularly voluminous sheet of furniture covering, hoping to find him beneath it. There was only a wardrobe. "I'm certain you haven't heard your conscience since you were a lad."

"That smarts."

His voice was directly behind her. She turned to find him towering over her, a dark and inviting figure. "It is merely truth." She did her best to curtail the breathless quality threatening to overcome her voice. Today of all days she did not want to show him a hint of weakness, for she sensed he was a hunter stalking his prey. She had few defenses against him other than her wits.

He stepped closer to her. "How did you find me here?"

"Fortune." She crossed her arms over her breasts, praying he wouldn't touch her and thereby crumble the infinitesimal wall she had built between them. "Or perhaps misfortune."

"Did you miss me, my dear?"

She had, and the realization troubled her. When had he become necessary to her, a man she chased? "Of course not," she lied. "Mrs. Keynes is uncertain of what she ought to send to dinner. Apparently, she doesn't wish to incur your displeasure."

"Indeed?" He was devastatingly near to her now. His hand caught her elbow, drawing her right arm away from her body. With practiced expertise, he trailed his fingers down the inside of her arm, catching her just where her sleeve gaped to reveal bare skin. He stopped at her wrist, raising her hand to his lips for a lingering kiss.

"What is this chamber?" She was determined not to be distracted by his blatant invitation to sin.

"It is nothing now." His grip tightened on her, in warning, she supposed.

She remained undeterred. "What was it before now?"

Abruptly, he went from teasing to stormy. "I don't wish to speak of it."

"I'm sure you don't. But there's a reason for secreting yourself away in here."

He dropped her hand, pivoting abruptly to give her his back. "I abhor your American sense of persistence."

"And I dislike your English sense of avoidance," she countered. "You cannot hide forever. Tell me, Simon. You can trust me."

"Can I?" He turned back to her. "In my experience, the fairer sex is furthest from trustworthy."

"How interesting, for I share a similar experience with their male counterpart." She wished she could see his eyes, but the dimness of the chamber rendered it impossible.

"Point well taken. You can't trust me, Maggie girl. Don't ever do it." His voice was bitter, self-mocking.

She didn't hesitate. "You can be certain that I won't. But you can trust me, my lord. I am not Lady Billingsley." His former mistress had hurt him. Maggie knew a pang of jealousy for Lady Billingsley's ability to wound him, for it meant he cared.

"You most definitely are not." His voice was solemn.

She couldn't tell if he paid her a compliment or an insult, but she decided on the former. "What is this chamber?" she asked again, refusing to allow him to dodge her question. There was a reason for him to have hidden himself away in a dusty old-furniture-laden room. She was determined to know what it was.

He was silent for a few heartbeats and she feared he wouldn't answer her. Then, his gruff voice split the uneasy quiet. "It was my mother's sitting room."

His mother. Surprise flitted through her, mingling with compassion. She knew little of the previous Marchioness of Sandhurst other than the facts related to her by Mrs. Keynes, who had been a retainer at Denver House for nearly forty years. Simon's mother had died in childbirth when he was a lad. Beyond that stark truth, she hadn't much information.

She placed a hand on his arm, the need to comfort him an impulse as strong as it likely was wrong. "How long has it been closed?"

"Fifteen years, I suppose." The breath escaped from him in a long, weary sigh. "I was but a lad. I've never had the heart to change it. This is the first time I've been inside this chamber since her death. Damn odd how so many years can pass and yet upon return, it's as if no time has gone at all."

His sadness was palpable. This rare show of emotion from her otherwise guarded husband moved her. For one ridiculous moment, she thought of taking him in her arms before dashing the notion away with her common sense. He wasn't worthy of her comfort, and she mustn't forget it.

She pulled her hand away, needing to put some reason and distance between them. "Memories are like a book you've already read. You may forget the details, but once you delve back into the pages, it all returns to you."

He considered her through the half-light. "You're surprisingly sage for a woman of your tender years."

She was twenty-two, and she didn't think that to be

terribly young, particularly since he was only seven years her senior. "I do have a mind," she pointed out. While she was aware that it wasn't always fashionable for women to possess sharp wits, she had never been wont to hide her intellect.

"And it is indeed a worthy one. I begin to see just how gravely I underestimated you, my dear." He startled her by reaching out and caressing her cheek.

A small shiver laced through her at his touch. "Have you been hiding away in here the entire day?"

"No. I've been wandering. Confronting old ghosts, I suppose." His thumb brushed her lower lip.

She stilled, her heart thumping madly. "Perhaps you ought not to confront them alone."

"Christ." He took her in his arms then, crushing her to him and burying his face in her neck. "How can you be so bloody kind?"

"I'm not kind." She tried not to be affected by his lips on her skin and failed horridly. "My younger brother and sister would attest to that."

His grip on her tensed. "I had a brother as well. My mother died bearing him, and he died two days later."

She embraced him despite herself, putting aside her pride's frantic call to treat him no better than he had treated her. How could she deny him solace when he was showing his humanity for the first time? He seemed fragile, the complete opposite of the cool man she'd known. "It must have been difficult for a boy to lose his mother and brother so abruptly."

His face remained pressed to her throat. "My mother was a gentle soul. She deserved far better than to die alone in the countryside while my father was gadding about with his paramour."

Maggie rubbed his back in soothing motions. He wore only a shirt, no jacket, no waistcoat, entirely divested of his polite trappings. Wildness emanated from him, as if all the pain he'd buried boiled to the surface now. She felt as if she understood him—perhaps better than he understood himself—for the first time.

"I'm sorry, Simon." It was all she could say. Words could not rewrite his past, the sadness that had run through his life as if it were a river. Likely, it had washed away much in its path.

"You needn't be sorry. Life has its way of righting wrongs. My father died the year after in his mistress's arms. Apoplexy, the doctor said. A fitting end."

"Leaving you alone," she finished for him. "Had you no one else?"

"I had myself. That was all I required."

Maggie had possessed a childhood that, while far from perfect, had never been lonely. Her days had been filled with siblings and love, albeit with a healthy portion of bickering. Her disillusionment had begun later, along with the inevitable awful realization that she must leave the comfort of her family behind. She felt sorry for him, for what he must have suffered as a boy suddenly bereft. "You have me now as well," she told him, hating that he had ever felt as if he were on his own, though she knew well she shouldn't care one whit.

"Have I?"

She thought of the lad who had lost his mother, who had been left without comfort and love, and her heart crumbled for the boy he must have been. Tears stung her eyes, and she blinked them away. "For the next month, you do," she said before she could think better of it.

"Why the devil are you here, Maggie?" He pulled away to look down at her, his gaze dark and searching.

She wasn't certain she knew what he asked of her. She frowned. "You brought me to Denver House."

"I'm well aware." He paused, seeming to collect his thoughts. "What I meant to ask is why are you in this chamber with me? Why are you being so good to the man who never wanted you?"

She'd known, of course, that he'd never wanted her as a

wife. He'd made that abundantly clear with his desertion and ensuing silence. But hearing him confirm it aloud still stung. Maggie allowed her gaze to travel over his handsome face as she searched for a response. "For the next month, it is my duty."

"Duty." His tone went lifeless.

Was it possible she had actually hurt him? Though she knew she ought to possess a heart of hardest stone when it came to him, she couldn't quite bear to. He had a way of creeping into her heart when she least expected it. At Lady Needham's party, they had fallen into each other's arms little knowing what was to come when their true identities were uncovered. In so doing, they had become inextricably linked in a way their marriage had never managed to accomplish.

"I don't want to be your duty, Maggie," he intruded upon her thoughts, his voice low and intense. "I want more from you."

"How much more?" she dared to ask although she told herself she had nothing left that she was willing to give him. He'd already taken too much.

"I don't know." Pent-up emotions made his voice ragged.

It wasn't an answer to any of the questions thudding around in her mind, but it was somehow all she needed. She hooked an arm around his neck and pulled his handsome face closer to hers until their mouths barely touched. He didn't require further encouragement. With a groan, he claimed her lips in a long, searching kiss.

Maggie's fingers sank into his hair as she opened for him. His tongue slipped into her mouth and she sucked it, a hot surge of want nearly toppling her over in that moment. How was it that she could be irritated with him one minute, and yet in the midst of a dusty room, she could long for him so much the next?

He broke the kiss at last, resting his forehead against hers. His breath draped warmly over her lips. "Tell me how it is that you continually surprise me."

She stared. "I could ask you the same."

"Thank you for finding me."

That gave her pause. She hadn't anticipated his gratitude. "I reckoned you needed finding."

He dropped a soft, sweet kiss on her lips. "It would seem you have an uncanny knack for finding me when I need it most."

"If you're speaking of our meeting at Lady Needham's, it was you who found me," she pointed out, trying to maintain the tentative grip she had on her judgment. "You thoroughly trounced my train."

"Trains are nuisances," he quipped. "You ought to have had it tied up properly, by God."

Maggie's smile widened. "I did. You ought to have watched where you were placing your overly large feet, by God."

She enjoyed their banter, and the realization startled her akin to a pinprick to the thumb. To her amazement, she was beginning to like him. A paradox, he was filled with passion one moment and yet cold and calculated the next.

He blustered without meaning it. He had loved his mother. He had loved another woman who had not been worthy of that love. She knew now that beneath his façade there hid the boy who had been left alone in the world, that the boy had grown into a man who still possessed the same fear of being alone. He was imperfect, it was true, but so was she. And his kisses made her mad. His touch set her aflame.

No. She had to stay the course of her reckless mind before it took her deeper down the path to ruin.

"Now I've overly large feet, have I?" There was a grin in his voice.

"It's amazing you can even walk with those unwieldy fellows," she teased, running her hands down over his broad shoulders. She could trust in desire, if little else. That was the only emotion between them that made any sense.

"You're a minx." He found her bottom through the

layers of her gown, sliding beneath her bustle with unerring accuracy. He pulled her snugly against him.

"What if I am?" she challenged.

"I shall have to make you pay."

"Do you promise?"

He kissed her again. "Absolutely."

When their mouths broke apart at last, Maggie gathered her common sense, forcing herself to recall her initial reason for seeking him out. It wouldn't do for them to become fodder for belowstairs gossip on their first day in residence. She had never been treated as the lady of the house, and she didn't want to lose the tentative respect she'd won from her housekeeper. As much as she wanted to allow him to drag her to the bedchamber, it wouldn't do. Not now. "Your retribution will have to wait, I fear, for it's likely nearly time for dinner by now. Will you join me?"

He inclined his head. "I shall."

"Thank you." She stepped away from him, smoothing her hands down over her skirts. "Poor Mrs. Keynes must be beside herself wondering what to send to table."

"I'm certain she will find something suitably delicious." He took her hand, lacing their fingers together in a startling show of solidarity. "I meant what I said, Maggie. Thank you for finding me."

She squeezed his fingers, an unexpected twinge of emotion shooting through her. If she wasn't careful, she would soften toward him too much. And when their agreed-upon month was over, there was no telling where he would choose to go. She would do best to remember that their truce was not lifelong, she warned herself. Her maudlin thoughts of moments before were just that, sentiment rather than reality. They didn't know each other. Not at all.

But she couldn't quite tamp down the desire to know him better. "You're welcome," she whispered past the tension that threatened to close her throat. *You mustn't grow to care for him too much*, she reminded herself as he escorted her from the chamber.

If only she hadn't already begun to do so.

Maggie woke to find Simon had gone for a ride. A week had passed since their arrival at Denver House, and they had spent each night in sensual abandon. Heartened by the note he'd taken care to leave her, she enjoyed a small breakfast before deciding to further her explorations. One room called to her more than all the others she had yet toured, and it was the library. She found it again with the aid of the redoubtable Mrs. Keynes, and once inside its immense book-lined confines, she was quite in love.

The library was cavernous, its high ceiling and ornate shelves carved from luxurious walnut. Large gothic windows allowed bright sunlight to illuminate the room at its far end. A thick carpet ran the length of the room. Chairs and settees were scattered throughout, along with a massive desk and a stunning marble fireplace. She could have happily lived in this entire room alone. Rendered breathless by the effect, she strode to the nearest wall of shelves, curious to see what sorts of books might await her there. It had been so long—too long—since she'd last lost herself in reading.

She discovered a great deal of Latin, as was to be expected. Nothing caught her eye until she moved on to the next set of shelving. He possessed a surprising number of poetry tomes, and it appeared that his taste was modern rather than the typical collection of century-old poets. She ran her finger idly across the spines, discovering that their interest in poetry was markedly similar. And then she stopped, shocked at the name on a particularly small volume.

M.E. Desmond.

She knew the name well, as well as she knew the contents of the book itself. For she was M.E. Desmond, and the poems were her own. Had he actually read her poetry? It seemed impossible that he even owned it, for the volume had been printed in New York with a limited number of volumes. Curious despite herself, she plucked it from the shelf. The physical embodiment of her words never failed to humble her.

"Are you in need of entertainment, my dear?"

She gasped at the sound of Simon's deep voice behind her and spun to face him. Unfairly handsome, he wore a pair of muddied riding boots with tweed trousers and coat. A rakish air emanated from him with enough potency to make her drop the book from her limp fingers.

Longing sliced through her, sending an ache directly to her core. She entirely forgot what she'd been about. Forgot everything except the tall, lean man stalking across the study to her. He stopped a scant foot away, smelling of leather and outdoors and his familiar, beguiling scent. His eyes burned into hers.

"Have you lost your ability to produce a sharp retort?" He grinned, melting her even more. "Let us mark this day down for perpetuity."

He was teasing her, she realized, and she liked this side of him. It provoked a sense of intimacy and easiness between them that all the lovemaking in the world could not. She was staring as if she were a lovestruck girl holding on to her mother's skirts. Maggie attempted to gather her wits, wishing he weren't so unutterably gorgeous, his grin not so infectious, that he didn't make her stomach feel as if it were about to drop straight to her toes.

"You're a wit, aren't you?" she forced herself to quip at last, wishing she didn't sound breathless.

"Whenever possible," he returned, bowing and retrieving the dropped book all in the same fluid motion. He looked down at the volume in his hand. "Ah, I see you've discovered a favorite. Have you read Desmond before?"

She swallowed, uncertain of how she ought to answer. With honesty, she supposed at last. "I have, yes."

He raised a brow, his interest clearly piqued. "What do you make of him? He's only ever put out the one collection, but I've rather enjoyed it."

Oh dear. "Why do you suppose the author is a man?"

"Why do you suppose the author is a woman?" He exhibited perfectly flawless logic.

She wasn't prepared to answer that particular question just yet. There was something that she wanted to know first. "What is your favorite poem?"

"I'm especially fond of *Empire*," he answered without hesitation. "Though there are a great many sonnets I admire. He's a clever fellow, to be sure."

Empire was one of her favorite poems she'd written as well. It was a confluence of the world she knew in New York and the early days of her childhood, the days when her father had been a man with the burning dream of building an empire instead of a man who owned one. As a young woman, she had many times wished to return to her life of simplicity, for the wealth her father had amassed with his hotels and stores had trapped her as surely as any gilded cage. With wealth had come responsibilities and ultimately a life far away from everything she'd ever known.

She stared at Simon, wondering if she should tell him the truth. If he would even believe her. But she was proud of her work, and she wouldn't hide it. Not from him. "I've always been fond of that poem as well. I wrote it, after all."

Confusion clouded his eyes. "I beg your pardon?"

"I wrote the poem," she said in a quiet voice. "I'm M.E. Desmond. Or rather, I was, for I have not written a poem in some years now."

"You cannot be." He searched her face, looking for an answer he apparently found. "My God. You're deadly serious, aren't you?"

"Margaret Emilia Desmond." She held his gaze, unflinching.

"Bloody hell." Simon stared at her with an inscrutable expression. "When were you planning on telling me,

Maggie?"

She shrugged. "I wasn't going to tell you. I don't write poetry any longer. It hardly seemed important."

"You don't write any longer? Why the hell not?"

She hadn't anticipated that sort of response. Crossing her arms over her bodice in a defensive gesture, she met his gaze without flinching. "I'm no good at writing poems. It was a childish fancy, nothing more."

"A childish fancy?" He held the book to his heart, and she couldn't be certain if it was an unconscious act or an intentional one. "Surely you can't be serious, Maggie. These are some of the finest poems of our age."

She frowned at him. "Flattery is the worst sort of compliment."

He frowned back at her. "I'm not flattering you, by God. I wouldn't."

Maggie thought about that for a moment and had to acknowledge the kernel of honesty his words held. He had never been a man of easy charm. He was handsome and seductive, powerful and attractive in ways she couldn't entirely comprehend, it was true. But he had never paid her the sort of odious obsequiousness others had in the past.

"Very well," she allowed. "But yours is merely one opinion. The only reason I was able to publish this volume at all is that my father is wealthy and he paid a publisher a handsome sum to do the deed. I dare not fool myself into thinking I'm a true poet."

"Rubbish. Others have read your work and admired it as I do."

They had? She didn't dare to hope. After she had discovered that her father had bought her way into the world of poetry and literary aspirations, she'd sworn to never write another poem. Her damnable pride, she supposed, or perhaps vanity, but if her poetry wasn't good enough on its own, she didn't wish to ever see it in print again.

"What others?" Of course, she knew she ought not to

entertain any such thoughts. From the time she'd first been enrolled in school—the one-room schoolhouse of her youth rather than the private tutors and finishing school she'd later endured—she had wanted nothing more than to be a poet. But she had given up that dream, knowing it to be a fruitless one.

"Lord Egglesfield, for one," he told her, his tone grave. "And lords Ridley, Cavendish and Tyndale as well. Mr. Tobin also."

Dear heavens. While she hadn't heard of all the peers he mentioned, she had certainly heard of Mr. Jonathan Tobin, for he was an extraordinarily talented poet in his own right. It baffled her that such a distinguished group of men had deigned to read the scribbling of her youth. And admired it.

She fanned her flushed cheeks with her hand. "Mr. Tobin? You know him?"

He scowled. "Yes, and he's ugly as a bear's arse."

Did she sense jealousy? A small smile flirted with her lips as she contemplated him. "Why have I never heard any such kind words regarding my poetry?"

"No one knows who M.E. Desmond is," he pointed out, once again the soul of common sense. "Tobin is given to fat as well."

"Of course. I hadn't thought of that." Her smile blossomed into a grin as the last bit of what he'd said permeated her whirling mind. "I've seen an engraving of Mr. Tobin. He didn't appear at all plump to me."

"Fat as a hog," Simon snapped, his lips compressing in his irritation.

"I thought him rather handsome." She couldn't resist pushing him.

He pulled her flush against his hard chest. Somehow, even his glower was charming. "I'm going to have to punish you for that." His mouth swooped deliciously near to hers, his hot breath cascading over her lips in temptation. "Why did you not tell me about your poetry?"

She struggled to focus on his words rather than his sinful

mouth. "When was I to have told you? You scarcely spoke to me until Lady Needham's."

"You've had ample time since then." One of his hands slid around her waist and then upward to cup her breast over the fabric and corset barrier separating them.

She arched into him, unable to help herself from seeking out the exquisite sensation of his touch. "I didn't think it mattered. As I've said, I haven't written in years. I'm no longer a starry-eyed girl led by silly dreams."

Simon was intent, his gaze as seeking as his wandering hands. "Why?"

Maggie wasn't entirely certain what he was asking of her. She swallowed, barely holding on to her wits. "Why should you care so much?"

"I admire your work." He reached up to caress her cheek. "Truth be told, I admire you. I didn't want to, but I do."

His confession stole the breath straight from her lungs. Admiration was not love, but it was something more than nothing at all. She skimmed her palms up over his chest, resting her right hand above his thudding heart. "I never thought to hear those words from you, of all men."

He winced. "I suppose I've earned your cynicism."

"You have." She drew no quarter. Their ugly past would never be completely forgotten.

"Think what you must of me, but know that I speak only truth when I say that you have a gift, Maggie. You should write again, for yourself as much as for others." His tone was solemn.

She had not thought of writing in a long time. While she had continued to read poetry and to enjoy the works of others, she had truly felt that part of her was closed off forever. She was no great poet. "I cannot write. The music isn't in me any longer."

He caught her chin between his thumb and forefinger, tipping her head back so that she could not look away from him. "What has stolen the music from you?"

She didn't know what to say, and he was so terribly close. Desire unfurled within her like a ripe blossom. "I can't be certain," she forced herself to say, and it was true. "My life has turned out to be quite different from what I fancied it would be when I was a girl. Sometimes we must give up the dreams of our youth."

She heard the sadness in her own voice. Her life had altered so much since that carefree time when she'd been given to dreams and whimsy. She had been free to write as she wished, live as she wished. And then, her world had disappeared, replaced with finishing school and French gowns, a trip to England from which there proved no return.

Before she'd known what she was about, she had been left in a strange land with a new husband who didn't want her and with precious few friends for support. Poetry had most certainly not been foremost in her mind. She had done her duty to her father. He had wanted nothing less than a title for his daughter, and she certainly hadn't wished to disappoint him, not even at the risk of disappointing herself. Not even at the risk of losing a man she'd cared for very much. Richard was, like her past, forever out of reach for her.

"I hope you will consider writing again," he said, his expression inscrutable as always. "Not every dream needs to be abandoned."

It was apparent that he was a child of the aristocracy. Oh, to have been born a man with all the power in the world at his pinky finger. Maggie frowned. "I'm too rational to have dreams now."

Her father had taken her aside before sending her to England with her mother. He had told her that dreams were for men and not for women. She had been devastated by his last words to her before she'd been sent away to England and to a marriage that would serve to enhance his New York status while leaving her utterly miserable. She knew now that her father must have known what he was sending her away to face. And it hurt, for once she had been his treasured child.

As a girl and the eldest of her siblings, she had always been close to him. He had taken great care to show her the intricacies of his business dealings when she was quite young. But when she'd turned twelve, her mother had finally birthed the son he'd been wanting. And almost instantly, or at least as soon as it was known that her brother would be a healthy baby, Maggie had been cast aside, replaced. At seventeen, she'd been sent to finishing school. She'd returned and had fallen in love with Richard, the sweet younger son of a New York clergyman. Her father had disapproved immensely, and she had bowed to his will. He'd sent her off to marry a title in a faraway place instead. She'd been forgotten.

Now, her father didn't bother to send her more than the occasional letter, and even those correspondences were written by his secretary's hand. Merely because she hadn't been born a son, and although she was every bit as intelligent as James would one day prove to be. It was all so horridly, dreadfully unfair. She'd forced herself not to dwell upon the disappointments her relationship with her father had produced, for if she lingered over them, it would hurt her far too much. But now, Simon and his surprising concern were deconstructing the walls she'd built between her past and her present.

"Why do you frown so fiercely, my dear?" Simon's voice interrupted her troubled musings.

"I'm thinking of my father." She felt an odd sense of comfort with her husband now. They had shared their most intimate selves with each other. And they were husband and wife, which united them more completely than any other man and woman could possibly be joined. Even if that bond had never been truly sealed before, since their sudden relationship, she couldn't deny their deep connection. Nor did she want to deny it any longer. He was awakening her heart and her passion, and perhaps it was dangerous but she didn't think she cared.

"What of him?" Simon's tone was gentle.

"I was thinking of how my father raised me to have dreams, but only until it was clear that he would have a son. When my brother was born, my father promptly forgot I existed. No more sessions in his study. No more teaching me arithmetic and philosophy. No more encouraging me to read the great poets."

"It would seem we share a commonality of sorts then," Simon said, surprising her with his revelation in turn, "for my father never gave a damn that I existed."

"I wonder if that wouldn't have been a better fate," she said, "than having been close to your father and then knowing that he treasured a sibling more than you for no reason other than his sex. I cannot help that I've been born a woman. I am still every bit as worthy as James."

"Of course you are, my dear." Simon gathered her to his chest then, embracing her in his strong arms and seemingly trying to erase the troubles in her heart.

She leaned into him, soaking in his strength. How odd it was that he had the power to bring forth feelings in her that she hadn't known she'd been hiding. "A woman is every bit as worthy as a man." Why, after all, should her baby brother be touted the heir to her family simply by virtue of his sex? Females could be every bit as intelligent, if not more so than their male counterparts.

"Don't cry, darling." He caught her tears on the pad of his finger. He was unbearably handsome looking down at her, the light of the far-off windows illuminating his aristocratic features. His eyes were what haunted her most, pinning her to the floor upon which she stood.

"I'm not." She sniffed, trying to hide her embarrassment. How had they gone from speaking of her old poetry habit to this deep, emotional conversation? She didn't want to linger over wounds that didn't have a ready bandage. "My father was not particularly kind to me as I grew to become an adult, but that is hardly your affair. I'm sorry, my lord."

She licked her lips, embarrassed that she had allowed herself to sink so low in the mire of her past. It was hardly his fault that her father had bartered her for his title. For the first time in her life, she recognized her father's machinations for what they were. She could be as angry at Simon as she chose, but the truth was that her father had orchestrated it all. He had sold her for a title, and once she was gone, he no longer had a need for her. All the happy childhood memories in the world could not supplant that bitter fact.

Simon brushed a kiss over her forehead. "I'm sorry, my dear. My father was an utter bastard as well. All he left me was a mountain of debt and no true solution."

No true solution. Maggie winced, for she knew she'd been the solution. Or rather, her father's willingness to provide him with a fat dowry had been. "I suppose we are both the victims of our circumstances." She'd never looked at the situation from such a perspective, but the more time they spent together, the more she'd come to see him differently. She felt a deep empathy toward Simon, who was a man who'd been set adrift on the ocean of life every bit as much as she.

"I suppose we are." His expression was as solemn as his gaze was searching. "Perhaps we ought to begin again, toss away the old hurts between us. What say you, my dear?"

If he'd surprised her before, he shocked her now with his unexpected query. The lonely life she'd led since her marriage could not have prepared her for this moment, for the discovery that her husband wasn't wholly the cad she'd believed him to be. That he was just a man who had made unwanted decisions the same as she.

"I would like that very much." The words were torn from her, an admission she didn't want to give but one she needed to give. She could only hope they wouldn't prove her undoing.

chapter six

"YOU CANNOT POSSIBLY BE SERIOUS."

Simon stared at his fiery-haired wife and decided that, whilst she looked particularly exquisite in a brilliant-blue afternoon frock, her American sensibilities were rotting her brain. Exceptional ability as a poetess or not, she was fit for the madhouse. She appeared quite sincere, her violet eyes huge and bright, pinning him to the spot. From her elaborately styled curls to her silk shoes, she looked every inch the proper marchioness. He longed to muss her up, undo a few of her buttons, bend her over a settee and sink inside her hot, wet flesh. Devil take it. He shook the thought from his mind. He bloody well couldn't always be making love to her. Could he?

"Of course I'm serious, Sandhurst." She smiled and he wanted her all the more. "So are you. That's the problem. It's occurred to me that I've never even heard you laugh."

Hadn't she? He pondered her statement for a moment, supposing that he didn't find much levity in the world. "Laughter is for fools," he snapped, irritated. She had invaded his home, his thoughts and, dear God, nearly his heart. Why did she have to be so damn lovely, so sweet and kind? It would have been better had she been a shrew.

Maggie gave him a look that he fancied she saved for motherless kittens. "Laughter is for people who are happy."

What was he to say to that? He frowned at her, thinking he should have acted on his instinct and ravished her. "What on earth has happiness to do with walking about in the rain?" he demanded, returning to her ridiculous idea that they go for a walk in the rainstorm that currently soaked the countryside. "I daresay drowning one's self in thunderclouds and mud puddles isn't going to incite either laughter or happiness."

She had the cheek to whisk away his statement with a gesture of her small hand. "Nonsense. It's not thundering and you've never lived until you've danced in the rain."

"I suppose you've never contracted a lung disease either." Christ, he was actually beginning to be charmed by her madness. Somehow, she was at her most fetching when she was smiling and daring him to step beyond the boundaries behind which he'd lived his entire life.

"Truly, Simon." She pursed her luscious lips together in that way she had that made him want to crush her in his arms and kiss her. "What good is life without a spot of fun?"

He scowled, confounded by his intense reaction to her. It was mad. Ludicrous. There was no reason he should want this woman he'd sworn never to bed, fewer reasons to be enthralled by her odd sense of adventure. She was everything he was not. Young, idealistic, filled with laughter and hope and innocence. Ready to give in to her desires, to forget about the strictures of society that said a husband and a wife ought not to love each other. She cared for him despite his abandonment of her, despite his admittedly cool nature. She was the fire to his ice and, damn it, she was melting him. He had to take care or he'd be burned.

He forced his mind to focus. What had she said? Ah, yes. More mutton-headed prattling about fun, of all things. "That sounds as if it's something Nell would say."

Pink blossomed over her cheeks, telling him he'd trapped her in her own game. "She did say it. But she was utterly right."

"If you want fun," he rumbled, closing the distance between them and sliding his arms about her sweet wasp waist, "I've something else in mind. It doesn't involve rain, but it does involve undoing all seven hundred of your buttons."

Her eyes widened, darkening with the passion he'd come to recognize. She was not immune. He slid his palms over the silk of her back, moving up to her nape. Her hair was so damn soft and smelled of roses. His cock went painfully erect. To hell with rain and dancing. He wanted her on the carpet of the library, beneath him, his cock slipping deep inside the slippery pink depths of her cunny.

"I believe you're making a jest, my lord," Maggie said, sounding as breathless as he felt. "Your eyes are almost twinkling with merriment."

Perhaps she made him maudlin. Perhaps he was just as touched as she was. Whatever the case, he rather found he didn't mind. Desire slid through his body, mingling with anticipation. He gently tipped her head back. "Nonsense. You know very well I don't jest, and if my eyes are shining, it's merely because I'm imagining you in the nude."

Her pretty lips parted. "You won't have me nude until you've gone out in the rain with me."

Again with the rain nonsense. Very well. She could have him standing in an icy rain for the rest of the afternoon, and he didn't think it would cool the fervor roiling through his blood. He wanted to have her, and if it meant doing as she asked, he gladly would. Anything to ease the persistent ache in his trousers. "You win, my dear. I'll venture into the weather with you."

She clutched his arms in her excitement, apparently shocked that she'd managed his surrender. "You will?"

"I will." He dropped a quick kiss on her mouth, unable to help himself. But with one kiss, he inevitably wanted more. "Only for a moment, you outlandish woman." He couldn't resist another kiss, this one lingering longer than the first. She opened to him and his tongue swept inside, tasting her, claiming her. She was his, by God. His senses were filled with her, the sweet scent of her perfume, the softness of her lips, her breathy sigh filling his ears, the sensation of her hands finding their way to his chest. Dear God. Perhaps the rain would dampen his ardor. He certainly hoped so, for she was growing more necessary to him than air, and it scared him like the devil. With great reluctance, he broke off their kiss, even if he suspected she would have allowed him to prolong the interlude.

He looked down upon her, his odd little wife who had come to mean so much to him in such a short amount of time. The wife he hadn't bothered to see in over a year. It seemed impossible now as he gazed at her brazen beauty. She looked back at him, mutual passion reflected in her glazed eyes. She caught her full lower lip between her teeth, almost as if she were struggling to compose her thoughts.

"Shall we?" he asked, wanting to get her peculiar request out of the way as soon as possible to make way for more pleasant pursuits.

She blinked. "Truly?"

Did she think him that much of an arse? He supposed he couldn't blame her. He had not been kind to her for most of their marriage. In truth, he wasn't sure he could be kind. Part of him couldn't believe he was deigning to indulge her silly fancies.

He cleared his throat, his insides all bollixed up. "Truly."

"You won't be sorry," she promised, even though he was altogether certain he would.

But somehow, none of his reservations mattered. "Let us be done with it," he said solemnly, not wanting to allow her to see just how deeply she affected him.

She wriggled free of his grasp, much to his dismay, appearing suddenly like a fairy. Her entire face brightened, becoming even lovelier, if at all possible. She grabbed his hands, tugging him in her wake. "Come along," she tossed over her shoulder as she headed for the double glass doors at the end of the library that led into Denver House's extensive gardens. "If you tarry any longer, I fear the rain will stop."

"That would be the greatest shame," he said dryly, allowing her to pull him as if she were a horse and he the carriage. He wasn't accustomed to following anyone, to bending to another's whims. In the past, even with Eleanor, he had always had his way. She had deferred to him in all matters. Indeed, now that he thought on it, Eleanor hadn't seemed to have any whims of her own. She had wanted to please him, but in a completely different way. Maggie wanted to see him happy. By God, she wanted to make him laugh, of all things, and she thought to accomplish it with raindrops. But as harebrained as her idea seemed, what warmed his cold heart was that she cared.

"Don't be a milksop, Simon." Maggie tugged him to the door before stopping and glancing back his way, looking almost shy now that she was about to have her way. "Are you ready?"

He trusted she wasn't looking to his trousers, for if she was, she wouldn't have asked. He raised a brow. "Ready as ever."

"We must dance," she informed him. "Those are the rules."

"Ah, now we've rules?"

"Every good game requires rules." She threw open one of the doors and hauled him over the threshold in her wake.

The rain was as unrelenting as it was cold, but he dutifully followed Maggie as she led him a few steps away from the house to the gravel path leading into the manicured gardens. She stopped and turned into his arms, looking up at him as water slicked her face and flattened her glorious curls. She was even lovelier in the rain than she'd been in the dry confines of the library. There was something freeing, something ridiculously rebellious about being in the

115

midst of a thorough soaking with her. Before he knew it, he was smiling at her. He couldn't help it. Her good cheer was infectious.

"Now we must waltz." She smiled again, and it was transformative. "But take care, my lord. You almost appear as if you're enjoying yourself."

He laughed at that. He couldn't help it, and he had to admit, even if only to himself, that it was truly the first time he'd laughed in earnest in as long as he could recall. She was wild, his little wife. And he wanted more. "You're making me as mad as you," he said at last, still grinning like a fool.

"You laughed." She cupped his jaw.

The touch was so gentle and yet so arousing that he grew rigid again despite the chill and the moisture. His cock was hard as marble, aching for release that he could only find in her voluptuous body. His hair plastered itself to his forehead and he was sure he looked as if he'd escaped from an asylum for the frail-minded. But he didn't care.

"I believe you requested a waltz, my lady," he told her instead, enjoying every moment of their impromptu embrace in the rain. And with that, he began humming, leading them into a proper dance that would have done any ballroom shame.

She followed, grinning up at him and blinking through the raindrops that continued to inundate them. "I did indeed, my lord."

It wasn't long before she'd trounced on his toes. She was an abysmal dancer, he discovered, almost gratified to find something at which she did not excel. For it surely seemed to him that in most ways, his wife was perfection. She laughed up at him, the happiest he'd seen her, and it struck him that this was what she'd meant. Unabashed, raw happiness. Her cheeks were flushed, her coiffure hopelessly defeated, the silk of her blue gown perhaps ruined forever, and yet she was glowing, tilting her head back to laugh as if she didn't care who heard her. It was infectious, and soon he was laughing along with her as they twirled and she trod on his instep.

"Devil take it, you're a horrid dancer," he told her as she laughed at another misstep.

"I am," she admitted easily. "A proper gentleman would keep that observation to himself."

"I begin to think I'm not a proper gentleman." He stopped them and yanked her into his body, tipping up her wet chin with his fingers. "After all, a proper gentleman wouldn't do this."

He kissed her, through the rain and the cold and the fear that he was falling under the spell of the tiny American in his arms. Her hands flitted to his shoulders, her mouth opening to him. Their tongues tangled. He relished the crush of her breasts against his chest, the heavy weight of her skirts against his painfully hard cock. She smelled of roses and autumn.

He wasn't going to last much longer. He had to have her. He wanted to strip the wet silk from her, reveal pale curves layer by mouthwatering layer, lay her on the library floor and press his rain-slicked body into hers. He wanted to lick her sweet cunny, make her come on his tongue. God, how he wanted.

When he broke their kiss to gaze down at her, the laughter had fled from her beautiful face as well. He recognized the same passion claiming her that raged through him, the need to be one. Her breathing was heavy, her mouth open. Her eyes were the deepest violet he'd ever seen them.

"My God, Maggie," he rasped. "I need you desperately."

"Yes," she said, gripping his hand once more. "Come."

Once more, he allowed himself to be pulled back across the gravel path, through the torrent of rainfall to the library doors. He didn't know what had gotten into him. She'd done something to him, something irreversible, and it had nothing to do with dancing in the rain and everything to do with her. If he wasn't careful, he could love her.

Dear God. He wouldn't allow that to happen. Couldn't

allow that to happen. Besides, he didn't even know what love was any longer. Perhaps it was a fiction that didn't exist. As they reached the dry sanctuary of the library once more, he turned his mind to the task at hand. Getting his wife naked.

He kissed her again, then began working on her buttons. The limpness of the wet silk didn't wish to cooperate, and his progress was slow. Too slow. He'd ruined her train once, he reasoned. To hell with it. Grasping each side of her bodice in his hands, he tore with all his strength. Buttons fell to the carpet.

"Simon," she gasped, sounding shocked.

"I'll buy you a new bloody dress." He yanked again until her bodice fell open to her waist. "One without any damn buttons."

She smiled, sending a foreign emotion slicing through him, and helped him to remove her arms from her sleeves. "I should like to see such a dress."

"Better still, I shall keep you nude for the rest of your days." He gave her a wicked smile of his own, liking his idea immensely. "To hell with dresses."

She shivered as she opened the hidden placket on her skirts, dropping them to the floor. She stood before him in her undergarments, her breasts a creamy swell of temptation. He passed his still-wet hands over her smooth shoulders, wanting her with an intensity that frightened him. "Are you cold, darling?"

"No," she whispered, and he knew then that it was the same for her.

He pulled away the strings of her bustle and helped Maggie to shuck her corset cover. "Turn," he told her, wanting to undo the laces of her corset.

She spun as he commanded, giving him her back. Her curls sagged under the weight of the rain, but her hair was still impossibly vibrant and beautiful. Even her shoulders were sheer perfection. He pressed a kiss to her neck as he settled his hands on her nipped waist. So tiny, such a delicious contrast to the lush curves of her bosom. When she tilted her head to the side, allowing him greater access, he kissed a path to her jaw. His fingers unerringly found the knot her indefatigable lady's maid had tied in her corset and began undoing it. With great care, willing himself to go slowly, he kissed the rim of her ear. When she shivered again, he took her earlobe between his teeth and gently tugged, earning a soft moan from her.

Ah, hell. Just the sound was enough to make him thrust into her, pressing his cock into the ample curves of her bottom. She arched back into him, making him groan as he met with her softness. He kissed the patch of skin just beneath her ear, tasting her, licking the rain from her.

"Oh," she cried out, turning her head to nuzzle his. "Oh Simon."

His fingers at last met with success, opening the knot on her corset ties. He moved between the crisscrossing laces, pulling them apart, intent on his quest to have her gloriously nude.

"Darling." He nipped at her skin enough to make her shiver but not hard enough to leave a mark. "I can't wait to have your beautiful breasts in my hands, to take your nipples in my mouth and suck them until they're hard."

"Yes." She turned her head and kissed him, open-mouthed and hungry. "Please."

Enough. He couldn't wait a moment longer. He pulled away and spun her to face him. If this was what she'd had in mind from the start, he'd dance in the rain with her every bloody day. He was ravenous for her. He removed her corset cover and then pulled her corset open and flung it away, intent on revealing her gorgeous body. Only a chemise separated him from what he wanted.

His breath caught as he gazed down at her. She was soaked, her skin glistening with moisture, the linen of her shift clinging to her breasts so that her sweetly pink nipples were visible through the fabric. They were already stiff, calling to him. He pulled her against him, cupping her face in his hands and kissing her again, unable to help himself.

She kissed him back, and when he felt her fingers on the buttons of his shirt, he groaned. She was a wanton, his Maggie, and he couldn't be more pleased. He nipped at her lower lip, wringing an answering moan from her. She liked when he was a little wild, a little rough. The knowledge only heightened his desire.

Simon shrugged out of his jacket, allowing it to fall unheeded to the floor. The last button on his shirt popped open, aided by Maggie, and he tossed that garment away as well. Then, her hands were on his chest, caressing a path of fire that led straight to his cock. When she cupped him through his trousers, he couldn't keep himself from surging into her, wanting her touch, wanting to be inside her. Christ, she made him mad. He had to have her. Right bloody now.

He tossed a look around the library, having second thoughts about the wool of the carpets on her delicate skin. His eyes landed upon an oversize settee and a wicked idea formed in his debauched mind.

"Come, my love." He led her to the settee, their embrace never breaking. He backed her to the cushioned edge before stopping to draw her final garment up over her head. She was nude before him, her breasts a round and full temptation, her curves lush. His gaze dipped lower, to her cunny.

He knew what he wanted. "Sit."

"What in heaven's name?" Maggie blinked at him, dredged from the depths of her passion by his request. Of course she would question him. "Why?"

"Hush." He pressed a finger to her rose-pink lips that were swollen with his kisses. "No more talking."

"But," she began, attempting to speak past his finger until he interrupted her.

"Do you trust me, Maggie?"

Her violet eyes were huge, piercing through to his very soul. She pressed a kiss to his finger before tipping her head back so that she could speak. "Yes."

Something inside him shifted, sending a warmth through him that had little to do with desire and everything to do with the emotions she stirred within him. She trusted him. She trusted the man who had left her while he spent an entire year with his mistress. He could admit it now, for if he hadn't a conscience before, he bloody well did now. Maggie had done that for him. She'd changed everything.

He gently guided her into a sitting position, needing to show her with his actions what he could not reveal in words. She was his. He was hers. And he wanted to make her scream. He wanted more than just a goddamn month. He sank to his knees.

She watched him, holding her hands over her breasts as she sat awkwardly. She looked dreadfully uncomfortable. He placed his palms on each of her bare knees, hungering to go higher and sweep over her luscious thighs but restraining himself.

"Have you ever sat naked on a settee before?" he asked her.

"You know I haven't."

"Another day of firsts for us. I danced in the rain for you." He bowed his head and pressed a kiss to first her left knee, then her right. Something occurred to him then. "You weren't wearing drawers."

A rosy flush crept over her cheeks. "It often seems I don't require them when you're about."

"A lady who plans ahead." He winked at her, showing her the lightness of heart she'd accused him of not possessing. He had it, by God. There merely hadn't been need of it before. No other woman had longed to hear his laughter. "I am once again in awe of you."

"What are you doing?" she asked again, her voice breathy. Not precisely concerned, but nevertheless a trifle on edge.

"Making love to my wife." He relished the word on his tongue for the first time ever. He skimmed his hands up her thighs ever so slowly, kissing the insides of her knees as he did so. "My turn for a question. Why are you hiding your lovely breasts from me?"

He glanced up at her to find her still flushed, watching him with an expression he'd never seen from her. "Would you prefer to see them?"

Ah, she was back to the teasing wanton once more. His cock was hard as stone, pressing against his trousers despite the cold, damp fabric. "I would."

Meeting his gaze, she removed her arms. Her breasts were perfection. "There you are." Her air was as breezy as if she complimented the fabric of the curtains across the room.

She had courage, his Maggie, a backbone as rigid as a brick wall. "I love your breasts." His hands slid ever higher until he reached her upper thighs. "Will you open your legs for me, darling? I want to pleasure you so very badly."

Wordlessly, she allowed her knees to fall apart, opening herself to him. No hesitation. She was a match for him in every way. His eyes devoured each inch of creamy skin revealed to him, lingering on the folds of her cunny. He could already smell her sweet, earthy scent. She was aroused, her cunny pink and glistening, ready for him.

Yes, this was what he wanted. He struggled to rein in the desire careening through him. He wanted to go slowly, to torture them both with anticipation, with pleasure. He ran his hands back down her voluptuous legs, loving the feel of them, the freedom of touching her as he pleased.

"Put your legs over me," he directed her quietly, showing her where he wanted her at the same time.

She did as he asked without further question, allowing him to place her legs as he wished so that the backs of her knees rested upon his shoulders. Bloody hell, yes. He grabbed her rump next, scooting her to the edge of the settee until her cunny nearly touched the bright gilding holding the upholstery in place. He hoped she soaked the damn settee so much that he needed to replace it.

Looking up at her, he placed a kiss on the inside of each

thigh. She watched him, her lip caught between her teeth. Her violet eyes were dreamy, half-closed. She wanted this every bit as much as he did. Still keeping her gaze trapped by his, he at last lowered his head to the prize he sought. He gently pulled back her mound until the plump bud he wanted jutted proudly forward. And then he took her in his mouth, sucking.

She moaned above him, her fingers sinking into his hair, running over his scalp. A hot surge of lust went directly to his cock. He loved the way she tasted, of muskiness and something innately hers. Delicious. His tongue flicked over her, up and down, side to side, before he sucked her again. She bucked against him, pressing her wet cunny into his face. Perfect. God. He was going to lose himself in her and he didn't give a damn.

With a growl against her eager flesh, he pulled back, glancing up at Maggie to find she'd closed her eyes, her mouth open. Her breasts were erotic as hell. She was a Venus on display. His. He wanted to fuck her with his tongue first and then with his cock.

He lowered his head and sank his tongue into her slippery cunny, again and again. She cried out, twisting against him, and he knew she was nearing her climax. He wanted to make her come as she'd never come before. He reached up, pressing a hand against her belly and slipping his thumb back to her pearl. He worked it back and forth, exerting as much pressure as he dared, as much as he knew made her writhe even more beneath him, all the while plunging his tongue deep inside her.

She shook and he felt a rush of wetness on his mouth. Ah, yes. She cried out his name, nearly sobbing with the power of her release. Now he was going to fuck her again. Fuck her until she came all over him once more. She was so wet. He couldn't wait to be inside her. Not another breath. He fumbled for his shirt, opening it over the carpet.

"Here, darling." Simon took her small hand in his. She was still dazed, the perfect picture of a wanton with her mussed hair, slack mouth and shining eyes. He pulled her to her knees, helping her to arrange herself on the softer fabric of his shirt. "I want you desperately."

She opened for him, holding her arms out. "I want you too."

Her words sent a new arrow of heat searing through him, the kind that pierced his heart. Damn it. He tore open the fastening of his trousers, releasing his rigid cock. In the next instant, he was inside her with one long thrust. She was hot and slippery and tight. Heaven. When she wrapped her arms around his waist and drew him even deeper, he was lost. He pumped into her, again and again. Out, then in, a delicious rhythm designed to make them both mad. At last, she constricted on him, her cunny wringing the last bit of sanity from him. He lost himself, spending so hard his heart nearly leapt from his chest.

Dear sweet Christ. Panting as if he'd just run for his life, he collapsed against her, pressing a kiss to her perfect lips. He touched his forehead to hers, completely bemused by what she'd done to him.

She framed his face with her hands, her eyes twinkling up at him, an impish smile on her mouth. "Perhaps next time you won't be so disagreeable about taking a walk in the rain."

He couldn't help himself. He threw back his head and laughed. Bloody hell. She was right.

"Tell me, what is your favorite poem?"

Maggie leaned back on the coverlet Simon had spread across the grass for their impromptu picnic and considered him. He watched her with an open expression as he nibbled on a sandwich prepared for them by his redoubtable cook Mrs. Gaston. She still couldn't believe she'd managed to convince him to join her for a picnic luncheon so easily. She knew it was often *de rigueur* at country house parties, but

Simon always seemed so staid, so fussy and incapable of levity. He had changed. He'd opened himself to her.

"You're staring at me," he observed, frowning. "Have I asked such an odd question?"

Oh dear. She was mooning over him, and she'd quite forgotten what he'd asked. She thought for a moment, trying her best not to look like a silly miss. Ah, yes. Poetry. She found their common interest heartening. It was one more thing that drew them together whereas before, one rather large and unfortunate thing had drawn them apart.

"How can I choose just one?" she asked him. "Perhaps you have a favorite?"

His eyes darkened. "I find that I prefer the poetry written by my wife."

She flushed, unable to fight back a smile. He certainly knew how to charm her. "Thank you, Simon, but I fear you're merely trying to woo me."

He raised a brow. "I didn't know I needed to woo you. I've already won you, after all."

But his actions had belied his words. Unless she was mistaken, he had begun doing his best to win her. "I'm beginning to think perhaps you already have."

A slow, knowing grin curved his sensual lips. "The sentiment is mutual, my dear."

Dear heavens. He was certainly charming when he wished to be after all. She found she had a difficult time resisting him. In fact, she didn't want to resist him, truth be told. "I'm glad. I hope you're finding marriage to me isn't as horrid as you once supposed."

"Do you truly care?" He cocked his head to the side, considering her in that intense way he had that made her feel as if he could see all the corners of herself she'd prefer to keep hidden. "I rather fancy you ought to loathe me. I wouldn't blame you, truly, and yet you're so bloody sweet to me."

His insight startled her. He'd gradually begun to open himself to her, and she had discovered a great many things about her husband thus far. One of them was that he had been searching for a family to belong to ever since his boyhood. She suspected he didn't realize it himself, but she fancied it was why he'd been so ensnared by Lady Billingsley.

But now that Maggie was a true part of his life and not a faraway dust mote occasionally flitting through his conscience, she hoped she could give him the family he'd been seeking. It was a frightening realization for her, just how connected she'd become to him. She didn't just want to settle for a month and then return to New York. Not any longer. She'd changed. He'd changed. Together.

"I've told you before I'm not the angel you think me." She thought of all the moments in her life where she had been unkind, had made mistakes. She thought of Richard, of how she had left him devastated when she had broken off their romance to leave for England. No indeed, she was altogether not an angel.

He shook his head. "I don't believe you."

She smiled sadly at his insistence. "I wish I were perfect."

"You already are perfect, Maggie." He picked up a dark-red hothouse strawberry, held it to his lips and took a bite. She watched, entranced. "And you make me perfectly mad with wanting you every time I so much as think your name."

Desire unwound within her. She liked that she at least possessed the power to make him long for her. It was something, a small battle won in the war she hadn't realized she'd wanted to wage. She wanted to win not just his passion, his kisses, his admiration, but also his heart. There it was, with such awful clarity it made her throat nearly close. She was going to pry it from Lady Billingsley's inglorious clutches. If she hadn't already done so. Maggie had to wonder as she watched him slowly devour his strawberry, making a burn start deep inside her.

"But you dislike me." She licked her lower lip, a force of habit.

"I disliked the notion of you, yes," he said agreeably. "As I daresay you did me. For me, however, that dislike has changed immensely."

"How has it changed?" she dared to ask him.

He sent her a wicked grin. "Shall I show you?"

Oh dear. He was such a tempting man. It was the midst of the day and they were in the open air. Anyone could happen upon them at any moment. Surely it would be foolish to indulge in the wickedness he promised. She ought to tell him no.

She caught herself grinning back at him. "Yes."

He was on her in an instant, pressing her all the way to the coverlet with his muscled body. He kissed her as if he'd been starving for it, long and passion-fueled. Her hands went into his hair, knocking his hat from his head. Her jaunty headpiece too fell to the wayside, half crushed beneath her back. She didn't care.

The day was alive with sunshine, singing birds, and endless possibility. It was a feeling she could get lost in forever. A feeling she never wanted to end.

chapter seven

$\mathcal{S}$ IMON STRODE INTO THE MAIN HALL OF DENVER HOUSE after an invigorating ride, a grin on his face. He didn't know why the devil he was grinning, but damn it, he was. An entire fortnight had passed since he'd brought Maggie to his country holding, a place where he once never thought he'd feel at home again. Something had changed, shifted inside him. The ghosts had been banished.

Maggie had done that for him.

Yes, perhaps the reason he was grinning like a bloody fool was blatantly apparent. His wife. Somehow, the woman he'd once resented had become the woman he desperately wanted. Even now, thinking of her made him hard. Christ. It was the midst of the morning and he was covered in muck. He'd just had her mere hours before, but the prospect of locating her and dragging her off for an impromptu bout of lovemaking was too potent a lure.

"My lord."

The somewhat aggrieved voice of his butler disturbed his pleasant musings. He slowed his steps, realizing he'd failed to notice the staid Milton standing sentinel. "Good morning, Milton. Whatever's the matter? You look as if someone's eaten your lunch."

Milton blinked at him, perhaps startled by his unusually good cheer. After all, the Marquis of Sandhurst didn't joke. At least, not the old Marquis of Sandhurst. "You've a *guest*, sir."

Bloody hell. He didn't like the way his butler spat out the word as if it tasted poorly. This surely didn't bode well. "Who can it be and where have you put him?"

"I have placed her in the drawing room, my lord."

Her? His guest was a woman? A leaden weight descended in his stomach, effectively crushing his former high spirits. There was only one woman who would seek him out. He had no relationship with his mother's sister the Countess of Northrup and his father had been the sole living child in his family. Lady Northrup made no secret of her disdain for him. No indeed, it would not be she who had called upon Denver House.

He swallowed, his throat gone dry. "Thank you, Milton. I shall see to her," he managed to say before stalking straight for the room in question.

It couldn't be *her*, he thought, his mind swirling with the possibilities and ramifications. What if it was? Good sweet God. Feeling as if he were trapped in a bizarre dream, he crossed the threshold to the drawing room, his heart about to gallop from his chest.

A woman stood with her back to him, her blonde curls artfully piled beneath a dashing hat so typical of someone he knew all too well. He took in her tiny, cinched waist and the frothy pink afternoon gown draped with lace. Recognition traveled through him with the force of a heavy stone being rolled downhill. The lady adored pastels and hats twice the size of her head. He knew she smelled of lavender and sneezed at the slightest hint of rose water. He knew she adored poetry, hated prose, and wrote lurid letters that once had made him mad with wanting. Ah yes, there was no mistaking her.

Eleanor.

He knew her silhouette as he knew his reflection in the mirror. After all, she was the woman he'd spent a few years of his life loving. Or at least, he'd thought he loved her. Now, he wasn't sure. She turned when she heard his footsteps approaching, a welcoming smile on her Cupid's bow lips. The time they'd been apart fell away for a moment. He almost crossed the room and took her into his arms as he'd done so many times before.

But he did not. Time and undone secrets had come between them. He had not forgotten Nell's revelation and what it meant for him, for the woman he'd once professed to love. He had not forgotten Maggie, his wife. He stopped, body rigid with tension, and fixed her with a cutting stare. She flinched, her smile fading. She had been expecting a far different welcome, then. What the hell was she doing here? He hadn't been prepared for this, for her.

"Why have you come, Lady Billingsley?" He was careful to keep all traces of emotion from his voice. In truth, he didn't know what he felt at seeing her again. Betrayal? Excitement? Hurt? It was likely a combination of all three. But he would not show her a hint of weakness.

"I've left Billingsley."

A few months before, the words would have been enough. Now they left him feeling oddly emotionless. "You've left him." His mind fumbled to comprehend the meaning of her revelation for him. Much had changed. He thought of Maggie. What did he feel for her? Not love, certainly. But something. Thoughts of what Eleanor had done swirled through his mind, questions he needed to ask her. But he wasn't certain if her betrayal with Lord Needham mattered any longer. Or if *she* mattered any longer.

She crossed the polished floor, her heels clicking, until she reached him. An expectant expression transformed her undeniably beautiful face. "I cannot live without you, Simon. I tried. I tried to do my duty to his lordship."

Thoughts of her husband, the bulbous-nosed Billingsley, sweating and straining over her to produce an heir, made him ill. She'd made her choice, duty over love. All too often in their world, duty trumped all else. Somehow, he'd expected a different outcome with Eleanor. She had proved him wrong. "I wish to God you had never tried at all," he told her honestly before he could stop himself.

But she had, and her sudden appearance in his drawing room could not alter that fact.

"I'm sorry." Her lower lip trembled in that way of hers that once infallibly brought him to his knees. "You know what a beast he is, Sandy. I had no choice."

He stiffened at her use of the diminutive only she had ever called him. It took him back to when he had cared for her. But had he every truly known her? He couldn't be sure any longer. "You betrayed me, Eleanor."

"Never." She appeared a sad, small figure to him suddenly. "I would never betray you."

But he knew differently. "What of Lord Needham?"

She grew pale, her entire form going utterly still. "What of him?"

He almost pitied her. But not quite. "Nell told me. You needn't lie."

"It was a long time ago, Sandy, and a dreadful mistake. We were both in our cups. It never meant anything. You remain the only man I've ever loved, the only man I shall ever love as long as I live."

Simon was gratified that she at least deigned to acknowledge the truth, however she attempted to minimize it. He would have thought she might prevaricate further. Even so, he couldn't allow her to reappear in his drawing room as though she hadn't abruptly told him to go to the devil. Still, he had to admit that her words of love affected him, however much he wished they did not.

"What of now? We were sworn to each other," he reminded her. "I promised to keep my wife in name only just as you promised you would never again go to your marriage bed."

Her blue eyes pleaded with his. "Billingsley gave me no other option. I did not want to tell you, but he has raised his hand against me."

He couldn't help it. Her words brought a rush of instinctive rage thrashing through him. He grasped her elbow. "What did you say?"

"My husband prefers to hit me rather than bed me," Eleanor said, her dainty hands landing upon his chest as if they were a pair of butterflies. "I could not suffer him any longer, Sandy. I thought I could, but I'm no match for his fists."

Fists. Rage skewered him. His hands went to her wasp waist as they had so many times before, finding their familiar home. Perhaps Nell had been wrong in her gossip, for Eleanor didn't feel *enceinte* in the slightest to him. She was trim as ever. He searched her gaze, hoping she lied. "Tell me that bastard didn't hit you."

A sob rose in her throat but she seemed to stifle it, biting her lip. "I cannot. He caused me to lose my babe."

"I'll kill him," he vowed, anger a wave overtaking him, threatening to bring him to his knees.

"No." Eleanor reached up to cup his jaw. "You mustn't. I've left him for good now, and that is all that matters."

"Simon?"

Christ. The lilting feminine tone with its undeniable American accent belonged to Maggie. He released Eleanor and turned to face his wife. She stood in the door, looking characteristically magnificent in a day gown of navy silk that complemented her alabaster skin to perfection. Her flame curls were caught up in an elaborate coiffure that rendered her ordinary elegance utterly striking. A stab of lust went straight to his cock.

It didn't escape his notice that it was Maggie who aroused him, Maggie he wanted with a ferocity that still shook him. His physical reaction to Eleanor had been tame by comparison. Confused, even. Belatedly, it occurred to him that Maggie appeared shocked. Hell, he couldn't blame her. She had just walked in on him in an intimate embrace with an old paramour.

But was Eleanor an old paramour? The question ate at him with an aching persistence. She had to be, yet how could she be? Comfort lived in familiarity, even if that familiarity was wrong. What could vanquish the years he'd misspent in her arms?

"Who is she?" Eleanor demanded of him in a near hiss at his back.

He met Maggie's gaze, all too aware of the hurt he read in the violet depths. She raised her chin, her countenance taking on a formidable air he'd never seen.

"I am Lady Sandhurst," Maggie proclaimed loudly in a brash American drawl that somehow made him want to drag her straightaway to their chamber, no matter the old feelings that had once again sparked as if coals in the grate. "*Sandy's* wife," she added, lest they be mistaken, he supposed, that she hadn't happened upon a great deal of their conversation.

Damn it. She had likely heard far too much. He strode to her. After all, she was his wife above all else, and he'd finally accepted the duty that rode along with being her husband. He suspected there wasn't a particular rule for introducing one's wife to one's mistress. But even he could recognize precedence with his mind awhirl.

He offered Maggie his arm as he gained her side. She refused to take it, so he pretended as if he were inspecting his coat sleeve instead before performing the necessary. "Lady Sandhurst, I don't believe you have yet made the acquaintance of Lady Billingsley," he said, all too aware he sounded awkward as a stripling attempting to woo his first maid.

"No, I have not." She held herself regally, pinning Eleanor with a queenly glare. "Nor can I honestly say that I have ever wanted to make her acquaintance. She is not anyone I would care to know. Why is she in our drawing room just now, *Sandy?*"

He didn't like the way she said his name. Such scorn. He frowned at her for both her rudeness and impertinence, though he couldn't truly blame her for either. "She is visiting, I suspect."

"Visiting," Eleanor echoed. "Pray, my lady, pay no attention to me. I am merely throwing myself on your husband's mercy as both an old and dear friend, and he has been kind enough to offer me his aid."

What the hell? He had done no such thing. Damn the woman. She was trying to force his hand and he didn't like it. Not one bit. Was this machinating woman truly the lady he'd fallen in love with? He couldn't shake the suspicion that he'd failed to see her for her true self. That he'd been blinded to her inconstant nature.

"His *aid*." Maggie repeated the word as if it were an epithet. "How exceedingly kind and generous of him. I've discovered that my husband is a most generous soul, Lady Billingsley."

"Indeed." Eleanor frowned, clearly not following Maggie's line of thought.

Simon was afraid he was following it all the way to its inevitable end. He had to admire her spunk. He wouldn't wish to be on the receiving end of her displeasure just now.

"Quite generous." Maggie tilted her head, gracing Eleanor with a lovely smile that hid quite a bit of bite behind it. "You are more than welcome to stay here at Denver House, my lady. But rest assured that his *generosity* will not be extending toward yourself during your tenure here."

He nearly choked as his fears came to fruition. "Maggie," he cautioned, knowing by now that his wife possessed a backbone that was as unpredictable as it was formidable. Still, he hadn't expected such a frank dressing-down from her. It was simply not done.

She didn't spare him a glance, intent as she was on her quarry. "I gather you understand my meaning, Lady Billingsley?"

Eleanor cleared her throat, looking quite like a bird choking upon a worm. "I must say that I do not, my lady."

"Well, then let us be clear." Maggie stalked across the room and stopped before Eleanor, fierce as a wild cat. "If you choose to remain here as a guest, I cannot stop you, but I will not tolerate adultery in my home."

"Adultery?" Eleanor sputtered. He suspected no one had ever before spoken to her with such lack of artifice.

"You will not be warming my husband's bed." Maggie paused before whispering something unintelligible into Eleanor's ear.

Simon wished he could have heard it. But he remained where he was, watching the tableau before him unfold as if he were an invalid. Or a complete duffer. And perhaps that was what he was.

Eleanor blanched, her eyes flying to his. Christ, what had Maggie threatened? A beheading? Then he read the hurt in her expression and he knew. His wife had revealed the extent of their relationship. His former mistress didn't care for the disclosure. He couldn't say he blamed her. He knew what it had felt like to think of her making love with her husband. It had been akin to a knife being plunged directly into his gut.

Time and space had lessened the pain. And if he were completely honest with himself, he had to admit that Maggie had as well. The pain had gone. He'd moved on. Just then, his wife gave him a seething look that didn't bode well for him later. He winced.

"I trust you will see that the staff gets your guest settled?" she asked. "I find I'm rather too weary to take on the task."

He bowed, feeling like a complete ass beneath her withering glare. She couldn't be expected to make preparations for the comfort of her rival. He would never ask it of her. "Of course, my dear."

She disappeared in a swirl of silk and riotous curls. He turned to Eleanor, wondering what in the hell he was going to do now. He supposed he'd have to allow her to stay on, at least for a few days. After all, she'd just told him that Billingsley had been mistreating her. He could not, in good conscience, turn her away. But neither was he certain that he wanted her here.

His mind was reeling, hopelessly confused by Eleanor, what he'd learned about her, the feelings he'd begun to develop for Maggie. By God, he'd just been about the business of restoring the order to his life, and now the one woman who could threaten to ruin it had appeared in his drawing room as if she hadn't been gone.

"I'm sorry, Sandy," Eleanor said quietly, interrupting his troubled thoughts. "I would have written you, but there wasn't time. I couldn't have known you'd have her in residence here."

"Bloody, bloody hell." He clenched and then released his fists as he fought to keep control over himself.

"Why is she here?" Her gaze probed his.

It was a question to which there was no ready answer. He paused, wondering how much he ought to reveal to her. "We are spending a month together as husband and wife," he said at last.

"You wish for an heir, then."

Simon didn't like the way she pressed him, as though he owed her the information she sought. In truth, he owed her nothing, not even a roof over her head to escape her husband's beating. Speaking of Maggie with her felt wrong. "It's none of your concern, Lady Billingsley."

She placed a tentative hand on his arm. "Is this your way of enacting revenge upon me?"

He raised a brow. "You flatter yourself, darling. I haven't thought of you in months."

She flinched, and he knew an instant of gratification, however small it was of him. "I know I hurt you, and I'm sorry for it. In time, you shall see that I had no recourse. I did what I had to, and at the first possible moment I came back to you."

"Much has changed." She was no longer his mistress, nor would she be ever again. Seeing her filled him with the blessing of finality. Their time together was at an end. "You may stay here for a few days whilst you find another refuge from Billingsley, but that must be all, Eleanor."

She gasped. "You cannot turn me out."

"I'm not turning you out," he countered. "I am merely warning you. Your stay will be temporary. You do not belong here."

Her grip on him tightened, her expression melting into desperation. "I belong with you."

"No." He shook off her hand, hardening his heart to her. "You don't, and you never have."

"You will change your mind." Her voice trembled. "I love you. Please don't act with haste."

"I'll give you a few days." He turned on his heel. "That is all."

For it had to be. He now had a wife who was more than a name and an unwanted presence in his life. The hard truth of it was that he didn't want to consider just how much Maggie had become to him in the last fortnight, for that scared the hell out of him. All he knew now was that he had to find her.

Maggie's hands shook as she awaited Simon in the luxuriously appointed salon that adjoined her bedchamber. She'd sent word for him to meet her directly following whatever he needed to settle Lady Billingsley, and for her own sake, she'd deemed it best not to meet him anywhere a bed could be found. His deadly good looks and wicked caresses had a way of disarming her every time. She couldn't afford to be so foolish this time.

She sighed. Although she had decorated the salon herself, the aesthetically pleasing confines did not bring her cheer at the moment. She had not been prepared to face the woman she had detested from afar, to see how lovely she was, how tiny her waist, how golden her hair. She had a penchant for overdressing, that much Maggie could see, but it appeared to be Lady Billingsley's only flaw. Damn her. What right did she think she had to throw herself into Simon's arms?

Every right, she supposed. Maggie frowned and paced the length of the room, worry a gnawing ache in her breast. Though she was reasonably certain she had exhibited confidence when confronting Lady Billingsley, the disheartening truth of it was that when it came to her husband, she had no confidence whatsoever.

Indeed, she feared he would return to his mistress. After all, he had admitted to loving her. She had been his paramour for longer than Maggie had known him. She still had a hold on him. That much had been apparent by the way he'd been leaning into her, his hands upon her waist when Maggie had intervened. The sight had nearly been unbearable.

In just over a fortnight, he had already become important to Maggie. Necessary. She fidgeted with her skirts, her nervousness increasing the longer it took for her husband to arrive.

At last, the door clicked open and he stepped inside. For a moment, she stared at him, their eyes interlocked. He was impossibly handsome, she thought again, wishing that he had a wart or perhaps a large nose, anything to mar his perfection. But he was debonair as ever despite the distressed expression he wore.

"I'm sorry," he said at last, lingering at the door when she longed for him to close the distance between them.

Maggie pressed her palms to her skirt, hoping she didn't look a fright. "Why?"

He sighed, the sound one of intense weariness. "I didn't know she would come here."

She wanted to trust him, but she didn't know if she could. "Did you invite her here?"

"Christ." He passed his fingers through his hair, leaving the too-long locks askew. "Of course I didn't. What do you take me for?"

The man who had ignored his wife while living openly with his mistress for the last year. She wisely refrained from saying as much. "I needed to ask. I can't think of why she would appear here unless you had asked her to come."

"She left her husband and claims she had nowhere else to go," he said tightly.

And he believed her? Maggie frowned. "Has she no friends or family?"

"I believe she does."

She wanted to shake him by his lapels. His sudden distance frustrated her. "She cannot go to them instead?"

"I expect she can, but I've told her she may remain here for a few days while she gathers herself."

"A few days." Her dismay could not be hidden.

He raised a haughty brow, looking every bit the arrogant nobleman she'd married. "Would you have me toss her out on her ear?"

"Yes." She knew not a hint of shame. "I would prefer that to having to see the woman you love sitting at my breakfast table."

He strode toward her then, breaking the unseen barrier he'd built between them. "It's no longer the same between us now."

"I saw how you touched her." She didn't want to press the issue for fear of what he might reveal and how deeply it would hurt, yet she remained unable to keep her tongue still. "It was very familiar." She hated the hitch in her voice.

"I can't deny what has already come to pass." He stopped before her, his scent wafting over her and rendering her heart weaker than it already was. "You know she and I were once close."

"A very old and dear friend," she repeated his words from Lady Needham's ball, unable to keep the bitterness from her tone. "She broke your heart. It was her choice to end things, not yours. And now she's back as if she was never gone at all."

He searched her eyes. "All that you've said is true."

A sharp pang of pain sliced through her heart. She spun on her heel, unable to face him for a moment longer. Did he not understand how much this killed her inside? She felt as if she were a delicate flower that had just been crushed beneath an unforgiving boot. "Please be kind enough to carry on your affair elsewhere. I cannot live beneath the same roof knowing you're making love to her." She pressed a hand to her lips as she stopped before the window, staring without seeing into the gardens below. Humiliating tears pricked her eyes and she furiously blinked, refusing to allow them to fall.

Simon had followed her. He settled a hand upon her waist, branding her through the layers of her linen and silk. "Look at me."

"No." She worried she would embarrass herself further. It was bad enough that he didn't care for her, but she feared she'd begun to feel something for him. Her heart couldn't withstand much more hurt.

"Maggie, please." He gripped her with both hands then, forcibly turning her. "Look at me."

She bit her lip and stared at the floor. "Get out of this chamber. I'm begging you. Leave me what little pride I have."

He tipped up her chin so that she had no choice but to meet his gaze. "I promised you a month, and I intend to keep that promise."

If he sought to reassure her, he was failing miserably. He confused her. He touched her as if he cared and yet he had touched Lady Billingsley in the same manner. What did he want? She couldn't tell. Perhaps it would be best to give him his freedom. After all, when had promises ever truly mattered between the two of them? She could go on with her life, return to New York. Forget him.

He would never have touched her if he'd known who

she was that evening at Lady Needham's. He'd never intended to make her his wife. After all, he had always loved another.

Maggie was numb. "I release you. You only have a fortnight remaining. I won't hold you to it."

His thumb remained on her chin, a hot brand. "Damn you, I don't want to be released. Why are you pushing me away?"

She stared, resentment and jealousy bubbling up within her. "I can't watch you with her. It hurts too much."

"I don't want her," he said, cupping her face in his palm. "I want you."

She was too afraid to believe him. "For how long? The next few days? The next few hours? Wanting is not enough any longer."

"I don't know." He sounded as frustrated and lost as she felt. "I never desired a wife, damn you."

His words stung. "Then you should never have married me."

"That's not what I meant to say." He paused, running a hand through his hair yet again. "I had to marry you to save the estates from ruin. My father left me with quite a burden of debt when he died and I was finally forced to act. I married you because I had no other choice. You had the largest dowry I could find, and your father was hungry for an English lord's title."

This was not news to her. She crossed her arms in a defensive posture. He'd married her for her father's money, and she'd married him for his title at her father's behest. "I knew that, Simon. I'm no fool. I may have initially thought differently, but it became apparent. People do talk, after all. I understand that you hated me because of that, but what I don't understand is why I must be punished for something over which I had no control."

"I'm not punishing you. I'm trying to explain that I'm giving you as bloody much of myself as I can." He dragged her against his hard chest. "A mere month ago, you never entered my thoughts, and now you're all I can damn well think about."

His admission moved her despite herself. She could clearly see that he wrestled with his attraction to her. Likely, had they never crossed paths behind the safety of anonymity as Lady Needham's, she never would have broken down the wall he kept around himself. But they had, and she liked to think that the passion they'd shared since that fateful night meant as much to him as it did to her.

"I can't stay away from you." His gaze lowered to her lips.

"Then don't." If only their lives were that unencumbered. But they were helplessly mired in a world more interested in money than love. A world more interested in the cut of a coat than the contents of a heart.

But Simon didn't seem about to allow her to wallow in her heavy thoughts. He looked at her as if he wanted to consume her. Thoughts of their unwanted visitor flitted from her mind, paling in comparison to the raw hunger she saw reflected on his face. The desire between them was real and true. A swift stab of heat coursed through her. There was only one thing she could do. She stood on her tiptoes and pressed a kiss to his sculpted mouth.

He angled his lips over hers, deepening the kiss with his tongue. His hands went to her bodice, tearing open the tiny line of fabric-covered buttons down the front. She didn't care if they tore the entire dress into shreds. She was as desperate as he, every bit as ravenous for him. She fumbled to help him pull it open to her corset cover. She wanted to claim him, her territory. Hers.

He broke the kiss. "Damn it, you've got to stop wearing so many bloody undergarments. Getting you naked shouldn't take longer than completing an eight-course meal."

She grinned at him, swatting his hands away to undo the fastenings on her corset cover as well. She managed to undo the first few hooks and eyes before he lost patience once more, pulling it apart to reveal her chemise. He pulled that thin scrap of linen down and bowed his head to suck a nipple into his hot, wet mouth.

Her fingers sank into his hair as she arched into him. Oh dear sweet heavens. She couldn't tear her gaze from the delicious sight of his sultry mouth on her breast. He glanced up at her, his glittering emerald eyes melting her as his tongue flicked out to tease her sensitive skin. She loved him when he was at his most sinful, torturing her with pleasure until she feared she'd splinter into a million shards of blissful woman. He sucked again, creating a tug of heady desire in her sex. She was already wet, ready for him.

"I want you to take me," she said, needing him more than she ever had. She wanted him to make her his in the most elemental sense, make her forget the awful reemergence of Lady Billingsley in their lives.

"Naughty darling," he said, grinning against the pale curve of her breast. He raked his teeth over her nipple, then blew upon it. "How much do you want me?"

Oh he was a devil, her husband. But a devil she increasingly feared that she loved. Dear God. It hit her then, with the blast of a pail of cold water over her head. Somehow, he was winning her heart. She froze, looking down at him, unable to recall what he'd asked her.

"Have I rendered you incapable of speech once more, love?" A knowing smile curved his mouth.

He had called her love. She was sure he didn't mean it in the way she wanted him to mean it. Heavens, she hoped her feelings weren't painted all over her foolish face. Surely there could have been a better time for her to realize her feelings for him. Of course, it would have been preferable for her to have not developed feelings at all. How she wished she was as wise and flippant as Lady Needham, who could flirt and throw wild parties as if she were doing nothing more natural than sneezing. But she was, in her heart, plain old Margaret. And she was losing her heart to a cad.

But was he a cad? She didn't want to think it.

She framed his face, running her fingers over the delightful abrasion of his whiskers. "Take me now," she urged him lest she embarrass herself by confessing her confusing jumble of emotions to him. "I need you, Simon."

He stood, towering over her once more, and pulled her to a settee in the middle of the room. "Christ, what you do to me, woman." He placed her hands on the gilt back and positioned himself behind her. "I have to be inside you."

"Yes." She needed him to make love to her so badly that she didn't bother to wonder how they would accomplish the coupling while standing. It didn't matter.

He pressed an open-mouthed kiss to the side of her neck and raised the back of her skirts, draping them over her arm. His nimble fingers untied her bustle pad and unhooked her drawers. They dropped to the floor with her petticoats and a whisper of sound. He continued kissing her neck, passionate caresses that made her knees threaten to give way. Cool air kissed her bare bottom, replaced in a moment by his knowing touch.

"Are you ready for me?" His fingers dipped into her sex from behind, toying with her before sliding inside.

She moaned, bucking into him for more. "Yes," she scarcely managed to say. She turned, capturing his mouth with hers. The kiss was plundering, devastating. Their tongues tangled. He replaced his fingers with his cock.

His hands went to her waist, holding her at the angle he needed as he plunged inside her again and again. A new wave of desire hit her, making her weak. She gripped the settee so hard her knuckles turned white as she struggled not to crumple into a puddle of lust at his feet.

He pumped into her, increasing his pace, and she came undone, reaching her pinnacle and crying out. She couldn't keep herself from half slumping over as the extreme sensation washed over her. He held her still, just where he wanted her, thrusting with a frantic need that soon had him filling her with his seed. She came again as he found his release, reveling in the completion of their joining, the incredible feeling of him losing himself in her.

He collapsed against her, his breathing ragged, their bodies still joined. She could feel his heart's frantic pace against her back. In the silence of their passion's aftermath, she silently prayed that she'd been wrong. That wanting would be enough to keep him by her side. She couldn't bear to lose him. New York was not where she belonged.

He woke from his dreams that night to a hand running down his chest, straight to his cock. Fingers curled expertly around his shaft, working him up and down. He moaned and arched into the capable touch, thinking that Maggie had tiptoed into his chamber through the darkness. He was hard and ready.

"Maggie," he muttered, "you want me again, do you?"

His hands went into her hair, but the texture was different, all smooth silk rather than soft curls. And then there was the scent. Lavender. The breasts pressed against his chest were all wrong. Too small. Her hips were narrow as well, her mouth on his neck all too familiar yet still somehow foreign.

"Eleanor." The realization startled him. He pushed lightly at her shoulders as wakefulness returned to him. "What the hell are you doing in my chamber?"

"I've missed you, Sandy." She writhed against him.

Once, the mere press of her naked body against his would have incited him to madness. But now there was something that kept him from rolling her to her back and fucking her as he had so many times before. He knew, after all, that she would be wet and willing as ever. They had been a perfect fit, the two of them. Lovemaking had been easy, passionate, effortless.

He thought again of Maggie and removed Eleanor's teasing hand from his cock. "We cannot. Maggie is in the chamber next door."

"I shall be very quiet," Eleanor promised, her lips near to his.

No. He could not. He flipped her to her back and rolled away from her, pulling the bedclothes around himself as a shield. "You must return to your bed at once. I will not disrespect Maggie, nor will I insult her by the servants being made aware of your presence here."

He was confounded, as much by her presence in his chamber as by her presence in his household. He owed Maggie his respect. His fidelity. Everything he'd refused to give her for the entirety of their union. They had forged a bond in the last month. It was different than what he'd shared with Eleanor. He had come to respect his wife. Yes, Maggie was an incomparable, from her poetry to her flaming curls to her willingness to open herself to him. She was special.

"Disrespect *her*?" Incredulity laced Eleanor's words. "What of me? Who is she to you, other than the funds you so desperately needed?"

He felt a great wash of shame then, and it made his cock wither more assuredly than a pail of cold water. She was only repeating words he had oft said to her. He recalled them now, a shower of shame pouring over his head. *The woman I've wed means nothing to me. She was a necessary sin.*

Disgust slammed into him. He stood from the bed, stalking through the darkness in search of his dressing gown. "I made a promise to her that I would be true to her for an entire month, and at the least I intend to keep that promise. You must go, Eleanor. I demand it."

"Very well." Her voice was drawn with hurt. "I shall go. But you will beg for me to be in your bed again, Sandy. This much I know."

"You're wrong," he said, his voice hoarse. Christ, he didn't know what to believe any longer. Part of him still longed for the Eleanor he'd thought he'd known. But a part of him wanted Maggie and the life he'd experienced with

146

her, filled with poetry and laughter and sensuality. Filled with freedom.

"You're wrong, Eleanor." he repeated, as much for her benefit as for his, and, throwing the sash about his waist, he strode from the room.

Maggie couldn't sleep. The ugly ramifications of the day taunted her so that even when she closed her eyes, she could see Lady Billingsley's fine-boned face, her tiny waist, the halo of blonde hair that marked her a true English beauty. Her head ached. Her heart hurt. She was alternately hot, then cold, uncomfortable trapped beneath too many coverings and then not enough.

With a sigh, she attempted to plump her pillow with perhaps more force than required of the task. Simon had come to her earlier in the evening, and their lovemaking had been slow and sweet, but she'd been almost too gripped with the sudden reappearance of the woman he loved to enjoy the simple mating of their bodies.

Dinner earlier had been an unbearably stilted affair. Lady Billingsley joined them, and while Maggie had yearned for nothing more than to hide herself in the private comfort of her chamber for the duration of the meal, she knew she could not allow the awful woman to see her weakness. Maggie was born from the stock of warriors, and she wasn't about to be beaten by a sylph who had broken her husband's heart only to return as if she could once again draw him back into her web.

She hoped she had retained her dignity. Twice, she had lost her head and had almost allowed her true feelings to billow forth. She had privately longed for Lady Billingsley to choke upon the soup course, much to her inner shame. But through it all, she had somehow managed to act the part of hostess, as if she weren't about to engage in battle with the woman seated opposite her at table.

Battle.

Maggie grimaced and turned to her left side, desperate to thrash the misgivings from her mind, at least for the night. Did she want to do battle? A few weeks before, the answer would have been a sure and steady "no". She had been disillusioned with life, with a husband who hadn't wanted her, with a life of solitude and longing for something more. And then Lady Needham's house party. Meeting Simon free of the encumbrances between them had been exhilarating. Her body had been awakened to desires she'd never imagined existed. Their bargain of one month in each other's arms had seemed fortuitous for the both of them.

But now it was all so hopelessly, painfully complicated. Her heart had somehow become involved. She cared for Simon, the man who she'd once thought cold and distant but who she'd discovered still wore the scars of his past beneath his elegant façade. She had not meant to allow him to make her feel so much.

A soft noise filtered through her troubled musings just then, putting a halt to her runaway mind for the moment. She held her breath and listened. It seemed to be coming from Simon's adjoining chamber. Filled with misgiving, she rose from her bed and padded across the carpet to listen at the door. A low rumble reached her ears, unmistakably Simon's voice. Then there was the softer voice of a woman.

Maggie pressed her ear to the door, not caring that it was an act better suited to a schoolroom girl than to a woman of her years. She was desperate to know what was being said, yet terrified to know at the same time. Unfortunately, she couldn't decipher their words no matter how hard she tried, but perhaps it was because of the blood rushing to her head. Anger took her over first. How dare the woman be so bold as to go to Simon's chamber? How dare Simon give her entrance?

Beneath the anger, an awful tide of hurt rose through her. How could he betray her in their home, and so soon after he had made love to her? How could he show her such passion only to give the same to another woman? *A mere month ago, you never entered my thoughts, and now you're all I can damn well think about*, he had told her, the rotten liar. Perhaps she had been wrong and he did not possess a heart after all.

Part of her wanted to throw open the door and confront them both, but the other part of her feared very much what awaited her on the other side. She couldn't bear to see him holding Lady Billingsley, kissing her, touching her. Feeling ill, she paced back to her bed and sank into it. She had nowhere else to go, no one to turn to, and for the first time in her largely unhappy stay in England, she felt completely and utterly alone.

Tears stung her eyes, and try though she might, she couldn't keep them from falling. After all this time, all the wisdom she had sworn she'd gained, he still had the power to hurt her, to crush her as if she were a paper doll beneath his boot heel. It was a horrible realization. She wanted so much to be impervious to him, to have been as worldly as Lady Needham. But she supposed that in the end, she was still the same dreamer with a poet's soul she had always been, a girl who naively believed in the promise of passion. A girl who felt too much, who saw the best in others even when it was not present, and who allowed a cad to strike too close to her heart. It had not been the first time Simon had hurt her, but as she lay in the darkness planning what she ought to do, she decided that it would have to be the last.

chapter eight

SIMON WAS THOROUGHLY INEBRIATED. SAUCED. In his cups. Whatever the words one preferred to use, he was claiming them all. He took a healthy swig of whisky, enjoying the burn down his throat. He'd been unable to sleep, so he'd spent the night in his study, drinking and wondering what in the hell he was going to do next. He'd never been more bloody confused in his life, torn between the past and a possible future with Maggie.

Maggie, his passionate poet who never failed to surprise him. Did he love her? The truth of it was that he had begun to believe love was more fiction than fact, that it was an impossible state invented by fools and romantics. He was drawn to her, to her responsive body and kind heart. She had shown him more generosity than he deserved, and he would always admire her for that.

"Christ." He took another drag of spirits. Libations were not the solution to his problems either, but they did a fine job of distracting him. His mind was lighter even if his heart was not.

A discreet tap at the door interrupted his solitude.

"Enter," he called out, assuming it was the butler with a breakfast tray.

Maggie swished into the room, looking formidably lovely in a day gown of aquamarine silk. Her flaming locks were styled simply, with curls cascading down over her shoulders. The bodice of her dress flattered her slim waist and full bosom to perfection. Damned if he didn't get hard just looking at her, whisky and all. A series of bows bedecked her skirts and sleeves, and he itched to untie them all, then peel her out of her dress, spread her over his *secretaire* and slide his cock deep inside her.

"My lord." Her tone was stiff as baleen corset stays.

Hell. The chill emanating from her luscious body was enough to dampen his ardor. Something was wrong. He belatedly realized her ordinarily full pink lips were pinched into an unhappy line. "Maggie," he returned, standing as he recalled his manners. "Good morning."

She stopped halfway across the room, hands clasped at her waist. She was a fiercely unique beauty. "I don't find it to be a good morning at all, I'm afraid."

He raised a brow, trying to fend off a looming sense of trepidation. "Indeed? And why would that be, my dear?"

"My slumber is frightful at best, easily interrupted." She stared at him in that knowing way she had. It quite stripped his soul bare. And he hadn't thought he possessed a soul any longer.

"Out with it, Maggie," he commanded, doing his best to sort out what was amiss even with his whisky-soaked brain. "What have you to say to me?"

She caught her luscious lower lip between her teeth before venturing into the dangerous waters before them. "I heard voices last night."

The weight of dread settled down upon his shoulders. How much had she heard? "Indeed?" Oh damn it all, he'd said that twice now. Now he was a cad and a twit in addition, of course, to being a drunkard.

"Indeed." Her expression was pensive, slightly

wounded. She had never appeared more beautiful to him, and the realization startled him. "I believe you were conversing with Lady Billingsley. In your chamber."

Bloody, bloody hell. He wanted to lie, but he could not. "She availed herself of my chamber whilst I was sleeping."

"And you did not see fit to summarily dismiss her?"

Of course he should have done. Not as a husband, for God knew that husbands and wives alike strayed when and where they would, but as her lover. He'd sworn to be true to her for an entire month. Although he had not made love to Eleanor, he had certainly not been true to Maggie for most of their marriage. He knew this in his black heart.

"I did not." He knew as he said the words that they could cost him more than he was willing to pay—everything he'd managed to find over the last fortnight, the tentative happiness he'd only begun to believe could be possible. "I removed myself when she would not comply."

Everything was too dear a price to pay, damn it. He wanted Maggie in his bed. The whisky rattling about in his troubled mind wasn't giving him a bit of clarity.

"Did you bed her?" Her voice broke.

"Christ no," he assured her. He wouldn't now. Couldn't. The act had once seemed so natural, his mind conditioned by society to do as everyone else did: marry for practicality, find love elsewhere. "I may be an utter bastard, but even I have morals when I need them."

"You wanted to, didn't you?"

Her blunt question shocked him, as much because she had dared to ask it as because it shook him. The plain truth of it was that if he'd wanted Eleanor, he would have taken her. At least, he would have in the past. His unfettered time with Maggie had changed him, and for the better.

"You still love her," Maggie said then without waiting for his response, her voice devoid of inflection save a slight tremor that he knew meant she was on the verge of tears.

Did he? The alcohol was muddled his already confused mind. All he knew was that he was hopelessly ensnared in

Maggie's violet eyes, their light filled with an accusatory glow. He had disappointed her. And that hurt him, smote him more than any other blow in his life. He was an utter failure. There it was, laid out before him. He had lived almost thirty years and yet this young scrap of American idealism had brought him low.

He was not worthy of her. He wasn't worthy to kiss her hem.

Didn't she know? Why did she dare to believe him better than what he was? He was nothing more than a broken, confused, bloody soused fool. "A fortnight cannot change a man as much as you hope."

"I will not stand in your way." Maggie bowed her head, composing herself with grace. Her beauty took on a fragile quality for the first time, her pale complexion fading into an ashen tinge. Her lips thinned. Even her elaborate upswept curls seemed to sag in defeat. She tucked her chin back up, defiance flashing in her gaze. "You must live your life as you see fit."

She was giving him freedom, he realized, the sort of freedom he'd once dreamt of owning. During his days of being her husband, long before he'd come to know her, the guilt had been at the edge of his conscience. Nagging him. Eating him alive. And now, she was telling him to pursue the woman he had loved. He should be thrilled. Overjoyed. Overcome with elation.

Instead, he felt only hollow. Eleanor was not the woman he wanted, not any longer. What of Maggie, the sweet wife he'd grown to care for over the last few weeks? She had inspired him, shown him new facets of life, brought him passion and joy. She had been giving and wonderful to him when he had only ever been unkind to her. The truth of it was that she deserved so much better than a bollixed-up horse's arse like him. Perhaps whisky was making him see straight for the first time.

"What of you?" he asked, hoping that she would not release him so easily.

He dared to think she might fight for him with that fierce American spirit of hers. That she might want him despite all his flaws and peculiarities. But she turned her back, taking a deep breath that bespoke emotions too raw to let loose.

"I expect I will find my way. I always have." She exhaled and turned to face him, her expression bearing a false cheeriness. "Perhaps I will write again. You've made me see that I ought not to have given up my dreams, and for that I will be forever grateful."

She spoke as if she expected never to see him again, and the thought of her disappearing from his life assailed him with a foreign sense of fear. His chest tightened. "What do you mean, find your way?"

"Oh, it is merely a figure of speech," she hastened to assure him. "You needn't fear that I will be underfoot. I can always go to London or to stay with friends."

"No," he bit out, perhaps faster than he ought to have. "You must stay here at Denver Hall. Why would you leave?"

He wanted her to stay. At least, he thought he did. He'd never felt so adrift in his life. He was a boat, bobbing upon the sea, no land in sight. Jesus, he didn't have a compass to tell him which direction he ought to take.

"Of course," she said with equal brightness. "I would never leave if you didn't wish it of me. Surely you must know that, Simon."

Feeling relieved, he nodded. "Very good, my dear." But when he would have closed the distance between them and taken her in his arms, she was already fleeing the room. He watched her go, helpless to stop her.

Maggie was reading in the comfort of the drawing room, trying to distract herself from the awful knot growing inside her stomach. She had sought out Simon in the hopes that he would tell her something that would give her reason to stay. She had hoped he would tell her that he didn't give a damn for Lady Billingsley, unlikely though she knew it was. But he had been conflicted as ever, his eyes bloodshot and his hair mussed. That he appeared to be in as much turmoil as she was left her little comfort. Even if he did care for her, he still had feelings for his old lover.

She feared she would have to leave Denver House. There was no earthly way she could remain, watching Simon fall back into Lady Billingsley's arms. She could go to London, she supposed, or perhaps seek out her dear friend Victoria while she booked passage to New York. She tried to tell herself it was for the best, but she couldn't quite muster the strength.

It hardly seemed fair that she would have discovered her feelings for her husband only to have the one woman who had kept them apart reemerge, determined to raze the fragile truce they'd built. As if on cue, her unwanted guest sauntered into the room, disrupting her peace.

Dear heavens, was there never a time when she could avoid the dreadful woman? She was everywhere. At dinner, in the drawing room, standing too near to Simon whenever she could, staring at him as if he were nude before her. She had only been at Denver House a day, and already it was one day too many. Maggie loathed her. With great reluctance, she looked up from the pages of Anthony Trollope into which she'd been attempting to escape.

Lady Billingsley was of course beautiful as ever, wearing an ethereal afternoon gown of rich lavender that emphasized her tiny waist. Maggie swore she was so heavily corseted it was a miracle she didn't faint whenever she seated herself. Her blonde curls were artfully arranged, golden as any angel's. But an angel she was not. She raised her nose ever so slightly as her gaze settled upon Maggie, as if to say Maggie's mere presence was an affront to her sense of English nobility. Maggie's brows snapped together into a frown. The feeling was mutual.

"Lady Billingsley, how lovely to see you." She was aware that she must at least uphold the pretense of being a happy hostess. It would never do for the woman to discover how much she vexed her.

"My lady," her foe acknowledged with a regally inclined head. "I'm delighted to find you here as it will save me the effort of seeking you out."

Dismay swept through Maggie. It didn't escape her that the woman had refused to refer to her as Lady Sandhurst. "Why should you need to seek me out?"

Her ladyship crossed the room, closing the distance between them, and reached into a pocket on her day gown, extracting a ribbon-bound stack of what appeared to be envelopes. "I have something I want to give you, something that I think will alter the way you must see me."

Maggie shook her head, eyeing the packet dubiously. "I'm sure it cannot. I don't want it, my lady."

"You must take them. I want you to have these." Lady Billingsley thrust the envelopes into her hands.

Maggie accepted them, but only because it was either close her fingers about them or allow them to drop to the carpet. She studied her adversary's face, wishing it was not nearly so lovely. "I don't want anything from you, Lady Billingsley, other than to never see you again."

"I understand that you despise me, but I love your husband," she said, startling Maggie with her candor. "And I know that he still very much loves me. I was wrong to leave him."

"But you *did* leave him," she pointed out, "and regardless of whether or not you accept that, it changed everything. Once, you had complete power over him. Now he no longer harbors even a hint of tender feelings for you."

Of course, she was blustering. Even if she knew this was not a war she could win, her pride demanded she not allow the woman to see it. In truth, she was terrified that her husband was still in love with the woman before her. After all, he had never given her any reason to hope for more than their month of passion. He had never spoken words of love to her. The letters in her hand burned into her skin in an awful reminder.

Love letters. Maggie knew it without bothering to read them. What made their existence all the more humiliating was that he had never written her a line. Not even to inquire after her welfare. Not even to ascertain whether or not she still existed.

"He is attempting to make me jealous," Lady Billingsley insisted. "You're a distraction to him. Read the letters, I implore you. You shall see how deep our connection runs. It cannot be broken by a mere American girl who has shared his bed for a month."

"I'm no mere American girl." Anger lent her new pluck. "I am a woman of her own fortune, a poet, a wife. What are you other than the woman who clung to a man who could never truly be hers?"

"He was," her nemesis hissed. "He has been mine and so he shall be again. Let him free. Can't you see how he feels trapped between us? He pities you."

Maggie looked from the insidious letters in her hand back to the woman's face. She was intent, her expression as if it had been chiseled from marble. But there was an underlying emotion in her voice, an urgency, perhaps. Her words rattled Maggie. *He pities you*, she'd said. Could it be true? She wouldn't allow herself to think it just now. "Let him free? I have no hold over him."

"This month you've made him promise to give you," she insisted. "He's told me all about it, and his sense of honor won't allow him to extricate himself. It is solely in your hands. That is why I give you these letters. You can never mean to him what I have meant to him. We have loved each other for years."

"I have been his wife for a year." She knew her protestation was a hollow one.

"In name only. You have been in his bed for a paltry amount of time."

It shocked Maggie that Simon had apparently shared the secrets of their relationship with this woman, the woman who had been a barrier between them from the moment she'd met him. Perhaps there was something to what Lady Billingsley told her. She had long ago lost her naiveté, after all, and that largely thanks to Sandhurst.

"My marriage is none of your concern," she forced herself to say through lips that had gone numb in her escalating fear. "You do not belong here, my lady. Indeed, you would do best to return to your husband."

Her ladyship's face transformed, her expression becoming smug. "I cannot. Sandy loves me, and I love him. I'll not make the same mistake twice. I must have him in my life or it's not worth living."

Dear God. What hope did Maggie have of winning against this woman? She had not been able to win before. Now, she had nothing more than heated embraces and wicked lovemaking to hold Simon to her. He had never spoken words of love, nor written them. She stared down at the letters, her heart aching. Disappointment sank through her. She knew what she must do.

She was gone.

The realization was akin to a punch directly in his gut. Simon nearly doubled over, so violent was his reaction. He threw open the door to her chamber and stalked inside, confirming what his butler had already told him. His wife had left in a flurry of hooves and portmanteaus. Her chamber still smelled of her perfume, but other than her scent and the handful of letters she'd left scattered over her bed, it was as if she had never been there at all.

Damn. He never should have allowed Eleanor to remain at Denver House, not even for a day. He scooped up a letter and scanned its contents, recognizing his youthful signature at the bottom of the page. Instantly, he knew what Eleanor had done. These letters were old. He'd never been one for dating his correspondence as he ought to have done, and he cursed himself for it now. Christ, he'd been a lovesick milksop, he thought with disgust as he read a particularly flowery line.

She had given these letters to Maggie, knowing she would read them and assume the worst. And then he found another letter, tucked into an envelope bearing his name. Maggie had left him a note, it would seem. He snatched it up far too quickly and tore it open.

She wrote that she was freeing him. She did not wish to see him ever again. She was going away, never to return. His fist tightened on the letter, crumpling it before he finished reading.

Damn her. How dare she think she could leave him so easily, without warning, without a word? She couldn't. He wouldn't stand for it. He had to find her. But first, he needed to confront Eleanor. Tossing the entire sheaf of papers to the floor, he stalked from the chamber, his former lover's name on his lips as if it were a war cry.

"Eleanor!" His vision had blackened with his rage as he realized the depths to which she'd sunk. She had been cruel, had hurt Maggie. "Eleanor, goddamn it, show yourself."

She refused. He knew which chamber she'd been assigned, neatly solving the immediate problem of giving her a tongue-lashing. Without bothering to knock, he threw open the door. Eleanor was seated at a writing desk but she stood hastily at his entrance, her eyes wide.

"Sandy, whatever is the matter?"

"You can dispense with the pretense of your innocence," he hissed, crossing the room to her and only stopping when he feared he may be capable of grabbing her arm and hauling her out the door. He wouldn't do her violence. "I know what you've done."

"Are you not pleased?" She frowned at him. "I've only made it apparent to the silly cow that she has no place here."

He had not been so enraged in a long time. He clenched his fists and took a breath, forcing himself to calm. "She has every place here. She is my wife."

"In name only." Eleanor sounded suddenly fragile.

But Simon was unmoved. "Indeed, Eleanor. Just as you have been wife to your husband. If he beats you, then you should not return to him. But you will need to find another roof above your head. You cannot remain here."

"I beg your pardon?" Her already wan complexion had gone paler.

"You must leave. I cannot countenance your machinations," he explained, realizing he had erred in ever allowing her to stay when she had first arrived. She had ever been a weakness of his, and he had pitied her, still moved by the tender feelings he'd had for her. But he should have urged her to seek other shelter. He had been too bloody stupid to see it.

"You love me." She came to him and placed a dainty palm on his chest. "You're angry. I only did what I thought you wished me to do. You mustn't permit yourself to feel sorry for her."

He shook her touch away. "No, Eleanor. I do not love you. I doubt now that I ever did. Nor do I think you love me. We were two people searching for something bigger than ourselves, naïve enough to think we'd found it."

Her expression disintegrated before him. "How can you be so merciless?"

"I might ask the same of you, madam," he reminded her tightly.

"Are you truly taking up the cudgels for that woman?"

Yes, damn it. He was. He had learned quite a bit about the wife he'd ignored. She was a poet, a wild lover, a kind heart. She hadn't deserved to be thrust into the position in which he had placed her. That much he knew for certain.

"I am," he said at last, feeling as if he had just taken up the first worthy cause of his life. "I have to, Eleanor. You made your choice a long time ago, and now I have made mine."

He'd known her for half his life. Each of them had been left in dire straits by their families. He'd needed to marry a fat dowry, and Eleanor had needed to marry a fat purse. But he was not the young buck she'd known any longer. Nor was she the girl he'd once admired. They had changed. Irrevocably.

"How could you?" Her hands fluttered about her as if they were lost butterflies before she pressed them to her mouth.

He had the uncomfortable impression that she was stifling a sob. He didn't want to hurt her either, but she had left him with a decision to make. He didn't know what would come of his marriage with Maggie, but he did know they were inextricably linked. He didn't want her to disappear from his life.

"I'm sorry." Rage seeped from him as if he were a torn sail. "I'm going to find her, and when I return, I want you gone from here. You may take my carriage."

Tears slid down her cheeks in earnest now as a sense of finality weighed upon the moment. "Where shall I go? Billingsley will not take me in now."

"If Billingsley hurts you, don't return to him. You have many friends, Eleanor. Seek them out." He gentled his tone as she continued to weep. "You chose your fate."

"He chose it for me," she argued.

"No." For Simon knew differently. He would have done anything to keep her, run away with her to the continent if he'd had to do so. He had told her as much then. She had still walked away. She'd done him the greatest favor of his life. He'd merely been too stupid to know. "You chose it. I begin to think you aren't at all the woman I believed you to be."

"But I love you."

"You also lie. Frequently and without compunction." He forced himself to think of Lord Needham and her indiscretion with him. How many others had there been? Likely, he would never know. "I'm sorry Eleanor, but our time together must be at an end."

"You're throwing me over?" Disbelief clouded her

voice. "Truly? You would be so callous as to chase after her and toss me out as if I were no better than rubbish from the dustbin?"

"Not rubbish," he corrected her. "Merely my past. I must go now. I hope when next we meet it shall be as friends."

He didn't wait to hear her response. He left the chamber, determined to find Maggie if it was the last thing he did.

The hired conveyance rumbled over the roads as Maggie pressed a hand to her roiling stomach. Perhaps her idea had not been a good one, she acknowledged now, for the carriage she'd been able to procure after sending Sandhurst's back to Denver House was appallingly creaky and old. It smelled of sourness, must, and horse dung. The combination of swaying, rumbling and odors nauseated her. To add to already dismal matters, the skies had opened up in a bitter torrent of rain, and the carriage had a leaking roof. But she hadn't wanted her husband to find her. She was not just leaving him, she was disappearing entirely. Oh, she didn't fool herself that he would bother to find her, but she didn't want it to be a possibility.

She certainly hoped they would soon reach Lady Needham's estate, for she couldn't bear to be trapped within the carriage for much longer. At least the unpleasantness of her surroundings was somewhat serving to distract her from the ache in her heart.

Maggie had never felt more broken in her life. She felt like a teacup that had been hurled from a rooftop to shatter into infinitesimal shards below. She was reminded of the poem by Elizabeth Barrett Browning, *My Heart and I. You see, we're tired, my heart and I. We dealt with books, we trusted men*, went the verses. Yes, Maggie's heart was tired indeed. She had trusted Simon, and in so doing had fallen headfirst into her own demise. *And in our own blood drenched the pen.* The poem rang so terribly true.

"Stop this carriage!"

A familiar voice, commanding and arrogant and yet beloved as ever, broke through her uneasy thoughts. Simon? *It cannot be.* She moved from the uncomfortable bench to press her face against the dingy window. She was afraid to hope, terrified that somehow she had conjured him. Perhaps she was dreaming, and any moment she'd fall to the dirty floor of the carriage and wake up to the awful realization that Simon still loved Lady Billingsley and he'd happily live the rest of his life without Maggie.

But no. There he was. Her foolish heart swelled with joy. Crouched low over his horse, a fierce expression etched on his handsome face, he looked like a marauder of old as the rains lashed him. A hero torn from the pages of a book she once sighed over.

He had followed her. Relief slipped over her. "Stop," she called to the driver. "Stop at once."

The carriage groaned to an unsteady halt and she was already on her feet, throwing open the door. Simon dismounted when he saw her, closing the distance between them in three long strides. He caught her waist in an almost punishing grip, hauling her down from her perch. Rains battered them. He was soaked. She didn't care.

"Damn you, Maggie. What the hell were you about, leaving me without a bloody word?" The question was almost a snarl.

She searched his face, finding not a hint of tenderness there. He was all harsh lines and unforgiving angles. Somehow, she hadn't anticipated his anger. As she'd played out his reaction in her mind, she had expected his relief. She had hoped for his sadness. She had not thought of rage, but it was an irate husband glaring down at her now, demanding answers.

"I wrote you a letter," she managed, holding on to his arms.

"A wrong-headed nonsensical piece of shite," he

declared.

His words, however gruff, should have heartened her. But they left her cold, questions clamoring within her. Why had he followed her? Pride? His rage? She decided to begin with the heart of her leaving. "Lady Billingsley gave me your correspondence. I read it all, and I couldn't bear for you to be apart from someone you obviously loved so much."

"You might have asked me," he countered. "You could have come to me, Maggie. Why did you not?"

"You never wanted me from the first." Fat droplets of rain landed on her cheeks, rolling down in a rude mimicry of tears. She dashed them away, not wanting him to think she cried for him. "I know you certainly never loved me."

"A man can change, by God." His grip on her tightened as he gave her a slight shake as if to shock some reason into her. "Haven't you ever thought of that?"

The vibrant-green depths of his gaze trapped her. "I thought you had changed. But then Lady Billingsley appeared, and you seemed so torn. I won't stand in the way of your happiness."

"Don't you see?" He took her face in his palms then, drawing their mouths impossibly near. "You are my happiness."

Her heart soared. "Me?"

"You," he confirmed. "I don't know how the devil it happened, but somehow you've managed to rot my brain."

Oh dear. That didn't sound romantic at all. She frowned at him. "I've done nothing of the sort."

"The hell you haven't. Before I stepped on your train at Lady Needham's, I was perfectly sane. I didn't need laughter or dancing in the rain or a wife at my side. But then a beautiful poet with hair the color of fire had me making love to her in the bloody library and on a hill in the middle of my estate and on the breakfast table and everywhere else I possibly could. And she made me realize I'm not the man I thought I was."

She flushed at his mentioning of their lustful adventures.

"You're not?"

"No." He shook his head. "Because the man I thought I was could live without Margaret Emilia Desmond, a woman who is kind when she bloody well shouldn't be, who made me feel at home for the first time in years, a woman who broke her arm when she was a girl and never once cried."

Tears pricked her eyes. He had remembered. He had remembered everything. And perhaps he had felt an answering love growing within him as well. It wasn't a declaration, but it would do.

"I thought I could live without you," he said again. "But I cannot. Come home with me, Maggie."

He wasn't asking, but she didn't care. That was Simon's way, all gruff blustering without a hint of persuasion. No, he had not told her he loved her. But he had followed her, and he wanted her back. It would definitely do, she decided again.

"Yes," was all she said, and then she was in his arms, his mouth on hers. She was precisely where she wanted to be.

Something was amiss. Maggie could detect as much the moment the hired carriage rolled to a stop before Denver House. The rains had at last ceased, and servants milled about outside in an uncharacteristic flurry. Before she could think, the door to the carriage flew open to reveal the shocked face of their butler, Milton.

"My lord." His voice carried a distinct thread of worry. "I regret to say there has been an incident."

"What the devil is it?" Simon demanded.

"I'm afraid it's Lady Billingsley," Milton intoned. "She has fallen."

"Christ," he bit out. "From what?"

The ordinarily formidable butler swallowed. "From a window, it would appear, Lord Sandhurst."

Shock speared her. Lady Billingsley had fallen from a window? Dear heaven. Judging from Milton's grim visage, she was either grievously injured or worse. And then something sinister occurred to her. Lady Billingsley would not have merely fallen from a window. It was architecturally impossible. No indeed, she would have jumped on her own accord.

"Is she..." Simon allowed his question to trail away, seemingly incapable of completing it.

"I've sent for Dr. Williams, but I'm afraid his attendance will not be necessary, my lord."

"Where the bloody hell is she?" Simon shot out of the carriage as if he were a cannon ball, leaving Maggie to be handed down in his wake.

"In the east garden, my lord," Milton called after him, but Simon was already running.

Her heart plummeted. Maggie gathered her skirts up in her fists and hurried after him as quickly as her mules would allow her feet to travel. She was terribly afraid of what she would find but neither did she want him to face the awful scene on his own.

She had to stop twice on account of pebbles working their way into her shoes. By the time she reached the edge of the immaculate east garden, Simon had garnered quite a bit of a lead on her. Her corset bit her sides as she rushed to catch up with him, fear tangling with the growing knot of worry in her stomach.

And then she saw it, a billow of pastel skirts marred by the undeniable stark red of blood. The dress itself appeared to be suspended in the air, draped over the intricate wrought iron fencing on the garden's perimeter. Maggie's frantic pace slowed as comprehension filtered through her jumbled mind. Heavens. She pressed a hand over her mouth to stifle the horrified scream rising in her throat. The entire picture came together as she spotted pale arms and a blonde head hanging listlessly downward.

Dear God. Lady Billingsley had been impaled on the

fence when she'd fallen from the window. Her form was utterly still. Milton's words returned to Maggie as she watched her husband rush to Lady Billingsley's side. *I've sent for Dr. Williams, but I'm afraid his attendance will not be necessary...*

Simon ran straight to her anyway, not faltering for a moment as he attempted to rescue her, Maggie supposed, by lifting her limp body from the spiked fence. He struggled to free her, letting out an inhuman cry of grief. Maggie reached him as he at last pulled Lady Billingsley from her ignominious perch atop the fence. Blood seeped from her wounds anew. Her skin was the gray of a sky before a storm. Her eyes were open yet sightless. Red trickled from her mouth as Simon held her to him, sinking to his knees. All lingering questions were dashed. Lady Billingsley was indeed dead.

"Eleanor," he moaned. "Jesus, Eleanor. What have you done?"

A violent surge of nausea hit Maggie, forcing her to turn away from the grisly scene. She had never seen death in a way that was less than peaceful. Lady Billingsley's departure from the earth had been anything but. She thought of how frightened the woman must have been, falling through the air to her demise. How horrific.

"Simon," she forced herself to say through lips that had gone dry with the terror of the moment. "She is gone."

"No," he denied. "She's not, damn it."

She looked back to see him cradling Lady Billingsley's lifeless body as if she were his dearest possession on earth. It was clear to Maggie that his love for the other woman had never abated. He was devastated, his voice laden with wild grief. She felt like an interloper, watching without knowing what to do, how to help him.

"Simon," she said again, placing a hand of comfort on his shoulder. "You mustn't torture yourself."

"Where the devil is Milton? Get me Dr. Williams, damn you." He rocked Lady Billingsley in his arms. He looked wild, as if he were in shock. And no doubt he was. They all were. "She needs assistance."

Maggie's heart broke for him. She searched her mind for words, but what could she say that would ease his suffering? He held a dead woman in his arms, the woman he had loved. It was as if the tentative bond they'd forged had fallen from a cliff, dashed on the rocks below. Maggie was once again an unwanted wife who didn't belong before and who certainly didn't now.

But she hated to see him tear himself apart. "I'm so sorry, Simon." She took care to keep her voice low, comforting. It was quite a feat given the horrors before her. She never could have imagined returning to this.

"Leave me, Maggie." His voice was ragged. "Please. I need to be alone."

He could not have hurt her more had he slapped her fully across the face. She snatched her hand from him and spun away. The tears she'd been holding finally fell, tears for Simon as much as for Lady Billingsley. And yes, as selfish and horrid as it was, tears for herself as well. She knew instinctively that there could never be a recovery from such a tragedy. Never. This horrible death would change everything.

Milton stood behind her, his ordinarily expressionless face filled with open sympathy. She knew he had heard Simon's dismissal of her. He cleared his throat. "Come along with me, my lady. You ought not to linger here. I shall see you into the care of the capable Mrs. Keynes."

"Yes." She allowed herself to be escorted into a side door as if she were a child. "Thank you, Milton. You're most kind."

"Of course, my lady."

"Please stay close to him," she added. "He doesn't want me, but I very much fear he shouldn't be alone."

"I will do as you ask, my lady." With a bow, he handed her off to Mrs. Keynes, who hovered over her like a mother hen.

"Blessed angels, Lady Sandhurst. There now. You're horribly pale. Do sit down." Deep furrows of worry lined the housekeeper's kindly round face. "You didn't see anything, did you, my dear?"

Maggie swallowed, feeling ill anew at the thought of Lady Billingsley's bloodied, lifeless face. "I'm afraid I did."

"Oh, my poor dear." Mrs. Keynes patted her hand in an unusual show of caring. "Sit down and I will have some tea brought round for you. You mustn't think upon it. Not for another minute. God rest her ladyship's soul."

"God rest her soul," Maggie whispered, feeling as if she were far away. Her vision began to blacken. Then, there was the abyss of nothingness stretching before her, calling her name. She fell headlong into it.

The crashing, thumping, and sounds of breaking glass emerging from Simon's study told Maggie exactly where her husband was. It was late. Hours had passed since their return to Denver House and the horrible discovery of Lady Billingsley's lifeless body. Maggie hadn't seen Simon since he had told her to leave him. A pall fell over the entire household, even the servants wandering about with bleak expressions.

Dinner had been served with Simon nowhere to be found and Maggie unable to eat. The pervading silence at the table had been almost unbearable, and the entire time she sat alone with her laden plate before her, all she could think of was that a woman had killed herself. The woman Simon had loved. And Simon hadn't wanted Maggie's comfort. He hadn't wanted her presence.

It was hurtful, his turning away from her, especially since it followed so closely upon the heels of his desperate ride to bring her back to Denver House. She knew he was grieving, that he'd witnessed an unspeakable tragedy, but his defection remained nevertheless troubling.

Her feelings didn't matter at the moment, she knew, as she hovered near the threshold to his closed study door. Another loud bang could be heard from within, along with a muffled curse. She winced and took a deep breath, her hand wavering on the knob. Likely he still would not wish to see her, but she had waited in vain in her chamber for him to arrive. She hadn't been able to wait any longer. She couldn't shake the feeling that he needed her, whether he wanted to or not.

The door opened to reveal a dimly lit scene of inanimate-object carnage that undoubtedly reflected the tumult of his soul. She stepped inside and closed the door at her back, mindful of the shards of glass at her feet, perhaps the remnants of a decanter. Then she saw him, his back to her, his head hanging.

"Goddamn it, I told you I don't want anything for the remainder of the evening," he all but yelled.

Maggie jumped, stilling to contemplate the wisdom of her invasion. But it was too late for second thoughts. "Simon, it's Maggie."

He turned around at her voice, his face haggard in the poor lighting offered by the two gas lamps on the far wall. "What the devil are you doing here?"

Not the welcome she'd been hoping for, but Maggie was in for a penny, in for a pound. "I'm worried about you. I haven't seen you in hours."

"I'm not fit company just now." He raked a hand through his already askew hair. "You should go."

At least he hadn't tossed anything yet, she reasoned. "I cannot leave you like this."

"You ought to, by God. I don't trust myself. Damn it, I'm responsible for her death, Maggie. I killed her." His voice broke on the last word, a rare show of real emotion from a man who was often cold unless he was in the bedchamber.

Her heart broke for him just as surely as his voice had. She had no choice but to go to him, crossing the chamber

170

to his side before she could think twice. She slipped her arms around him and he surprised her by leaning into her, pressing his face into her neck. "You didn't kill her, Simon. You mustn't think such an awful thing."

"I all but pushed her from the window with my own hands." His tone was tortured. The wetness of his tears slid over her skin.

Dear God, he held himself responsible for Lady Billingsley's awful decision. Little wonder he was falling apart before her. "She chose this end, not you."

He shook his head, lifting it to look down at her. His hands tightened upon her waist with an almost painful grip. "I chose it for her. I left her. My God, if I had realized how delicate she was, I never would have gone."

The implications of his words were painfully clear. He would have allowed Maggie to leave if he'd known Lady Billingsley would kill herself. That stung, much as she knew that he was in a rough state of mind, blaming himself for something he'd had no power to stop. "She was not well, Simon, or else she would not have done what she did. It was not within your power to stop her." Surely no one would make such a final decision precipitously. She little knew Lady Billingsley other than the brief time she had spent at Denver House, but Maggie believed beneath her lovely exterior had been some ugly demons, demons that had nothing at all to do with Simon.

"I abandoned her when she needed me the most. Christ, I'm my father."

His despair hurt her heart more than what he'd said. "You're not a bit like him." He refused to look at her, his eyes a deep, pain-filled moss, staring unseeingly beyond her. "Look at me, Simon."

"No. You should go, Maggie. You should get the hell away from me," he snarled, his tone vicious. He caught her arms and pushed her from him.

She staggered back, flinching at the raw rage emanating from him. She'd seen him at his ugliest before, when he'd discovered he'd bedded his wife without realizing. But even then, he had not been as he was now, mercurial, filled with fury and pain. Ready to wound.

"I cannot leave you when you're like this," she said at last, all but wringing her hands as she watched him give her his back and stalk away. She couldn't shake the feeling that he was further away from her now than he'd ever been, lost in the regrets and sorrows of his heart. He must have loved Lady Billingsley deeply, more deeply than she had supposed.

Had it been nothing more than guilt that had prompted him to follow her and stop her from leaving him? She had to wonder now. Surely he must have felt something for her other than duty. He had said so, had all but confessed tender feelings for her mere hours before. That had to mean something yet. After all, he'd certainly never felt responsible for her a day in his life before. She shrugged the troublesome thoughts from her mind and followed him across the study, uncertain of what she ought to do yet unwilling to leave him alone.

"You should leave me," he called over his shoulder, stopping in his angry strides only when he reached the paneled walls. "Good Christ, you ought to have left me a long time ago. I'm a bloody curse." He pounded his fists against the wall with so much force she feared he'd injure himself.

Maggie rushed to his side, not stopping until she was near enough to entwine her arms about his lean waist. She embraced him as she had that long-ago day at Lady Needham's before she'd known he was the husband who'd abandoned her. This time, it was because he was the man she'd grown to love, and he was in pain. Somehow, nothing mattered—nothing could matter—more than that Simon was hurting, lost, and confused. He needed her.

"You're not a curse," she told him firmly, past the knot in her throat. She hated that Lady Billingsley had chosen such an awful end, that she had been spiteful enough to pitch herself from a window knowing Simon would find her. It had been a final act of exerting power over a man who had no longer wanted to be beneath her dainty thumb. And it had wounded Simon as mortally as any bullet could have. Surely Lady Billingsley would have recognized that.

"Go, Maggie," he ordered her lowly, resting his head against the wall. His breathing was deep and hitched, his heart a rapid thrum beneath her ear. He slammed his fist again, startling her. "Go now."

"No." She held on to him when he would have shrugged her away. She was afraid to leave him, afraid of what he might do in his anguish. If he injured himself in some way, she'd never forgive herself. She couldn't bear that. No, she needed Simon in her life, as impossible as that seemed. "I'm not going anywhere."

"Have you no notion the danger you're in?" His voice was deceptively quiet, laced with darkness. "I'm not myself. Jesus, I don't think I'll ever be myself again."

But Maggie remained undeterred. "I'm not here to make drawing-room pleasantries with you. I'm here because you need me."

There, she'd said it. He stiffened beneath her touch, and she feared she'd overstepped the fragile boundaries he had once again erected between them. But then he startled her by spinning around to face her, his hands sinking to her waist. He hauled her up against him, her breasts pressing into his chest.

His gaze seared hers, raw agony and grief starkly reflected in his eyes. "Perhaps you're right. Perhaps I do need you. What will you do for me, Maggie?"

She wasn't sure she liked the implications in his tone. She didn't know what to say. It was as if the passion that always burned between them had spun into rage. She didn't want that to tarnish what they'd shared. But still, she wanted to show him she was here for him, an anchor of support in a storm-tossed sea. "What would you have me do for you?"

"Nothing. There's not a thing you can do." He drew away from her, gripping her arms, and shook her with enough force to catch her breath. "I keep seeing her face, her body hanging impaled on that damn fence. I caused it. I'm responsible."

She cupped his face, trying to comfort him, knowing she couldn't. He was in pain, blaming himself, lost in the depths of his agonizing grief. There was no place for her in his heart after this. Everything he'd said to her earlier that afternoon outside the carriage seemed to have fallen away. Now there only remained the jarring shock left to survivors. *I don't think I'll ever be myself again*, he'd said. Thinking of it struck fear within her, fear that all they'd accomplished would be whittled down to naught. That the love she possessed for him would forever go unanswered.

But she couldn't think of herself, for that was selfish and weak. She needed to be strong for her husband, to help ease his suffering. "You mustn't punish yourself," she told him. "You did nothing wrong."

He closed his eyes for a moment. "I did everything wrong."

She flinched, supposing he referred to the last fortnight they'd shared together. His words stung. "Perhaps I'm at fault. If I had never decided to create a scandal, none of this would have happened."

"I wish to God it wouldn't have happened." He sounded incredibly weary, as if he spoke from his very soul. "But it has, and it is our heavy mantle to live with. Christ, I've got to send word to her family, to Billingsley. They need to know what's happened."

"I can write the letters for you," she volunteered, numb. Maybe he blamed her as well as himself. If so, it was possible he'd never forgive her.

"No." He pushed her away from him. "It's my duty. Jesus, Maggie, just get out of here before I hurt you. There's nothing you can do but leave me to my misery."

She rushed after him as he stalked away from her, placing a staying hand on his arm. "Please, Simon. Don't keep me at a distance."

174

He shrugged away from her touch with such violence that she lost her balance for a moment and stumbled over a book he'd thrown in his rage. It sent her sprawling to the floor, the breath knocked from her lungs. Her head smacked off the carpet before she could catch herself.

"Damn it." He dropped to his knees at her side. His expression had softened to one of concern. "Are you hurt?"

"I'm fine," she said, feeling merely shaken and horribly sad for him, for Lady Billingsley, for herself. "I tripped over the book."

"Devil take it." He took her hands in his and hauled her to her feet, severing the contact the instant she stood. "Leave me now, Maggie. I don't trust myself."

"But—"

"Now." His tone was as fierce as his expression had become. "Go at once."

There was no arguing. No winning. He didn't want her company or her comfort. No, he didn't want her at all. "Very well," she allowed. "I shall go."

As she left his study, she couldn't help but feel she was making a terrible mistake in leaving him alone. But what choice did she have? Pride would not allow her to force herself upon him when he didn't want her there. All that remained for her to do was to grant him the solitude he desired. He didn't want her, and he'd made that more than apparent. How quickly, she thought as she cut a somber path back to her chamber, the world around her could change. How quickly it could crumble, never to be mended.

When Maggie woke in the morning, it was to a heavy heart and an empty bed. Simon had never come to her. She had spent a nearly endless vigil waiting for him until, exhausted and puffy-eyed from the tears she'd been crying, she finally gave in to slumber. The awful events of the day before seemed as though they'd been a nightmare to her as she allowed her lady's maid to dress her. But the evidence remained in her reflection, the pinched lips, pale cheeks, still-swollen eyes.

Her lady's maid was uncharacteristically silent as she dressed Maggie's hair into a subdued style. Her morning dress was a somber black. Yes, there had been a horrible death. She'd woken in the night twice, swearing she'd heard screams. It was terrifying to think of what Lady Billingsley must have experienced in the final moments of her life. There would have been the stomach-churning fall, the impalement on the fence. Maggie prayed she had passed instantly, that she had not lingered in pain overly long. And she prayed too that Simon would somehow recover.

After a final errant curl had been tucked into place, Maggie thanked her lady's maid and descended to the breakfast room. She wondered what it would be like to face Simon by the grim light of day. Had he slept? She doubted it. Likely, the days to come would only prove more difficult. He had lost the woman he loved and he felt responsible for that loss. Maggie knew her own guilt for her part in the bitter affair. She never would have wished for Lady Billingsley to commit such an act, but she little knew now how she would react if she were to do it over again. Would she pursue Simon? Would she leave knowing he would follow?

It all made her head spin and her heart ache.

As she rounded a bend in the lower hall, she nearly collided with Mrs. Keynes, who appeared unusually flustered, her time-weathered cheeks flushed with the exertion of her frantic pace. Maggie stopped herself short of the petite woman, startled and a bit flummoxed herself.

"Mrs. Keynes, good morning," she greeted, although she didn't feel a drop of cheer.

"I'm afraid it's anything but, my lady," Mrs. Keynes returned, sounding uncharacteristically worried. "Haven't you heard the news, then?"

News? Dear God. Maggie's heart plummeted to her toes.

She couldn't bear any more terrible news. "I have not," she said slowly, almost afraid to hear it. "What has happened?"

"It's his lordship." Mrs. Keynes pressed her lips together, taking a moment to compose herself, it seemed. "He's gone."

Ice crept into her heart. "What do you mean that he's gone?"

"I'm so sorry to tell you this, my lady, but he's disappeared. The head groom tells me he took a horse last night and never returned." She wrung her hands together, the picture of distress. "We've sent men out to search for him, thinking perhaps his horse went lame or..."

Maggie knew the ominous portent of the unspoken portion of Mrs. Keynes' words. Perhaps he'd been thrown from his horse. Perhaps he had chosen to hurt himself as Lady Billingsley had done. Perhaps she would never see her husband again.

"I'm sure he will return in no time, Mrs. Keynes," she forced herself to say through numb lips.

She tried to tell herself it was yet too soon to worry. After all, he could have only been gone for hours, not days. But fear still unfurled in her, a snake waiting to strike.

"Of course, my lady. He's likely to return before we know it." Mrs. Keynes gave her a kindly, almost pitying look. "Word of Lady Billingsley's incident has been sent to her husband at Elton Hall. I expect Lord Billingsley will arrive in the next day or two."

"Thank you, Mrs. Keynes," she said, grateful that the tragedy had at least been dealt with by their capable servants. She imagined Lord Billingsley would want to keep the facts surrounding his wife's death hushed. "Your efficiency in this is most appreciated."

"It is my honor, my lady. Pray forgive a woman in her old age for having a moment of sentimentality." She curtseyed, her countenance remaining pinched as ever.

Maggie suspected they both knew that the housekeeper's attempts to conduct business as ordinary only glossed over the fact that, at least for the foreseeable future, life at Denver Hall would be anything but ordinary. If indeed it ever had been to begin with.

chapter nine

One month later

"MAGGIE, READ YOUR LATEST POEM to Mr. Tobin, do. I fancy he'll love it every bit as much as I did." Nell's eyes danced with mischief as she made her request.

Maggie frowned at her once-again hostess, who had become a true friend to her. She wasn't prepared to share her work yet, and Nell knew it. Especially not to a brilliant poet like Jonathan Tobin. "I'm sure the company would far prefer to hear Mr. Tobin's poetry than mine," she deflected, occupying herself with the drape of her evening gown.

Although she would have once been thrilled to keep company with the likes of the eccentric man who had penned some of the finest contemporary verse, now she felt hollow. Unable to appreciate the world around her. She had sought out Nell in a moment of weakness, too tired of spending her days and nights alone, fraught with fear. The dear woman had thrown an impromptu house party in her honor, inviting every great artist, novelist, and poet she knew. It was a glittering, entertaining group of fine minds, but it was mostly lost upon Maggie.

A fortnight had passed without word from Simon. And then another. She had no way of knowing if he would ever return. She had nowhere to send her letters, no hope of knowing what had become of him. Perhaps she would never know. She'd written every known associate of his. No one knew his whereabouts. None had heard from him.

He was lost to her.

Lady Billingsley's suicide had been her final act of manipulation. And it had worked, for the tentative bridge Maggie and Simon had been building between them had crumbled into ash. She was once again alone.

"My lady?"

She glanced up from her lap, her hard thoughts disrupted by Mr. Tobin's deep, gentle voice. He was indeed a handsome man, she thought, wishing it wasn't lost on her. If only Simon's defection hadn't hurt as much, she would have been stronger. She would have been better off had he never trounced her train that fateful evening, for then she never would have realized her husband was a man she could love.

She shook herself from her troubles, forcing a smile to her lips. "My apologies, Mr. Tobin. I fear I was woolgathering."

"About a dark and storm-tossed sea, it would seem." He leaned closer to her on the settee they shared. "Do share. It simply isn't fair to keep all your troubles to yourself."

She relaxed a bit at his easy teasing. She rather liked him. He was enigmatic but humble, willing to appreciate a female poet in her own right. She found his way wonderfully modern. "I'm certain you don't wish to hear me wax on about the miseries in my life."

"But my dear Lady Sandhurst," he drawled, "miseries make for the best poems. Surely you must know that."

"It's true," Nell added, grinning in that unfettered way she possessed. "Miseries and lost loves were expressly created for the sake of beautiful poetry. Just as men were created for pleasing women."

Mr. Tobin raised a brow at their hostess. "Indeed, Nell? Others would swear it's the other way around."

It was Maggie's glum experience that neither women nor men pleased each other. "How can anyone truly please another?" she asked before she could stop herself.

"They say pleasure can be taught," Mr. Tobin said, his eyes and tone suggesting an entirely naughty meaning hidden behind his polite words and gentlemanly exterior.

He wanted to bed her. The realization struck her with devastating clarity. Once she would have been too naïve to note the subtle hints. But Simon had changed that for her. Now she knew the workings of men and women, but it all just left her feeling empty. She didn't want another man, couldn't think beyond the frantic worry that edged her mind. Where had Simon gone? Where was he now?

"Perhaps," she allowed, "but only if one wants to be taught."

Mr. Tobin inclined his head and retreated a few inches, apparently understanding that she was not a society wife ripe for the plucking. "Eloquently spoken, my lady."

"Shall we have a drawing room game?" Nell asked their small assembly at large then, trying to steer the conversation in a safer direction.

"I bloody well despise games of all sort," offered Mr. Sedgewick, a well-known artist whose talent rivaled that of Burne-Jones. He was as thin as he was tall, his slight frame belied by a raffish air.

Maggie laughed at his response, grateful for the distraction of Nell's house party. At least here she could tamp down the fear, the ache in her heart for a time. Surrounding herself with people wasn't a panacea, but it was something. It was life rather than death.

"I've heard you don't despise chamber games, Sedgewick," ribbed Lord Montford, whose most recent poetry volume had set tongues wagging and books flying from the shelves.

The ladies tittered and the men snickered.

Mr. Sedgewick pressed a hand to his heart, affecting an air of affront. "Truly, Montford, I'm shocked at the suggestion. I fear you've got it all bollixed up, and the man in question is truly Mr. Tobin."

Nell made a dismissive gesture with her hand, ever the imperious hostess. "Gentleman, please do calm yourselves. I'll not have blood drawn in my drawing room unless it's for a worthy cause."

"Pray tell us, Nell. What is your idea of a worthy cause?" Mr. Tobin gave Maggie a rascal's grin. "I've a notion to impress Lady Sandhurst, and if bloodletting is required, I've no compunction."

Oh dear. She supposed she ought to have known that Nell's gathering might take a wicked turn. But she wasn't prepared for flirting and feigned courting. She wished she could stop loving Simon as easily as he'd disappeared. Life would have been much simpler. Easier, for certain.

"Poetry impresses me," she returned. As did a strong man, an honorable man. One willing to fight for her. Simon had not fought. He'd given up and rode away. Perhaps it was better in the end. He never could have loved her, just as she never could have stopped loving him. Love had proven to give her all the joy of a festering wound.

"A recitation is in order," Nell decided. "Jonny, you must recite one of your poems for us if Lady S. shall not."

Mr. Tobin obliged her by standing. "Very well. You win, Nell, just as you always do."

But before he could begin, a commotion sounded just beyond the drawing room. A door flung open. Lady Needham's butler stood there, attempting to bar the path of an unseen foe behind him.

"His lordship, the Marquis of Sandhurst," he announced grimly.

Maggie's head swirled. It couldn't be. Had she heard correctly? A gasp caught in her throat as the butler moved to reveal the man standing behind him. He was tall, slightly disheveled, and most certainly not wearing evening finery. In fact, he was muddied and looked as if he'd just slid from his horse after a two-hour ride. He was thinner than she recalled, his face a trifle more gaunt and covered in whiskers, though handsome as ever.

It was him. Like a ghost, he loomed over them, his green gaze scanning the faces of those in attendance until he reached her. The breath seeped from her lungs. Simon had finally returned. Relief hit her. He was alive.

Nell was the first to react. "Sandhurst, whatever are you doing here?"

"I'm here for my wife," he all but growled.

He had come for her. She wanted to rejoice, run into his arms and kiss him. But she remained seated, wary, watching him. Because he was too late. Far too late in remembering he had a wife. And she had already closed and locked the door inside herself. She wasn't about to give him the key.

Simon was in a grim mood. He'd just had to ride across the countryside in the dark and muck to find Maggie. He was cold and miserable whilst there she sat, looking brilliantly beautiful in a black evening gown with diamonds in her red hair and a man at her side. By God. He knew he'd been gone for a time, but did that give his wife the right to cavort with a gaggle of lecherous poets? Of course it didn't. He was going to rip off one of Tobin's arms and beat him with the bloody thing.

Nell gaped at him as if he'd grown a second head atop his shoulders. He wanted to shake the woman for her interference, the audacity she had to spirit his wife away. He had finally been able to return to Denver House. It had taken him some time, some railing and raging and bottles of whisky. But he had returned because he'd known Maggie waited there for him. He had needed her sweetness, her warm embrace, the comfort of her ready passion and easy caring. Yes, by the time he had fought off the demons chasing him down and the fog of whisky had lifted from his addled mind, he'd known he'd made a terrible mistake in leaving her in the first place. He needed her more than he needed air to breathe.

And then she had not been there. Coming home to Denver House, with its ghosts, had been hell enough. Without Maggie there to welcome him, he'd been lost. At least Mrs. Keynes had known her whereabouts, for he may have well and truly lost his bloody mind if he hadn't discovered where to find her.

So here he was, cooling his heels while the company stared at him in dazed bemusement. He wasn't accustomed to being the odd man out, to making scenes or wearing his emotions on his bloody sleeve, but none of that mattered now. He had come for his wife. He couldn't *not* have her. He needed her. Desperately, he'd come to realize. He needed her to make him laugh again, to shore the loose pieces inside himself. But she remained seated, looking more as if she were about to leap into Tobin's bloody embrace than his.

Damn it all. He'd regained his sanity too late.

"Welcome back, Sandhurst," Nell said at last into the shocked silence that had descended over the drawing room's inhabitants.

"Thank you." The words felt rusty as he said them. He had been alone for many weeks, speaking to no one, lost in grief and blame and drink. "I apologize for intruding on your merriment." *There, that ought to do.* He realized he'd bungled things a bit upon his entrance.

"Think nothing of it," Nell said, smiling oddly at him. "You know I don't stand on ceremony."

Devil take it, did he look that poorly? He supposed he ought to have allowed his man to shave him. Suddenly, the audience felt as if it were going to rob his breath. He wanted to speak to Maggie. Alone. A glance in her direction found her watching him stiffly, her expression indecipherable. She looked more beautiful than he'd ever seen her, every inch the marchioness, from her perfect coiffure to her beautiful evening gown. She was at home here, and for the first time he felt the interloper.

"Lady Sandhurst," he said to her, "might I have a word?"

Christ, he couldn't wait to dispense with the formality, to take her in his arms and bury his face in her soft curls, to kiss her sweet mouth, to lose himself inside her body. He was expecting her compliance—he *needed* her compliance—so when she said something that sounded suspiciously like "no", he was certain he'd misheard her.

"I beg your pardon?" he asked, noting she remained immobile.

"No," she said again, more loudly this time so that there was no mistaking it.

She was denying him, by God. He stared at her, dumbfounded. This was not what he'd imagined. Not at all. She turned her head away, gazing down into her lap as though she couldn't bear to look at him. Tobin smirked at him as if he'd already taken her to bed. Yes, he was going to tear off one of the bastard's limbs, he decided, starting forward.

Perhaps he was indeed a madman. He didn't know who he was any longer, but he did know that he wasn't about to let some fop of a poet run off with his wife. Who the devil did he think he was, sitting so near to her? Why, his bloody thigh was nearly touching her skirts.

"Haven't you ever heard of propriety?" he asked Tobin, infuriated by the man's insufferable air of smugness. "Your poetry is drivel, sir. Complete shite."

He heard a few gasps at his lack of manners. He didn't care. He'd been through nearly all the circles of hell, and he damn well wanted what he'd come here for. He stopped before Maggie, who was once again gazing at him with large violet eyes as if she didn't know who he was and what he was about to do. But he supposed she was in good company, as neither did he.

He held out a hand to her. "Come with me, Maggie."

Tobin stood, puffing out his chest in a barnyard cock style. "Leave the lady alone, Sandhurst."

"Mind your own bloody business, Tobin." He looked back down at Maggie, forcing her to meet his gaze. He didn't want to plead before everyone, but bloody hell he would. "Please, Maggie."

"Whatever it is that you need to tell her can be said right here," Tobin demanded.

The man was an annoying fly buzzing in his ear despite repeated attempts to swat it. "No," he said slowly, turning to his nemesis. "It cannot."

Forget the arm. Before he realized what he was about, he took a lusty swing at Tobin's chin. And connected with a satisfying crunch of knuckles on bone. It smarted, but he was too pleased with his handiwork to pay it much mind. Tobin keeled backward, his eyes rolling.

Maggie gasped and shot to her feet, her eyes snapping with accusatory fire. "You've knocked Mr. Tobin out, you lout."

Well, bloody hell. That wasn't quite the response he'd been hoping for from her either, but it seemed that he didn't have much choice. If he wanted to speak with her alone, there was only one way for it to get done. He bent, pressed his shoulder into her midriff and his arm behind her skirts, and hauled her into the air.

"Put me down at once," she insisted, though her voice was a trifle muffled. She actually had the temerity to strike him on the arse with her fist.

He ignored her. He also ignored the men and women rushing to their feet and trying to stay his progress from the room. He wouldn't allow it. Nothing was stopping him now. He may have completely ruined what little emotion Maggie had once felt for him, but he had come too far to offer an olive branch now.

Nell threw herself in his path, twin patches of scarlet staining her cheeks. "Sandhurst, you cannot carry her off as if you're a Hun."

"Of course I can." He gestured with his free hand to demonstrate the faulty quality of her logic. He already *was* carrying Maggie off, after all.

"Don't be an oaf." She walked backward as she continued to try—unsuccessfully—to halt his movement. "You mustn't hurt her."

"I promise not to hurt her." He frowned at Nell. "You must know I'd never do that."

She studied his face, her expression pinched, before nodding. "Very well. Take her to the study if you must."

Maggie began pummeling his arse anew. "I don't wish to speak with you," she called out.

"You're not," he told her. "You're speaking with the floor." That earned him another swat. Good. Anger was an emotion he could appreciate. With a nod of thanks to Nell, he hauled his wife from the room.

Her husband was a maddening, arrogant, rude, heartless, blustering fool. Maggie pummeled him with all her might as she hung upside down. He'd tossed her over his shoulder as if she were a bundle of rags and carted her about Nell's home as if he were a vagabond about to abscond with the family silver. He wasn't about to take her anywhere, not if she had a say in it. She gave him another sound swat as the blood rushed to her head and dizziness began to settle over her. Her ears hummed.

"Sandhurst, cease this nonsense. You're behaving like a barbarian," she shouted. Dear Lord, the servants were sure to be witnessing this inglorious display. Mortification heated her cheeks. This was not the homecoming she'd envisioned, the one she'd longed for.

"Perhaps I *am* a barbarian." He stalked over a threshold and kicked a door closed at his back.

Good heavens. They were alone. "You certainly are.

Now cease carrying me about and put me down."

As suddenly as he'd snatched her up, he crouched down. Her feet met with the carpeted floor of Nell's study. At last. Heaving a breath, she stood and attempted to shake her dress back into order. Her silk was hopelessly crumpled. Her hands trembled as she righted the fall of her skirts. She was afraid to look up at him, afraid that doing so would ruin her defenses.

She still loved him. That would not change, even if he would never love her in return. She still ached at the way he'd left her, with no word, no warning, not even a change of heart. Not a single letter.

"There you are, on your feet again." An indefinable emotion rendered his voice harsh. "Why the devil won't you look at me?"

She clenched her fingers. "You're thundering at me."

"Bloody hell," he all but yelled, quite proving her point. "I'm doing no such thing."

Ever arrogant, ever Simon. Bracing herself, she gazed up at him at last. "I won't be hollered at, Sandhurst."

"Cease calling me by my title, will you?" He frowned down at her, ferocious in his pique. "I won't have you acting as if we're strangers."

"But we are strangers." She allowed her gaze to run over his face, at once hauntingly familiar and yet also different. He had not eaten well in his absence. His cheeks were nearly sunken, his powerful frame reduced to a wiriness he hadn't before possessed. His hair was longer than ever, his whiskers in desperate need of trimming. He looked, for himself, awful. But yet still so handsome. Still so beloved. "I am sure I never knew you at all, my lord."

His eyes burned into hers, unrelenting. "Have you forgotten just how well you know me?"

His question stirred a month-long-buried ache within her. She didn't want to think about making love with him, for it would reduce her to a puddle of weakness. She couldn't be weak before him now. He had left her, hurt her.

She would not forgive so hastily. If ever she could.

She raised her chin, a small show of defiance. "There are other ways of knowing a man. Those are the ways I speak of, and I certainly never knew you as I'd thought I did."

"I daresay the same could be said for you, madam," he returned, his tone as cold as Wenham Lake ice. "I've scarcely been gone, and already you're cavorting with poets and rakes."

She gasped at his effrontery. "Cavorting? How dare you?"

"What else would you call it, my dear?" He gripped her elbow and dragged her against his body in a punishing grip. "I need to know something. Is Tobin fucking you?"

His crudeness took her by surprise. She had dreamt of Simon returning to her, but she had not dreamt of this cruel stranger with the taunts and the dead eyes. He had come back to her as the same man he'd been in his study that awful night, someone almost frightening to her.

"Of course not," she denied. "How dare you suggest such a horrid thing?"

"I'm a man, darling. I know the ways of the world. Why would you come to Nell's if you weren't seeking a man for your bed once I'd gone?"

The "darling" he'd used for her sounded empty, a mere husk. If she had been hurt before, she was devastated now, crushed by his accusations and his desire to see the worst in her. "I am not Lady Billingsley," she told him fiercely. "Nell has told me everything, you know." It had been a small comfort, learning that the paragon who had taken Simon away from her was, in fact, a mere mortal after all. A deceptive, manipulative mortal who had done her best to ruin that which was not hers. "I would not betray our vows, not after what we shared."

"I'm more than aware that you're nothing like Eleanor." His stare remained hard upon her, his touch hot through the layers of her gown and undergarments. "You speak as if our marriage is at an end. We are inextricably bound to each other, Maggie."

She shook her head, sadness threatening to crush her heart. "We are wed, yes. But there's no reason why we cannot continue to live separate lives just as we've done throughout most of our union."

When she would have extricated herself from his touch, he held fast. "To hell with living separate lives. I forbid it."

She had a notion to knock him over the head with a heavy object. His superciliousness knew no bounds. Had he truly believed she would fling herself into his arms when he had treated her as if she were no more significant to him than a piece of furniture? "You can't return after disappearing for an entire month and expect me to act as if you've never been gone."

"I didn't disappear." His brows snapped together, making him appear more grim than he had before. "I took some time to get my bloody head back into working order."

Did he not realize how agonizingly long the month had been during which she'd had no word, no hope he'd ever come back to her? She searched his gaze, trying to understand him. "You left me without word."

"I needed to, Maggie. After what happened the night of Eleanor's death, I didn't trust myself not to hurt you." The admission appeared to be difficult for him to make. His expression was pained, his voice tinged with something like regret.

But her ice would not melt so easily. "Why could you not have at least left me a letter? Some sort of explanation as to where you'd gone? When or if you'd return? I feared the worst."

"I wasn't thinking properly. Everything was a jumble in my mind, but the last thing I ever wanted was to do you harm. I had to leave as quickly as possible. I didn't trust myself, not after what had happened with Eleanor and not after I practically threw you to the floor in my study."

"I could have helped you," she said, giving voice to the thought that had been a constant, painful reminder during

190

his absence. "You pushed me away when all I wanted was to lessen your suffering."

His grip tightened upon her. "You would have thrown yourself beneath an oncoming carriage for me. I saw it in your eyes that night, and I couldn't bear it. I had already hurt Eleanor, and I couldn't bear to hurt you too."

Had he truly been motivated by fear that he would do her harm? It would explain his abrupt departure, certainly. She wanted to believe him. He looked forlorn, the fierceness of his anger drained from him, replaced by a vulnerability he'd never exhibited.

"Your leaving hurt me more than anything else could have done," she told him quietly, taking pity on him but not enough to relent.

"I'm sorry."

The simple statement shocked her. The Marquis of Sandhurst, the man who had once lived with his mistress in flagrant disregard for their marriage, stood before her, thin and sad, utterly humbled. She never would have thought she'd see the day. Oh, he had apologized to her before, but only for trifling matters, and it had never been so complete, so earnest. In a sense, she was vindicated. In another sense, it was still far too little from him, given far too late.

When she didn't respond, he continued. "I'm sorry I began our marriage as I did. I'm sorry for every hurt I ever inflicted upon you. And I'm sorry as hell that I left you in the manner I did. I have nothing to say for myself, Maggie. I don't blame you if you can't find it in your heart to forgive me. I've done wrong by you, and I know it."

His admission startled her as much as his apology had. She longed to show him a sign of tenderness, to cup his bristled cheek, to draw his mouth down to hers. But she could not. Her heart wouldn't allow her to trust him. Another blow would be too much.

"I'm afraid your apology, while appreciated, is too tardy to be of consequence," she forced herself to say, feeling numb.

"Goddamn it, Maggie, what would you have me do?" He reverted to the stern stranger who had strode through the doors of Nell's drawing room not long before.

"Return to your life just as I shall return to mine," she said, though it was truly the last thing she wanted. It had become a matter of what she must do instead. The choice was a heavy one.

"No." His lips compressed into a firm line. "I don't want my old life. I want a life with you. I want what we were beginning to have, damn it."

So had she. Once. Now she couldn't trust herself with him. She struggled to remove herself from his grip and succeeded this time. After taking a step in retreat, she hugged herself protectively. "If you require me to live with you, I will have no choice but to acquiesce. However, I'm afraid that our month as lovers is all we shall ever have."

"If I require you?" He clenched his jaw. "What the devil do you think I am, some sort of tyrant?"

She stared at him, wishing it were easier, that they could go back and avoid all the misery between them. Wishing she did not have to remain so steadfast in her determination not to allow him back into her life in any way that truly mattered.

"I suppose I should be glad you didn't answer," he said grimly. "Christ, I won't force you into anything you don't wish. You ought to know that much."

"Very well," she said firmly. "Then I want to remain here with Lady Needham for the time being."

"With that reprobate Tobin slobbering all over you like a dog in heat? I think not," he scoffed.

"Sandhurst." She grew frustrated.

"Damn it to hell, call me by my given name," he bit out. "If you want me to fight for you, I shall. But at the least you can cease your pretense of unfamiliarity."

He wanted to fight for her? A foolish spark of hope ignited in her breast. She forced herself to snuff it out. "You've proven to me that it's not a pretense."

He raised a brow, his eyes hot upon her. "Need I remind

you, my love?"

There it was again, a glimpse of the polished gentleman she'd known still hiding beneath his rough exterior. How she wished none of the awfulness had ever happened. If only Lady Billingsley were still alive and well, if only Maggie had never left that day, if only Simon had not followed her, if only they had found love immediately instead of a year too late. The possibilities were innumerable for how they might have never reached this current, desperate crossroads.

But they had.

"I don't require reminding," she told him stoically.

"I think perhaps you do," he returned, closing the distance between them in two strides.

He reached for her, his hands clamping on her waist this time, drawing her body flush against his. She couldn't fight her response. She had missed him, his touch, his kiss, his glittering green eyes, everything about him. Even his arrogance and his bluster. Despite her misgivings, she slid her arms around his lean waist, splaying her palms on his back. He felt different now than he had before, harder, stronger. Her gaze never left his.

With a surprising show of gentleness, he caressed her cheek. She could almost believe that he cared for her. Emotion flickered dark and demanding in his eyes. Perhaps he had missed her as she had missed him. Perhaps he too had suffered in his self-imposed exile.

"My God, Maggie," he groaned.

Before she could manage further thought, he lowered his lips to hers. She kissed him back because she had to, couldn't not, and as much as she knew she shouldn't allow him to breach her defenses, she reveled in the feeling of his mouth on hers. She hugged him to her, her breasts smashed against his chest, wishing she could wrap herself around him, cling to him always. Wishing there wasn't so much melancholy hiding beneath the simmering desire between them.

His tongue swept inside her mouth, toying with hers,

tasting and claiming as she longed for him to do. Her resistance unraveled, a great ball of yarn tossed down a mountainside. He sank his fingers into her hair, undoing her lady's maid's elaborate pinning of earlier in the day. She didn't give a damn. They kissed again and again, neither one of them particularly caring for taking a breath. She remembered. She remembered everything, every glorious moment of being in his bed, in his arms.

Her breasts tightened, her aching sex going wet. She wanted him still. Wanted him more than she wanted to write another poem or take another dance in the rain. Wanted him more than anything, even after all that had transpired between them. Dear heavens. She had to stop the madness before she lost her head and her heart both.

She turned her face away, breaking the seemingly endless kiss. When she would have disentangled herself from his embrace, he held her fast with the hand that still clung to her waist. He pressed his cheek to hers, his whiskers a not entirely unwanted abrasion on her skin. His nose sank into her hair just behind her ear as he inhaled deeply of her scent. She tried not to notice that he held her as if she were precious to him. As if she were necessary.

"I need you." He said this into her ear, his breath hot, his lips grazing the delicate shell. "You haven't any idea just how much."

Maggie squeezed her eyes shut against the tears that threatened to fall. So many emotions coursed through her that she couldn't make sense of what she felt, what she ought to be feeling. Her heart was decidedly at war with her mind. "I cannot do this," she managed to say.

"You can." The hand that had undone her coiffure slid to the nape of her neck, gently caressing. "I won't lose you, not now."

"You already have." She hated herself for saying the words, wished she could recall them the moment they'd been spoken. But it was compulsory, wasn't it? She had to force him away, keep him at a safe distance while she

194

rediscovered her defenses.

He drew his head back and looked down at her, pinning her with his gaze. "I haven't, Maggie. I can feel it in your response to me."

She wished he wasn't so perceptive. "I will always treasure the time we shared, but it's over now and can never be again."

"Look in my eyes and tell me that you feel nothing for me," he demanded, unrelenting in his quest to win the battle if not the war.

She couldn't. He knew it. Her gaze went past his shoulder, focusing on the *escritoire* on the far side of the room. "Please release me."

He surprised her by doing as she asked, removing his embrace and stepping away from her. She felt the absence of his touch immediately. "I'll release you for today. But not for forever. You're mine, and I'm bloody well going to win you back."

Wrapping her arms protectively around herself, she turned to flee the room. She couldn't remain in his presence a moment longer, for if she did, she feared she would lose herself to him again. And surely that would be the greatest mistake she'd ever make, even if resisting him would prove nearly impossible.

chapter ten

WELL, GOOD SWEET CHRIST. He was going to
have to court his wife. Simon hadn't anticipated
that. He had expected—foolishly, he
acknowledged—a warm homecoming, a happy wife who
threw her arms about him and took him promptly to bed.
Instead, he'd been met with a rigid spitfire who refused to
bend even after he'd kissed the bloody hell out of her.

She hadn't been unmoved, of course. He'd felt it in her
response to him, the way her body had melted ever so
slightly into his. He had seen her determination wavering in
her eyes. But she had remained firm in her resolve to keep
him at a distance. In the end, she'd walked out of Nell's
study, slamming the door at her back and leaving him in her
dust with nothing more than a hard cock and a battered
heart.

But he certainly wasn't defeated. His gracious hostess
had given him a chamber, and he'd had a bath and change
of clothes. Admittedly, he should have seen to the two latter
items before striding into Nell's drawing room in a frenzy
of fury. But he had been desperate, his mind whirling with

the implications of Maggie leaving Denver House for Nell's den of iniquity, and he hadn't stopped to think about the vagaries of polite society. It had been foolishness fueled by a lack of sleep, he realized. He'd been stupid and cruel to her, ass that he was.

Now it was a new day, and he was prepared to undo his first disastrous attempt at winning back his wife. He stopped before her chamber door and delivered a series of loud knocks. He'd learned from Nell that Maggie had been hiding herself away from the company since his arrival the previous day. She hadn't been to breakfast. It was time for her to emerge from her cocoon.

The door opened to reveal her lady's maid's plain, frowning visage. "My lord?"

"Is Lady Sandhurst within?" he asked, trying not to allow his irritation to show. He felt as if the woman were acting the part of a guard at the castle doors.

The maid blinked. "I'm afraid Lady Sandhurst isn't receiving visitors."

Giving her a frown of his own, he caught the door in his hand lest she attempt to close it on him. "I'm afraid that I'm not a visitor. I'm her husband, and I require an audience with her at once."

"I'm sorry, my lord." The woman's expression went from displeased to anxious. "She's given me express instructions not to allow anyone to enter."

"Well, where the devil is she?" Christ, this was bordering on ridiculous. He didn't appreciate being treated like a vagabond at his wife's bloody chamber door.

"She's at her bath," the maid responded.

The simple sentence brought a host of sensual images to mind. Maggie sleek and glistening, her breasts bare, her glorious red hair down about her creamy shoulders. He imagined her soaping herself with a cloth, his hand replacing hers, imagined rubbing her stiff nipples. Oh bloody hell. He was getting hard already. He forced his mind back to the moment.

"Excellent," he snapped, putting his shoulder to the door and creating enough leverage to push the unwanted female aside. He stepped over the threshold and into Maggie's chamber.

"But my lord—"

"Your services are no longer needed," he interrupted her smoothly. "Her ladyship shall ring if you're required."

He could tell the instant she knew she'd been thoroughly routed, for her eyes lowered to the floor and her face went ashen. She had been torn between loyalty to her mistress and the knowledge that he was her employer, he knew. He had won. She dipped into a curtsy. "Yes, my lord."

Simon waited for her to hastily exit the chamber before turning to the closed door that undoubtedly led to a bathing chamber. And his naked wife. His cock twitched. He forced himself to rein in his desire for her. She needed time. Wooing. He had hurt her again, and he understood that. He damn well couldn't rush into the room, pull her warm, slippery body from the tub, bend her over, and sink deep inside her sweet cunny. No matter how much he wanted to.

No.

Winning Maggie back would require far more tact and control than that. If he even could win her back. The unwanted thought struck him like a lead ball to the gut. He'd meant what he said. He couldn't lose her. He hadn't managed to make sense of much in the time he'd been gone other than to realize that he couldn't be without her. He needed her smile, her silliness, her passion, her poetry, and every other dizzying American bit of her.

He crossed the chamber and opened the door keeping him from her, taking care to be as quiet as possible. The tub was large and deep, dominating the small tiled room. Her back was to him, her hair not unbound as he had imagined but piled high atop her head. He took in the graceful sweep of her neck and shoulders. Her bare arms stretched over the lip of the tub on either side of her. In the silence, he recognized the hushed sound of her breathing.

She was asleep. Simon crossed the threshold, thinking perhaps it was a boon. After all, if he took her by surprise, she wouldn't have the chance to throw her soap at his head. When he reached the tub, he sank to his knees behind her. The delicious, floral scent of her bathwater reached him. Roses. He pressed his face into her hair, inhaling. He'd never get tired of her sweet scent. Unable to stop himself, he ran his palms over her bare shoulders, down her arms, stopping when he reached her hands. He tangled his fingers in hers as he kissed her ear. No one had ever made him feel as passionately as Maggie did.

No one would.

She shifted suddenly, jolted awake by the contact, and turned to face him. Water sloshed over the side of the tub, some of it landing on his boots, but he didn't care. The expression on her face flitted from frightened to taken aback.

"Simon?" She sounded breathless as she eyed him with undisguised trepidation. "Where is Osborn? What are you doing in here?"

He almost smiled at her quick round of questions. The lady was not immune, that much was apparent. Good. His gaze traveled hungrily over her face, appreciating the undeniable beauty she possessed. She was rare, his Maggie, like a wildflower bright and defiant amongst the weeds.

"That's rather a lot of questions," he remarked slowly, wanting to touch her again but not wishing to make her retreat any farther than she'd already gone, to the opposite end of the tub.

"It's only two," she said, licking her luscious lips in her obvious nervousness.

"Three." He ignored his knees as they began to ache from remaining so long upon the hard floor.

Her brows snapped together. "Did you come here to quibble over arithmetic?"

Ever stubborn, his Maggie. "Of course not."

"Then perhaps you'd care to answer one of my three

questions," she rejoined.

And ever the quick wit, even nude and gorgeous, attempting to shield her breasts from his gaze. Too late. He'd already caught a mouthwatering glimpse of her pretty nipples. "I came here to ask you if you'd like to accompany me on a ride," he said honestly. "But when I arrived, you were at your bath."

"I haven't any idea why Osborn would allow you in here." Her vibrant eyes narrowed in suspicion. "What have you done with her?"

He would have smiled were the tension between them not so deep. "I've dismissed her."

"You had no right to do so. I still have need of her assistance." Twin patches of red marred her cheeks as her ire grew.

"I'll assist you," he said helpfully. "I shall do a most thorough job of applying soap to your breasts."

She stared. "Are you making a jest?"

Well, Christ, he supposed he was. Fancy that. Being back in her presence did things to him. Warmed his cold heart. Made him feel as if he weren't so unbearably alone in this life of his. He cleared his throat, wondering if he'd truly gone mad in the wake of Eleanor's death or if it was that Maggie somehow cast aside everything he'd ever thought he'd known about himself. Perhaps a bit of both, he decided.

What the devil had she said? He was having difficulty focusing with her breasts barely shielded by her arms and her luscious legs visible beneath the water. Ah, yes. "I would be happy to help you," he offered again.

"That's not necessary," she denied quickly. "I can do for myself."

She didn't want him to touch her, he realized. He hoped that it was because she couldn't trust herself and not because she despised him. He knew he had never treated her with the respect and consideration she deserved. He had hurt her too many times to hope she could forgive him, but he was a selfish bastard and he was willing to try to earn her forgiveness anyway.

"Nonsense," he countered. "Tell me what assistance you need, and I shall but give it."

She pursed her lips together, looking as if she smelled something rotten in the chamber. "I need you to leave."

Certainly not the answer he'd been seeking. He'd had enough of the peculiar game they played. He stood, deciding to press his advantage after all, and then walked to the opposite end of the tub. She stared up at him with wide eyes, but didn't slide away from him immediately as he'd thought she might. A small victory. He sank to his knees so that they were once more gaze to gaze. She was near to him, close enough to kiss.

"I'm not leaving," he said at last. "It would seem I've done rather enough of that."

"Yes," she agreed softly, "you have."

If he'd felt like a bastard before, he felt like a criminal now. He needed to explain to her, if he could. He didn't entirely understand himself, but he couldn't bear for her to think the awful muddle he'd created of his life was in any way her fault. "It was never because of you."

She studied him in that way she had, seeing straight through him. "Thank you for admitting that."

"I don't deny that I've been a horrid husband to you," he continued, knowing that he would have to lose his pride to regain her. He was at fault, and he bloody well knew it. "I should never have abandoned you when we first wed. If I hadn't, I would have seen that what I'd been seeking was right before me."

"You were seeking Lady Billingsley," she reminded him tartly.

He inclined his head, acknowledging that he deserved her every bitter barb and more. "I thought I'd found a woman I could love. But I'd found a broken woman with a shallow soul, a woman who couldn't love me because she'd never loved herself first."

Maggie remained unmoved, her face impassive. "What has this to do with me?"

"It has everything to do with you." He couldn't restrain himself any longer then, reaching out to brush a fallen curl from her cheek. His fingers lingered on her soft, warm skin. She didn't shrug away as he'd expected her to. He forced himself to continue. "When Eleanor decided to return to Billingsley, I thought I'd lost the only woman I could ever love. But then I trounced the train of a beautiful woman at Nell's ball, and I realized I was wrong."

He stopped, almost afraid to continue. He hadn't allowed himself to think it, to ponder the notion during his month away. But now that he was back in her presence, it was all too clear to him. He loved Maggie. He loved the poet, the temptress, the violet-eyed, flame-haired wanton who brought him to his knees and made him dance in the rain. He loved that she'd been kind to him when she shouldn't have, that she'd cared enough to want to hear his laughter, that she was without artifice, at home in her skin.

Damn it all, he hadn't intended to do things this way, to kneel before her on a floor that was surely a form of torture, to open himself for scorn or rejection. He'd wanted to take her riding, flirt with her, perhaps steal a kiss. But she was naked in the bath, more glorious than he'd imagined, and he couldn't seem to stop from making a complete fool of himself. He stared at her, afraid to say more, afraid not to.

Her eyes were wide, trained upon him. "What are you saying?"

"I'm saying," he began, only to pause and take a steadying breath. Christ, he'd never intended to reveal so much to her. Not today, perhaps not ever. "I'm saying that I love you, Maggie."

Once again, she didn't produce the sort of response he may have hoped. She shook her head, her expression turning sad. "No you don't. I'm not certain you know what love is."

The bloody hell he didn't. He stiffened. "Of course I

know what love is."

"You think you know what love is," she countered. "Love most certainly doesn't involve flitting from woman to woman and disappearing for an entire month, leaving the woman you profess to love to suppose you've gone forever."

They were back to his leaving. A stalemate. Devil take it, didn't she see he'd had no choice? When she'd fallen to the floor in his study, he'd been disgusted with himself. It had been as if he'd transformed into a monster before his eyes. He'd been out of his mind with guilt, drink, and grief, and he hadn't been certain of what he'd do. Given time and distance, his sanity had returned. He was in a far better place now. He'd even shaved, by God.

"I had to leave," he repeated. "I couldn't trust myself."

Her lips compressed in a stern line that told him she was vastly displeased. "You could have left word. You could have returned the next day. You did neither."

He supposed he shouldn't expect her to understand. Christ, he didn't understand himself. All he knew was that he'd been lost in his grief and his guilt. "I'm sorry. I cannot say it any other way. I was not myself."

Her expression softened ever so slightly, but she maintained her defensive pose, her arms crossed over her delicious breasts. "I know it was difficult for you, losing the woman you loved."

"It was a tragedy." He repeated the only answer he'd been able to find in his self-imposed search. "It never should have happened."

"No, it should not have," she said quietly. "But it did, and we must now forever live with its mark on our hearts. On yours especially."

It was time, he realized, to tell her the truth he'd only recently uncovered himself. "Maggie, I haven't loved Eleanor in some time. In truth, I'm not certain I ever did. She was a way to keep from feeling so bloody alone." He paused, trying to find the proper words. If there were any.

"Then what was I?" she asked, her voice hushed, eyes watching him.

He wanted to look away but could not. Maggie was so much more to him, more than he ever could have imagined she would be. More, certainly, than he had ever wanted her to be. Hell, he'd never intended to consummate their marriage, and now he bloody well couldn't live without her.

He swallowed. "Initially, you were a necessity. Then, you were a beautiful stranger I couldn't help but make love to. Finally, you became something intoxicating, something I knew I ought not to have but that I couldn't resist. Like whisky. But in all the time we spent together, you were one thing above all others."

"What?"

"The woman I love," he told her again, more determined now that he'd already said it to her once. And he meant the words, damn it. Meant them as he'd never meant them in his life. "My wife. A woman who made me dance in the rain, who made me laugh, who taught me that life need not be so very serious after all or so very lonely." He reached out to her again, cupping her cheek. He was heartened when she didn't shrug away. The scented water of her bath clung to the air between them, teasing his senses. "Tell me you feel nothing at all for me, Maggie. I asked you yesterday, and now I ask you again."

She was silent for a beat, still staring at him as if she couldn't be sure what to expect. "You know I cannot tell you that. Of course I have feelings for you. It is simply that I can't afford to have them. The price is too great."

Relief blossomed in his chest. She couldn't deny she still cared. He had hope, then, that if he pressed her, the wall she'd been doing her best to build between them could be broken.

"What is the price of love?" he asked, sliding his hand to the nape of her neck and drawing her face closer to his ever so slowly.

"Dear." She shook her head. "Please don't, Simon. It

hurts too much."

But he couldn't. He couldn't shake the feeling that stopping now would cost him the one thing he wanted most. Her. And he couldn't bear that great a loss. Not now, not ever. "I can't stop," he said honestly. "Push me away if you must."

He knew instinctively that she would not, that she couldn't resist him any more than he could her. It was there in her eyes. She was at the edge of a cliff, needing just another tiny nudge to throw her off balance. He had to win her back, by God. There could be no losing her. And how better to win Maggie the poet than with words?

"'Ask nothing more of me, sweet'." He recited the lines of the poem that had been plaguing him for days. "'All I can give you I give. Heart of my heart, were it more, more would be laid at your feet'."

Unshed tears glistened in her vivid eyes. "'Love that should help you to live, song that should spur you to soar'," she returned, her voice rather shaky. "Algernon Charles Swinburne."

He inclined his head, a small smile quirking his lips. He was aware he'd never possessed a great deal of levity. But Maggie had changed him. She made him smile, made him laugh, brightened his dreary life with her fiery hair and stubborn nature, her beautiful body and equally beautiful soul.

"You know the poem as well," he remarked, shaken by the powerful emotions churning through him. He had never expected to feel so much, to be moved by the simple act of a poem's recitation.

A small, answering smile blossomed on her luscious mouth. "I do."

"I'm giving you all I can," he told her. "I'm not an angel by any man's standards, but I do love you. I want to make amends for everything." He didn't know what else to do, save drag her from the bath and take her to bed. That particular idea held increasing appeal. He shifted as the thought of a naked, wet Maggie beneath him sent a wave of hunger to his rigid cock. No, this time was different. As much as he wanted to seduce her, he also wanted her to believe him. While their passion was undeniable, she meant far more to him than lovemaking ever could. She had become a necessary part of his life, and he'd be damned to hell rather than give her over to some slobbering rake like Tobin.

Maggie's mind was as jumbled as a seamstress's back room after a fire. She thought of another of Swinburne's poems, this one decidedly dark. *Dead love, by treason slain, lies stark.* She felt stark, trapped between the equal thralls of protecting herself and giving herself to Simon. She stared at him, his handsome face so unbearably near to hers, falling into the compelling green of his eyes. She wanted him with a fervency that shook her even now.

"You can make amends by ringing for my lady's maid," she told him, clinging to her battle defenses as best she could.

"Damn it, woman," he growled, "why must you insist on being so bloody stubborn?"

He was difficult to resist ordinarily, but for some reason, when he grew blustery, he melted her heart. She loved him, after all. Had never stopped. "I'm afraid," she admitted quietly, aware that her bath had long since grown cold and that she was naked and vulnerable before him. He could easily whisk her from the tub, lay her on the bed and persuade her with his clever hands and mouth. But he had not, and she rather admired his restraint.

"Afraid?" He appeared genuinely puzzled at her response. "Afraid of what, darling?"

She hesitated, fearing she was about to reveal too much to him and yet unwilling not to say the words clamoring to be heard. "Afraid that you shall leave me again."

"I'm not leaving," he vowed. "Not today or ever again. You're bloody well stuck with me, my love."

His love. Was she? She thought back over the time they'd had together. He had indulged her whims, had comforted her, listened to her, had shown her pleasure. He had chased after her that fateful day too. She realized suddenly that she had to know something now before she could proceed any further.

"I must know something, Simon," she said, almost hating to ask for what the answer might be.

He caressed her cheek with the pad of his thumb, warming her with the simple touch. "What is it?"

"You told me that you regretted chasing after me the day Lady Billingsley died." Perhaps it was selfish of her to broach the topic. Certainly, it was selfish of her to need to know. But she couldn't help it. "Do you still? Do you wish you had allowed me to leave you had it meant sparing Lady Billingsley?"

He stared at her, and she knew he had not expected the question. His expression was unreadable. She wished at once that she could redo the moment, that she had not dared to ask when she likely didn't want to hear the answer. And then came the deep rumble of his voice, one word only.

"No."

She blinked, certain at first that she'd misheard him. Her foolish heart swelled with hope. "You don't?"

"No," he said again. "Eleanor made her choice, and I've made mine. 'Tis you, Maggie. It will always be you."

Always.

The admission was what she needed to hear from him, and once again she supposed it was down to the poet in her. Words were ever the most potent lure. Perhaps she was a fool for believing in him, but she did. His expression was unguarded, his feelings for her worn on his expensive sleeve. There was no doubt he meant what he said. After all, Simon wasn't a devil-tongued charmer. He was serious, blunt to a fault, and hopelessly arrogant.

207

But he could humble himself before the wife he'd never wanted. He had loved her enough to return to her, even after the horrors of Lady Billingsley's death. He had followed her, again and again. And she loved him all the more for it.

Before she could contemplate the wisdom of her actions, she threw her arms around his neck and pulled him to her for a kiss. Water sloshed all over his riding clothes, splashing on his boots and the floor about him. She didn't care. His mouth on hers was heaven.

It had been far too long, and this unfettered embrace was like coming home after a difficult journey. She melted into him with a sigh, opening to his claiming tongue. He broke their kiss to scoop her from the tub with an unabashed whoop. She was nude and dripping, completely soaking his riding clothes. He didn't seem to mind as he stalked back into her chamber to lower her gently to the bed.

She waited for him, watching as he hastily discarded his wet garments. How she loved him, she thought as her gaze traveled over his dark hair to his beautifully masculine face to his broad chest. She almost didn't dare believe that this time he was well and truly hers. That he loved her.

But it was there in the glittering brilliance of his gaze, and the realization quite took her breath. As impossible as it seemed, the Marquis of Sandhurst, the man whose heart had infamously belonged to another, was lovestruck.

By her.

This time, his love was for his unwanted American bride, plain old Margaret Emilia Desmond.

Maggie smiled, opening her arms to him as he joined her on the bed. His body was hard and delicious, pressing into her soft curves precisely where she wanted him. His large, knowing hand swept over her waist, stopping at her hip. With his other arm, he propped himself up, looking down upon her.

"Do you forgive me, Maggie?"

His wicked fingers dipped into her slick folds then, momentarily robbing her of breath as a spike of desire shot through her. She arched into him, wanting more. "Of course I do." How could she not, when he had so plainly bared the darkest part of himself for her to see? She thought again of the glimpses she'd seen of the lonely boy he'd been, and her heart ached. She wanted to make him whole, to erase that part of his past. To fill his life with so much love and laughter that he no longer felt alone.

He lowered his head so that their foreheads nearly touched, his hot breath fanning her lips. "Bloody hell, woman. You'll be the undoing of me."

Feeling bold, she reached between them to where his cock was rigid and insistent against her belly. She curled her fingers around his length, stroking him as she'd come to learn he liked. "I certainly hope so," she returned, gratified when she heard his sharp intake of breath. She ran her thumb slowly over the head of his cock. "For you have already become the undoing of me."

"Have I, my love?" He dropped a lingering kiss on her ready mouth.

When he would have pulled away, she pressed him to her with her free hand, opening her mouth for his tongue. An answering surge of pleasure hit her, making her hungry for more. To claim him. To be claimed by him. She was undeniably his, and she wanted him to take her hard and fast, to make her explode with her climax and wash away the last remnants of pain between them.

To make a fresh beginning.

She wanted to show him just how much she wanted him, how deeply she cared. Maggie broke away from the kiss and pushed at his shoulders, urging him gently to his back. He stared at her, comprehension dawning in his vivid eyes.

"Maggie, you needn't."

She smiled at him before lowering her head to press a path of kisses down over his chest, to his lean stomach. When she reached his cock, she kissed slowly down his length. His strained groan told her she was giving him the same pleasure he so freely gave her.

"But I must." She took the tip of him into her mouth.

Her jerked against her, his hand settling into her hair as another moan left him. She licked, sucked, loving the taste of him, the musky scent that was innately his. At his guidance, she took him deep into her throat.

"Enough." He gripped her arms to pull her back up against him. "I want to come inside you, darling, not in your mouth."

His words sent a wave of desire over her. He caught her to him for another ravenous kiss. Their tongues tangled. He rolled her to her back, his hands sliding down to her cunny. He played a lazy rhythm over her sensitive nub, working her into a frenzy. She gripped his cock again, imagining it inside her, wanting him so badly she ached with it. He sank a finger deep inside her, the small invasion a decadent tease for the one she truly longed for.

Simon broke the kiss, his breathing as ragged as hers. "Are you ready for me, darling?"

"Yes," she hissed on a quick exhalation. When he removed his fingers, she guided him to her. A tip of her hips and one swift thrust from him, and he was inside her. She reveled in the sensation, the overwhelming pleasure of it all.

He hooked her legs around his waist, and they both gave in to the abandon of their desire, straining against each other, hands in each other's hair. He thrust into her repeatedly, lowering his head to suck a nipple into his mouth. She was mindless, heedless to anything now but having more of him, all of him, faster, harder. She climaxed suddenly and violently, clenching down on his cock in a series of shuddering spasms.

He groaned, rocked into her and spent his seed. The hot spurt of him within her was enough to have her shuddering again. He lowered himself over her completely, his big body pinning hers to the bed as he gave her another lingering kiss. As the world slowly returned to normal, she clutched him to her, holding on to the love she'd never thought she'd find. He was unbearably precious to her, this stranger she'd crossed an ocean to marry. At long last, he was truly hers.

She realized that in the flurry of their lovemaking, she'd forgotten to tell him. It struck her that he hadn't required it of her, that he had been willing to love her without her loving him in return. The selfish lord she'd married had somehow become a selfless husband. The words she'd withheld from him rose past the lump of happy tears in her throat.

"I love you," she said into the sated silence that had fallen between them.

He raised his head to look down at her, cupping her face with a hand. "You do?"

The unadulterated hope in his voice was enough to make her inner dam burst. The tears broke free, slipping down her cheeks as she smiled up at him. "I do."

"Then why the bloody hell are you crying, my darling?" he demanded in typical, blustery Simon fashion.

She laughed then, marveling at the wonderful way life had of working out for the best when she'd least expected it. "Because you've made me a very happy woman."

"And you've made me the happiest man in England." He dropped another swift kiss on her mouth before rolling to his side and holding her tightly against him.

Sated and overwhelmed with love and joy, Maggie snuggled back against him, folding her arms over his. His heart thrummed deep and steady against her back, his cock nestled against her derriere. This, she thought to herself, was surely heaven.

The rumble of his voice startled her. "Maggie?"

She looked down at his possessive embrace over her bare midriff, finally feeling free from all the ghosts of their pasts. "Yes?"

"Do you think you would mind terribly saying it just one more time?"

She grinned. Yes, her blustery marquis had been tamed

indeed. "I love you."

"By God." An answering smile was in his tone. "I don't think I'll ever grow tired of hearing that. I love you, my wild and wonderful American. And if you ever leave me again, I'll bloody well chase you down and tie you to my bed."

Maggie turned in his arms, giving him another long kiss. "I'll hold you to that promise, my lord. For if you ever leave me again, I shall do exactly the same."

He threw back his head and laughed as she'd never heard him laugh before. "I wouldn't expect anything different, my love."

epilogue

"**D**ARLING."

With a sigh, Maggie looked up from the poem she'd been attempting to write. Ten of the fifteen lines she'd penned thus far had been summarily scratched off. Some days, poetry came easily to her. Most days, she needed to scrabble and claw for it.

Simon sauntered into the library in his riding clothes, looking debonair and sinfully handsome at the same time. Her heart gave a great pang of love. Each day that had passed between them in the months since he'd come to her at Nell's had only brought them closer together, making their love stronger. She didn't think she could ever grow tired of seeing his gorgeous head lying on the pillow each morning.

"How was your morning ride?" she asked, grateful for the interruption. She'd been writing a great deal of poetry recently, her love for the art renewed along with her happiness. She hoped to publish another volume one day soon, and Simon had been wonderfully encouraging to her.

"Most invigorating, but I do wish you'd joined me." He

strode across the room, eating up the distance between them in no time.

He took her hands in his and pulled her to her feet. These days, she appreciated the help, given the relative roundness of her stomach. "You know I can't properly ride in my condition."

Simon pulled her close for a hungry kiss before winking down at her. "As long as you continue to ride me, I shan't complain."

She tried to suppress a smile at his wicked words but couldn't maintain a properly staid façade. "You're a devil of a man," she said without heat, "speaking to me so."

"You like when I'm wicked," he returned with ease. "I can tell by the way your eyes turn that lovely shade of dark violet, and the way you try to frown at me but really cannot stop smiling."

He knew her too well. She inclined her head, conceding the point. "Very well. I suppose I'm a book too easily read."

His hands tightened on her waist, or what remained of it given the ever-growing babe inside her. "Not easily read, my love. It is simply that I know all the best parts by heart."

She leaned into him for another kiss, thinking that her dratted poem could certainly wait. Why had she decided to pen something about love, anyway? Each time she attempted to write about the man she loved, she either ended up turning into a quivering blob of sobs or throwing the entire thing away. She supposed that sometimes, the most wondrous aspects of life could never be properly written.

"You're frowning," he said, dropping another peck on her waiting lips before straightening again. He reached into his jacket and extracted a letter, handing it to her. "Perhaps this shall make you smile again."

Her curiosity piqued, Maggie took the letter from his hands and scanned its contents. Shock made her nearly drop it from her numb fingers. It couldn't be. How could he have done this without her knowing? "What have you done,

Simon?"

He grinned at her. "I sent away some of your poems to Livingston Press. I felt it was bloody well time for the world to once again see your work."

He was ever surprising her, this husband of hers. She hadn't known he'd had such a scheme in mind. He'd never said a word. The glowing language of the letter returned to her, buoying her flagging spirits. "And they want to publish a full volume?" She'd never dreamed of such a possibility. After all, it had been too long since she'd published a word, and even then, it had only been because of her father's influence.

"The publisher says he would be thrilled to print another M.E. Desmond book. Indeed, he considers it quite a rare find, for as you know, the mysterious Desmond has only written but the one volume." That penetrating gaze of his was trained upon her, gauging her reaction. "Are you happy?"

She threw her arms about him, laughing when her ungainly stomach wouldn't allow her to embrace him as she wanted. "Happy? I'm utterly thrilled. I can't believe you did this for me."

He caught her up in a nearly crushing embrace. "Much as I'd like to, I can't keep you all to myself, now can I?"

How she loved him. If she wasn't careful, she'd turn into a watering pot all over him. Heaven knew she'd done it a great deal since becoming with child. "Thank you, Simon."

"It is I who must thank you," he said against her ear.

"What must you thank me for?" she asked, puzzled.

He drew back to gaze lovingly down at her. His hands went to her belly, hidden cleverly in the layers of her skirts. "For loving me in spite of myself. For giving me the family I've always wanted. Finding a publisher for your poetry is the least I can do after all you've done for me, Maggie. You've made me whole again."

"No," she said softly, putting her hands over his as their baby gave a kick. She thought of all she'd left in New York and just how much she'd gained in England. She never could have imagined just how complete she'd feel in Simon's arms. "We've made each other whole again."

As he took her back into his embrace for another passionate kiss, she knew instinctively that the best was yet to come.

Dear Reader,

Thank you for reading *Her Lovestruck Lord*! I hope you enjoyed the second book in the Wicked Husbands series. Fiercely independent, dazzlingly beautiful, and married to handsome scoundrels, these American heiresses are ready to turn the tables on the insufferable English lords they've wed. What happens when their wicked husbands start falling for the wives they never thought they wanted? Corsets come off, bed chambers ignite, the passion sizzles, and more than one stubborn English rake gets reformed by love.

If you'd like to keep up to date with my latest releases, sign up for my email list at:

http://www.scarsco.com/contact_scarlett.

As always, please consider leaving an honest review of *Her Lovestruck Lord*. All reviews are greatly appreciated!

If you'd like a preview of Book Three in the Wicked Husbands series, do read on.

Until next time,

Scarlett

Her Reformed Rake

Wicked Husbands Book Three

She refuses to behave...

American heiress Daisy Vanreid prides herself on bucking convention at every turn. Equally well-known for her beauty and her rebellious nature, she has no qualms about entrapping the notorious Duke of Trent to avoid marriage to the aging aristocrat her father chose for her. But once she becomes Trent's duchess, he disappears. Now, she's on a mission to stir up enough scandal to force his return.

He refuses to be chained...

An elite spy, Sebastian, the Duke of Trent, is on a mission of a different variety, and his wild, trousers-wearing wife is creating the sort of distraction he can't afford. He returns to London to take the minx in hand, but the woman he married as a pawn proves a wilier opponent than any enemy of the Crown. His inconvenient attraction to her complicates an already tangled web of danger and deceit.

Love is the most perilous risk of all...

When Daisy uncovers Sebastian's secret life, she's swept into his world of intrigue and straight into his arms. Together, they become locked in a battle of passion and wits that they can only survive by trusting each other.

chapter one

London, 1881

*T*HE BRASH AMERICAN CHIT HAD NOTHING to
do with dynamite. Sebastian would wager his life
upon it. He watched her from across the crush
of the Beresford ball as she flirted with the Earl of Bolton.
He was trained to take note of every detail, each subtle
nuance of his quarry's body language.

Studying her wasn't an unpleasant task. She was
beautiful. A blue silk ball gown clung to her petite frame,
emphasizing the curve of her waist as it fell in soft waves
around lush hips down to a box-pleat-trimmed train. Pink
roses bedecked her low décolletage, drawing the eye to the
voluptuous swells of her breasts. Her golden hair was
braided and pinned at her crown, more roses peaking from
its coils. Diamonds at her throat and ears caught the light,
twinkling like a beacon for fortune hunters. She wore her
father's obscene wealth as if it were an advertisement for
Pears soap.

Everything about her, from the way she carried herself,
to the way she dressed, to her reputation, bespoke a woman

who was fast. Trouble, yes. But not the variety of trouble that required his intervention.

She tapped Bolton's arm with her fan and threw back her head in an unabashed show of amusement. Her chaperone—a New York aunt named Caroline—was absent from the elegant panorama of gleaming lords and ladies. Dear Aunt Caroline had a weakness for champagne and randy men, and provided with sufficient temptation, she disappeared with ease.

Sebastian wasn't the only one who was aware of the aunt's shortcomings, however. He'd been watching Miss Daisy Vanreid for weeks. Long enough to know that she didn't have a care for her reputation, that she'd kissed Lords Wilford and Prestley but not yet Bolton, that she only smiled when she had an audience, and that she waited for her aunt to get thoroughly soused before playing the devoted coquette.

As he watched, Miss Vanreid excused herself from Bolton, hips swaying with undeniable suggestion as she sauntered in the direction of the lady's withdrawing room. Sebastian cut through the revelers, following her. Not because he needed to—tonight would be the last that he squandered on chasing a spoiled American jade—but because he knew the Earl of Bolton.

His damnable sense of honor wouldn't allow him to stand idly by as the foolish chit was ravished by such a boor. Wilford and Prestley were young bucks, scarcely any town bronze. Manageable. Bolton was another matter entirely. Miss Vanreid was either as empty-headed as she pretended or her need for the thrill of danger had dramatically increased. Either way, he would do his duty and by the cold light of morning, she'd no longer be his responsibility.

He exited the ballroom just in time to see a blue train disappearing around a corner down the hall. Damn it, where the hell was the minx going? The lady's withdrawing room was in the opposite direction. His instincts told him to follow, so he did, straight into a small, private drawing room. He stepped over the threshold and closed the door at his back, startled to find her alone rather than in Bolton's embrace. She stood in the center of the chamber, tapping her closed fan on the palm of her hand, her full lips compressed into a tight line of disapproval. Her chin tipped up in defiance. He detected not a hint of surprise in expression.

"Your Grace." She curtseyed lower than necessary, giving him a perfect view of her ample bosom. When she rose with equal grace, she pinned him with a forthright stare. "Perhaps you'd care to explain why you've been following me for the last month."

Not empty-headed, then. A keen wit sparkled in her lively green gaze. He regarded her with a new sense of appreciation. She'd noticed him. No matter. He relied upon his visibility as a cover. He flaunted his wealth, his lovers. He played the role of seasoned rake. Meanwhile, he observed.

And everything he'd observed thus far suggested that the vixen before him needed to be put in her place. She was too bold. Too lovely. Too blatantly sexual. Everything about her was designed to make men lust. Lust they did. She'd set the *ton* on its ear. Rumor had it that her cunning Papa was about to marry her off to the elderly Lord Breckly. She appeared to be doing her best to thwart him.

He fixed her with a haughty look. "I don't believe we've been introduced."

She gave a soft, throaty laugh that sent a streak of unwanted heat to his groin. "You mean to rely on your fine English manners now when you've been watching me all this time? How droll, but I already know who you are just as you must surely know who I am."

His gaze traveled over her thoroughly, inspecting her in a way that was meant to discomfit. Perhaps he'd underestimated her, for in the privacy of the chamber, she seemed infinitely more wily than he'd credited. "I watch everyone."

Tap went her fan against her palm again, the only outward sign of her vexation aside from her frown. "As do I, Your Grace. You aren't nearly as subtle as you must suppose yourself. I must admit I found it rather odd that you'd want to spy upon my tête-à-tête with Viscount Wilford."

Miss Vanreid was thoroughly brazen, daring to refer to her ruinous behavior as though nothing untoward had occurred. It struck him that she'd known he watched her and had deliberately exchanged kisses with Prestley and Wilford, perhaps even for his benefit. She seemed determined to bait him.

He crossed the chamber, his footfalls muted by thick carpeting. Lady Beresford's tastes had always run to the extravagant. He didn't stop until he nearly touched her skirts. Still she held firm, refusing to retreat. Some inner demon made him skim his forefinger across the fine protrusion of her collarbone. Just a ghost of a touch. Awareness sparked between them. Her eyes widened almost imperceptibly.

"Wilford and Prestley are green lads." He took care to keep his tone bland. "Bolton is a fox in the henhouse. You'd do best to stay away from him."

She swallowed and he became fascinated by her throat, the way her ostentatious diamonds moved faintly, gleaming even in the dim light. "I'm disappointed you think me as frumpy and witless as a hen. Thank you for your unnecessary concern, Your Grace, but foxes don't frighten me. They never have."

Her bravado irritated him. Even her scent was bold, an exotic blend of bergamot, ambergris, and vanilla carrying to him and invading his senses. He should never have touched her, for now he couldn't seem to stop, following her collarbone to the trim on her bodice, the pink roses so strategically placed. He didn't touch the roses. No. His finger skimmed along the fullness of her creamy breast. Her skin was soft, as lush as a petal.

"You do seem to possess an absurd predilection for your ruination, Miss Vanreid."

She startled him by stepping nearer to him, her skirts billowing against his legs. "One could say the same for you. Why do you watch, Your Grace? Does it intrigue you? Perhaps you would like a turn."

Jesus. Lust slammed through him, hot and hard and demanding. He'd never, in all his years of covert operations, gotten a stiff cock during an investigation. Thanks to the golden vixen before him, he had one now. While he'd already decided she was not involved in the plot, he was still on duty until he reported back to Carlisle in the morning. He wasn't meant to be attracted to Daisy Vanreid, who was not at all as she seemed.

Still, he found himself flattening his palm over her heart, absorbing its quick thump that told him she wasn't as calm as she pretended. The contact of her bare skin to his, more than the mere tip of a finger, was jarring.

"Are you offering me one?" he asked at last.

Her lashes lowered, her full, pink lips parting. "Yes."

And he knew right then that he'd been wrong about Daisy Vanreid. She bloody well *was* the dynamite.

Her Reformed Rake is coming soon.

If you enjoy steamy Regency and Victorian romance, don't miss the Heart's Temptation series. Read on for an excerpt of Book One, *A Mad Passion*.

A lost love…

Seven years ago, the Marquis of Thornton broke Cleo's heart, and she hasn't forgotten or forgiven him. But when she finds him standing before her at a country house party, as devastatingly handsome as ever, old temptations prove difficult to resist. One stolen kiss is all it takes.

A proper gentleman…

Thornton buried his past and his feelings for Cleo long ago. He's worked diligently to become a respected politician with a reputation above reproach. The only trouble in his otherwise perfect life is that he can't resist the maddening beauty he never stopped wanting, no matter how devastating the cost.

A mad passion…

Cleo is hopelessly trapped in a loveless marriage, and Thornton is on the cusp of making an advantageous match to further his political ambitions. The more time they spend in each other's arms, the more they court scandal and ruin. Theirs is a love that was never meant to be. Or is it?

chapter one

"A beautiful woman risking
everything for a mad passion."
— Oscar Wilde

Wilton House, September 1880

CLEO, COUNTESS SCARBROUGH, decided there had never been a more ideal moment to feign illness. The very last thing she wanted to do was traipse through wet grass at a country house party while her dress improver threatened to crush her. Not to mention the disagreeable prospect of being forced to endure the man before her. What had her hostess been thinking to pair them together? Did she not know of their history? A treasure hunt indeed.

Seven years and the Marquis of Thornton hadn't changed a whit, damn him. Tall and commanding, he was arrogance personified standing amidst the other glittering lords and ladies. Oh, perhaps his shoulders had broadened and she noted fine lines 'round his intelligent gray eyes. But not even a kiss of silver strands earned from his demanding career in politics marred the glorious black hair. It was most disappointing. After all, there had been whispers following the Prime Minister's successful Midlothian Campaign that a worn-out Thornton would retire from politics and his unofficial position as Gladstone's personal aid altogether. But as far as she could discern, the man staring down upon her was the same insufferably handsome man who had betrayed her. Was it so much to ask that he'd at least become plump about the middle?

Truly. A treasure hunt? Gads and to think this was the most anticipated house party of the year. "I'm afraid I must retire to my chamber," she announced to him. "I have a megrim."

Just as she began to breathe easier, Thornton ruined her reprieve. His sullen mouth quirked into a disengaged smile. "I'll escort you."

"You needn't trouble yourself." She hadn't meant for him to play the role of gentleman. She just wanted to be rid of him.

Thornton's face was an impenetrable mask. "It's no trouble."

"Indeed." Dismay sank through her like a stone. There was no way to extricate herself without being quite obvious he still set her at sixes and sevens. "Lead the way."

He offered his arm and she took it, aware that in her eagerness to escape him, she had just entrapped herself more fully. Instead of staying in the safe, boring company of the other revelers, she was leaving them at her back. Perhaps a treasure hunt would not have been so terrible a fate.

An uncomfortable silence fell between them, with Cleo aware the young man who had dizzied her with stolen kisses had aged into a cool, imperturbable stranger. For all the passion he showed now, she could have been a buttered parsnip on his plate.

She told herself she didn't give a straw for him, that walking a short distance just this once would have no effect on her. Even if he did smell somehow delectable and not at all as some gentlemen did of tobacco and horse. No. His was a masculine, alluring scent of sandalwood and spice. And his arm beneath her hand felt as strongly corded with muscle as it looked under his coat.

"You have changed little, Lady Scarbrough," Thornton offered at last when they were well away from the others, en route to Wilton House's imposing façade. "Lovely as ever."

"You are remarkably civil, my lord," she returned, not patient enough for a meaningless, pleasant exchange. She didn't wish to cry friends with him. There was too much between them.

His jaw stiffened and she knew she'd finally irked him. "Did you think to find me otherwise?"

"Our last parting was an ugly one." Perverse, perhaps, but she wanted to remind him, couldn't bridle her tongue. She longed to grab handfuls of his fine coat and shake him. What right did he have to appear so smug, so handsome? To be so self-assured, refined, magnetic?

"I had forgotten." Thornton's tone, like the sky above them, remained light, nonchalant.

"Forgotten?" The nerve of the man! He had acted the part of lovelorn suitor well enough back then.

"It was, what, all of ten years past, no?"

"Seven," she corrected before she could think better of it.

He smiled down at her as if he were a kindly uncle regarding a pitiable orphaned niece. "Remarkable memory, Lady Scarbrough."

"One would think your memory too would recall such an occasion, even given your advanced age."

"How so?" He sounded bored, deliberately overlooking her jibe at his age which was, if she were honest, only thirty to her five and twenty. "We never would have suited." His gray eyes melted into hers, his grim mouth tipping upward in what would have been a grin on any other man. Thornton didn't grin. He smoldered.

Drat her stays. Too tight, too tight. She couldn't catch a breath. Did he mean to be cruel? Cleo knew a great deal about not suiting. She and Scarbrough had been at it nearly since the first night they'd spent as man and wife. He had crushed her, hurt her, grunted over her and gone to his mistress.

"Of course we wouldn't suit," she agreed. Still, inwardly she had to admit there had been many nights in her early marriage where she had lain awake, listening for Scarbrough's footfalls, wondering if she hadn't chosen a Sisyphean fate.

They entered Wilton House and began the lengthy tromp to its Tudor revival styled wing where many of the guests had been situated. Thornton placed a warm hand over hers. He gazed down at her with a solemn expression, some of the arrogance gone from his features. "I had not realized you would be in attendance, Lady Scarbrough."

"Nor I you." She was uncertain of what, if any, portent hid in his words. Was he suggesting he was not as immune as he pretended? She wished he had not insisted upon escorting her.

As they drew near the main hall, a great commotion arose. Previously invisible servants sprang forth, bustling with activity. A new guest had arrived and Cleo recognized the strident voice calling out orders. Thornton's hand stiffened over hers and his strides increased. She swore she overheard him mumble something like 'not yet, damn it', but couldn't be sure. To test him, she stopped. Her heavy skirts swished front then back, pulling her so she swayed into him.

Cleo cast him a sidelong glance. "My lord, I do believe your mother is about to grace us with her rarified presence."

He growled, losing some of his polish like a candlestick too long overlooked by the rag. "Nonsense. We mustn't tarry. You've the headache." He punctuated his words with a sharp, insolent yank on her arm to get her moving.

She beamed. "I find it begins to dissipate."

The dowager Marchioness of Thornton had a certain reputation. She was a lioness with an iron spine, an undeterred sense of her own importance and enough consequence to cut anyone she liked. Cleo knew the dowager despised her. She wouldn't dare linger to incur her wrath were it not so painfully obvious the good woman's own son was desperate to avoid her. And deuce it, she wanted to see Thornton squirm.

"Truly, I would not importune you by forcing you to wait in the hall amidst the chill air," he said, quite stuffy now, no longer bothering to tug her but pulling her down the hall as if he were a mule and she his plow.

The shrill voice of her ladyship could be heard admonishing the staff for their posture. Thornton's pace increased, directing them into the wrong wing. She was about to protest when the dowager called after him. It seemed the saint still feared his mother.

"Goddamn." Without a moment of hesitation, he opened the nearest door, stepped inside and pulled her through with him.

Cleo let out a disgruntled 'oof' as she sank into the confines of whatever chamber Thornton had chosen as their hiding place. The door clicked closed and darkness descended in the cramped quarters.

"Thornton," trilled the marchioness, her voice growing closer.

"Your—" Cleo began speaking, but Thornton's hand over her mouth muffled the remainder of her words. She inhaled, startled by the solid presence of his large body so close behind her. Her bustle crushed against him.

"Hush, please. I haven't the patience for my mother today."

He meant to avoid the dragon for the entire day? Did he really think it possible? She shifted, discomfited by his nearness. Goodness, the little room was stifling. Her stays pinched her again. Did he need to smell so divine?

"Argnnnthhwt," she replied.

She needed air. The cramped quarters dizzied her. Certainly it wasn't the proximity of her person to Thornton that played mayhem with her senses. Absolutely not. The ridiculous man simply had to take his hand from her mouth. Why, he was nearly cutting off her air. She could scarcely breathe.

Thornton didn't seem likely to oblige her, so she resorted to tactics learned from growing up with a handful of sisters who were each more than a handful themselves. She decided not to play fair and licked his palm. It was a mistake, a terrible one and not just because it was unladylike but because he tasted salty and sweet. He tasted rather like something she might want to nibble. So she did the unpardonable. She licked him again.

"Christ." To her mingled relief and disappointment, he removed his hand. "Say a word and I'll throttle you."

Footsteps sounded in the hall just beyond the closed door. If Cleo had been tempted to end their ruse before, her sudden reaction to Thornton rattled her too much to do so now. She kept mum.

"Perhaps you are mistaken?" Thornton's sister, Lady Bella ventured, sounding meek.

"Don't be an idiot, Bella," the dowager snapped. "I know my own son when I see him. All your novels are making you addle-pated. How many times must I implore you to assert yourself at more improving endeavors like needlepoint? Women should not be burdened by knowledge. Our constitutions are too delicate."

Cleo couldn't quite stifle a snicker. The situation had all the elements of a comedy. All that yet remained was for the dowager to yank open the door so Cleo and Thornton would come tumbling out.

"You smell of lavender," he muttered in her ear, an accusation.

So what if she did? It was a lovely, heady scent blended specifically for her. Lavender and rose geranium, to be precise. "Hold your breath," she retorted, "if you find it so objectionable."

"I don't."

"Then what is the problem, Thornton?"

"I find it delicious."

Delicious. It was a word of possibility, of improbability, improper and yet somehow…seductive. Enticing. Yes, dear heaven, the man enticed her. She leaned into his solid presence, her neck seeking. Even better, her neck's sensitive skin found his hungry mouth.

He tasted her, licking her skin, nipping in gentle bites, trying, it would seem, to consume her like a fine dessert. His hands anchored her waist. Thornton pulled her back against him, all semblance of hauteur gone. Her dress improver cut viciously into her sides.

She didn't care. She forgot about his mother. Their quarrel and complicated past flitted from her mind. Cleo reached behind her with her right arm and sank her fingers into his hair. He stilled, then tore his lips from her neck. Neither of them moved. Their breaths blended. Thornton's hands splayed over her bodice, possessive and firm.

"This is very likely a mistake," he murmured.

"Very likely so," she agreed and then pressed her mouth to his.

He kissed her as she hadn't been kissed in years. Strike that. He kissed her as she hadn't been kissed in her lifetime, deep and hard and consuming. He kissed her like he wanted to claim her, mark her. And she kissed him back with all the passion she hadn't realized she possessed. Dear heavens, this was not the political saint who took her mouth with such force but the sinner she'd once known. Had she thought him cold?

Thornton twisted her until her back slammed against the door with a thud. His tongue swept into her mouth. Her hands gripped his strong shoulders, pulling him closer. An answering ache blossomed within her. Somehow, he found his way under her skirts, grasping her left leg at the knee and hooking it around his lean hip. Deliberate fingers trailed up her thigh beneath three layers of fabric, finding bare skin. He skimmed over lacy drawers, dipping inside to tease her.

When he sank two fingers inside her, she gasped, yanking back into the door again. It rattled. Voices murmured from far away in the hall. "Thornton," she whispered. "We should stop."

He dropped a hot kiss on her neck, then another. "Absolutely. This is folly."

Then he belied his words by shifting her so her body pressed against his instead of the door. She no longer cared why they should stop. Her good intentions dissipated. Her bodice suddenly seemed less snug and she realized he had undone a few buttons. Heavens. The icy man of moments ago bore no resemblance to the man setting her body aflame. Scarbrough had never touched her this way, had never made her feel giddy and tingly, as if she might fly up into the clouds.

Scarbrough. Just the thought of her husband stiffened her spine. Hadn't she always sworn to herself she would not be like him? Here she was, nearly making love in who knew what manner of chamber with Thornton, a man she didn't even find pleasant. The man, to be specific, who had betrayed and abandoned her. How could she be so wanton and foolish to forget what he'd done for a few moments of pleasure?

She pushed him away, breathing heavy, heart heavy. "We must stop."

"Why must we?" He caressed her arms, wanting to seduce her again.

"My husband."

"I don't hear him outside the door."

"Nor do I, but I am not a society wife even if my conduct with you suggests otherwise. I do not make love with men in closets at country house parties. I don't fall to his level."

"Madam, your husband is a louse. You could not fall to his level were you to roll in the hay with every groom in our hostess' stable and then run naked through the drawing room."

She stiffened. "What do you know of him?"

"Plenty."

"I doubt you do." The inescapable urge to defend her wastrel, blackguard husband rose within her. How dare Thornton be so arrogant, so condescending when he himself had committed the same sins against her? And had he not just been on the verge of making love to a married woman in a darkened room? He was no better.

He sighed. "Scarbrough's got scads of women on the wrong side of the Park in St. John's Wood. It's common knowledge."

Of course it was, but that didn't make it any easier to hear. Especially not coming from Thornton, the man she'd jilted in favor of Scarbrough. "I'm aware Scarbrough is indiscreet, but that has little bearing on you and me in this moment. This moment should never have happened."

"We are once again in agreement, Cleo." His voice regained some of its arrogance. "However, it did happen."

Her name on his lips startled her, but she didn't bother taking him to task for it. After the intimacies she had just allowed, it would be hypocritical. She wished she could see him. The darkness became unbearable.

"How could you so easily forget your own sins? You had your pretty little actress all the while you claimed to love me."

He said nothing. Silence extended between them. It was obstinate of her, but she wanted him to deny it. Thornton did not.

"Aren't there orphans about somewhere you should be saving?" She lashed out, then regretted her angry words. That was badly done of her. But this, being in Thornton's arms after what he'd done...it went against the grain.

"I think you should go," she added.

"I would if I could fight my way past your bloody skirts. There's no help for it. Either you go first or we go together."

"We can't go together! Your insufferable mother may be

lurking out there somewhere."

"Then you must go first."

"I shall precede you," she informed him.

"I already suggested as much. Twice, if you had but listened." He sounded peeved.

The urge to stamp her foot hit her with fierce persistence. "You are a vexing man."

"And you, my love, are a shrew unless your mouth is otherwise occupied."

She gasped. "How dare you?"

"Oh, I dare lots of things. Some of them, you may even like." His voice had gone sinful and dark.

The dreadful man. She drew herself up in full countess armor. "I'm leaving now."

Then he ruined her consequence by saying, "Lovely. Though you might want to fasten up your bodice before you go. I should think it terribly difficult to convince my mother we were talking about the weather when your finer bits are on display."

Her finer bits? It was the outside of enough. She slapped his arm. "Has the Prime Minister any idea what a coarse scoundrel you are? None of my...person would be on display if you hadn't pulled me into the room and accosted me."

"You were well pleased for a woman being accosted," he pointed out, smug.

She hated him again, which was really for the best. He was too much of a temptation, too delicious, to borrow his word, and she was ever a fool for him. "You're insufferable."

"So I've been told."

Cleo gave him her back and attempted to fasten her buttons. Drat. She pulled. She held her breath. She tugged her bodice's stiff fabric again. The buttons wouldn't meet their moorings. "Did you undo my lacings?" she demanded, realization dawning on her.

"Perhaps." Thornton's voice had gone wistful. Sheepish,

almost.

Good heavens. How did he know his way around a woman's undergarments so well he could get her undone and partially unlaced all while kissing her passionately? Beneath his haughty exterior still lay a womanizer's heart.

There was no help for it now. She couldn't tight-lace herself. "I require some assistance," she mumbled.

"What was that?"

Cleo gritted her teeth. "I can't lace myself."

"Would a 'please' be in order?"

"You're the one who did the damage. It seems reasonable that you should repair it."

"Perhaps I can slip past your voluminous skirts after all," he mused.

"Please help me," she blurted.

"Turn around," he ordered.

Cleo spun, reluctant to face him again. She could barely see him in the murkiness, a tall, imposing figure. His hands slipped inside her bodice, expertly finding the lacings he had loosened.

"Breathe in," he told her.

She did and he pulled tightly, cinching her waist to a painful wasp silhouette once more. "Thank you. I can manage the buttons."

He spun her about and brushed aside her fingers. "I'll get them." She swore she heard a smile in his voice. "After all, it only seems reasonable I repair the damage I've done."

"Fine then." His breath fanned her lips and she could feel his intense gaze on her. She tilted her head to the side to ease her disquiet at his nearness. Was it just her imagination, or did his fingers linger at the buttons nearest her bosom?

"There you are." Thornton fastened the last one, brushing the hollow of her throat as he did so.

She closed her eyes and willed away the desire that assaulted her. This man was not for her. He ran the backs of his fingers along her neck, stopping when he cupped her jaw.

"Thank you," she whispered again.

"You're most welcome," he said, voice low.

The magnetism between them was inexorable, just as it had been before. Despite the intervening years, despite all, she still recalled the way he had made her feel—weightless and enchanted, as though she had happened upon Shakespeare's moonlit forest in *A Midsummer Night's Dream*.

His thumb brushed over her bottom lip. "If you don't go, I'll undo all the repairing I've just done."

She knew he warned himself as much as he warned her. Sadness pulsed between them, a mutual acknowledgment their lives could have turned up differently. So many unspoken words, so much confusion lingered.

"I must go," she said unnecessarily. She was reluctant to leave him and that was the plain truth of it. "I find my megrim has returned."

With that, she left, returning to the hall, to sunlight streaming in cathedral windows. More importantly, she hoped, she returned to sanity.

A Mad Passion is available now. Get your copy today.

Don't miss Scarlett's other romances!
(Listed by Series)

HISTORICAL ROMANCE

Heart's Temptation

A Mad Passion (Book One)
Rebel Love (Book Two)
Reckless Need (Book Three)
Sweet Scandal (Book Four)
Restless Rake (Book Five Coming Soon)

Wicked Husbands

Her Errant Earl (Book One)
Her Lovestruck Lord (Book Two)
Her Reformed Rake (Book Three Coming Soon)

CONTEMPORARY ROMANCE

Love's Second Chance

Reprieve (Book One)
Perfect Persuasion (Book Two)
Win My Love (Book Three)

Coastal Heat

Loved Up (Book One)

about the author

Award-winning author Scarlett Scott writes contemporary and historical romance with heat, heart, and happily ever afters. Since publishing her first book in 2010, she has become a wife, mother to adorable identical twins and one TV-loving dog, and a killer karaoke singer. Well, maybe not the last part, but that's what she'd like to think.

A self-professed literary junkie and nerd, she loves reading anything but especially romance novels, poetry, and Middle English verse. When she's not reading, writing, wrangling toddlers, or camping, you can catch up with her on her website www.scarsco.com. Hearing from readers never fails to make her day.

Scarlett's complete book list and information about upcoming releases can be found on her website.

Follow Scarlett on social media:

www.instagram.com/scarlettscottauthor
www.twitter.com/scarscoromance
www.pinterest.com/scarlettscott
www.facebook.com/AuthorScarlettScott

Made in the USA
Middletown, DE
07 September 2018